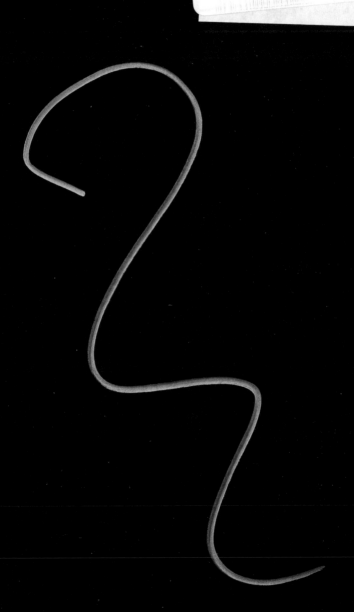

ALSO BY NATASHA BOWEN

Skin of the Sea

SOUL
OF THE
DEEP

NATASHA BOWEN

RANDOM HOUSE 🏠 NEW YORK

Text copyright © 2022 by Natasha Bowen
Jacket art inspired by the work of Jeff Manning
Images used under license from Shutterstock.com.

All rights reserved. Published in the United States by Random House Children's Books, a division of Penguin Random House LLC, New York.

Random House and the colophon are registered trademarks of Penguin Random House LLC.

Visit us on the Web! GetUnderlined.com

Educators and librarians, for a variety of teaching tools, visit us at RHTeachersLibrarians.com

Library of Congress Cataloging-in-Publication Data
Name: Bowen, Natasha, author.
Title: Soul of the deep / Natasha Bowen.
Description: New York: Random House Children's Books, [2022] | Series: Skin of the sea; 2 |
Summary: When signs of the eight ajogun begin to appear, Simi teams up with the corrupt trickster god Esu to stop the demon warlords before they enter the human realm and ruin humankind.
Identifiers: LCCN 2021053539 (print) | LCCN 2021053540 (ebook) |
ISBN 978-0-593-12098-9 (hardcover) | ISBN 978-0-593-12099-6 (lib. bdg.) |
ISBN 978-0-593-64488-1 (int'l) | ISBN 978-0-593-12100-9 (ebook)
Subjects: CYAC: Mermaids—Fiction. | Gods, Yoruba—Fiction. | Yoruba (African people)—Fiction. | Souls—Fiction. | LCGFT: Novels.
Classification: LCC PZ7.1.B6847 So 2022 (print) | LCC PZ7.1.B6847 (ebook) |
DDC [Fic]—dc23

Printed in the United States of America
10 9 8 7 6 5 4 3 2 1
First Edition

To my children,

who inspire me in ways

they don't even realize

CONTENT NOTE

Before you begin reading, please be aware that parts of this book may be triggering for some readers. *Soul of the Deep* blends fifteenth-century history with fantasy, and there are depictions of violence, enslavement, and death.

SOUL
OF THE
DEEP

CHAPTER ONE

THE BONES ARE buried deep, white against the velvet of dark water. I shudder in the cold press of the sea as I swim beneath giant rib cages. The chill has burrowed into my core, where it nestles in the pit of my stomach, settling next to the promise I made to Olokun. The promise I must keep, even though it colors my days in shades of midnight, of misery. Sometimes I let myself think of the sun, the perfect pink-and-orange rise of it, the fire of the way it sets. But then my mind always goes to Kola and the heat of his skin, the slice of his smile, and the way one touch can make my chest tight.

My choice.

My sacrifice.

I blink away curls from my eyes, trying to rid myself of thoughts that only make the lightless water harder to bear. Release them, I tell myself. Release what you cannot have and accept the present.

I adjust my grip on the terra-cotta pot I found resting in the sand, an offering from above that made its way down to the deep. At least I will be able to bring evidence that *someone* still worships Olokun. Flicking my caudal fin, its blush-and-gold pleats barely visible, I pass slowly under the last of the skeletons, their ivory arcs protruding from the silt.

When I emerge from the bones, I pause for a moment in water that grows warmer. The heat is a balm, and I spin once in the hot silk of a current, almost smiling at the relief it brings. Almost.

Ahead, on either end of the coral reef, the earth is split, emitting searing gases that bubble into the sea. A blue glow spreads over my skin as I draw closer to a large carved opening lit up by firefly squid. Smaller seeps of gases cause the water to shimmer and glitter, feverish swirls that escape, framing the entrance in the coral. The squid illuminate an archway draped with luminous sea moss and studded with mollusks.

I swallow thickly. The soft light makes my heart ache with its gentle beauty, but it's only a pale imitation of what I crave. Six months without the scald of a full sun and I find it hard to imagine the feel of sweat sliding down warm skin. I want air, even though I don't need it, even when it is dense with a coming storm or cut through with the chill of night. I want to see the stars again, their scattered flares puncturing the sky. I want to feel the earth beneath my feet, the rich black soil that turns to soft mud when the rains come.

Floating closer to the entrance, I run a finger over the etchings of fish, whales, and the peaks of the seabed. The last image is one of scales, curls, and the telltale beauty of Yemoja. My maker, my second mother, the most gracious of orisas. A sadness coils within me, but I don't let it take root. Instead, I focus on Yemoja's safety, on Folasade and the other Mami Wata, fulfilling their task of gathering the souls of those who die in the sea. If I hadn't asked Olokun for help, then the fracturing world would have broken entirely.

I am here so that they can be safe. And this is the price I must pay.

I touch the sapphire at my neck, its cold blue brighter than the rock around me. I think of blessing souls with Yemoja, honoring their journeys home to Olodumare. A different kind of service from the one that Olokun demands of me now.

But my choices were the right ones, and they don't change what needs to be done. I grasp the pot tighter and glide through the gases, chin tipped up, shoulders back. More warm water flows over me as I pass under the arch, giving way to much cooler currents when I emerge into a tunnel that stretches ahead. No firefly squid here.

My heart beats quicker, and I hold a cold hand to my chest. This part used to scare me, but months of making this journey now allows me to swim through the passage with faith, though there is still a slither of dread in knowing what awaits. I slip into the gloom, skin grazing the smooth black sides as I head toward the vague light in the distance.

The rock widens into a circular space. Hundreds of larger firefly squid are draped over the coral walls, their glow reflecting on the iridescent insides of cracked-open shells studded among them. The moss grows in abundance here, its thick glistening arcs looped around the walls. I squint through the dazzle of light, eyes narrowed against the sudden brightness.

A current tugs me farther inside and I let it, clasping the offering to my chest, allowing myself a glance upward at a ceiling peppered with more moss, its trails pulsing with soft white lights.

"I see that you have decided to grace me with your presence." The deep voice trickles out from the back of the hall, where the light stretches to reach. I feel a faint flicker of pride when I don't flinch.

A flash of a metallic gaze, and then Olokun leans forward, his mouth curled up at the edges. I swim toward the murkiness until I can make out the coil of the orisa's great tail curved beneath him. Olokun sits on a black coral throne, fingers curling over the armrests. He flicks his abede back and forth, the silver fan creating ripples in the water. Shadows cloak the muscled bulk of Olokun's body, but his eyes shine in a face with sharp angles. A thick golden chain wraps around his waist, its end tailing off into the sea.

"It's not yet time," I answer, the words slipping out like stones settling around us. The pot is cool in my arms, and I grip its handles firmly, teeth clenched so tight that my jaw aches. I want to remind the orisa of what I gave up to be here, but I bite it down.

Setting the vessel before Olokun, I touch my fingertips and forehead to the seafloor as a sign of respect before moving backward. The orisa's cape trails down to the sand and stones, black pearls bulbous and gleaming.

Olokun peers at the clay pot, a finger held against the cleft in his chin. "What is that?"

"An offering," I say, hands hovering over the tribute. "Shall I open it?"

"Let me." The water swirls, rocking me slightly as the orisa lunges forward and snatches up the pot.

Olokun wrenches the lid off and reaches inside, bringing out a bundle of waxed cloth, which he slowly unwraps. The whitish belly of the raw yam is exposed. The orisa's smile disappears as he covers the peeled vegetable and places it back inside.

"Another reminder of those who worship you," I say, my annoyance forming at the downward tilt of his lips. I know what he is thinking—that he will never be able to taste iyán this deep in the sea. Will never be able to dip it into ẹ̀gúsí, dig his feet into the hot earth, take sips of palm wine between each bite. He finds something lacking in every offering I bring.

Olokun shoves the pot against the wall with the others, and the golden chain around his waist rattles, its links clinking against the throne. He turns his gaze away from the discarded tributes I spent my days searching for, a frown puckering his forehead.

"Are you not pleased?" My voice wavers, the question shooting out before I can swallow it back down.

The orisa doesn't answer, but he kicks out at the pot this time, sending it crashing against the rock, where it smashes into pieces. I edge backward, welcoming the rise of my anger, using it to keep most of my fear at bay.

"It is not enough. You should be bringing me more. Find more!" Olokun roars, surging from his throne, tall in the glitter and gloom. When I don't speak, he sits back down, fingers testing each sharp point of his abede. "I do not ask much of you. Searching for tributes, your company at times, and overseeing the dead. These are small things."

My chest swells with anger. I think of the hours spent combing the bedrock until my fingers are numb, the relief when I do find something, the days when I dread returning empty-handed. The times when thoughts of Kola make me sink to the blackest part of the water, letting the arctic currents wash away my tears, when missing him hurts so much that it burns.

"You will never be sated!" The words fight their way up my throat, and I can't hold them in. "There's too much bitterness in your heart. It's not the people's fault that you are chained down here, and it certainly isn't mine!"

5

Olokun freezes, his abede held high. He slashes it once, twice, through the water, and then looks directly at me, a muscle in his jaw twitching. "If I had been shown proper respect from the beginning, then I would not be trapped down here."

"You sent wave after wave to destroy Ife!" I answer, a sneer in my voice. Obatala created land in the middle of Olokun's waters and gave life to humankind. But he did not consult Olokun, whose outrage at his shrunken kingdom and lack of worship grew. Lurking in the depths, the orisa became twisted with spite and jealousy, until he tried to erase the earth and its people by battering them with the sea. "Obatala had to chain you to save humanity. You have no patience. No care. You are here because of what you did!" I glare at him, my frustration taking over. A part of me used to feel some sympathy for Olokun, banished so deep, but his vanity is exhausting. "Was it worth this? The weight of water above us? A life without sunlight, the gnawing cold that eats away at your bones?" This is the most I have ever said, and I brace myself for his fury, my hands in fists.

The gentle swish of water is the only sound in the chamber. I hold Olokun's gaze in a way I never have, my heart thumping.

"You made your choice, and now you dare to complain?" Olokun's voice is low, laced with menace. He snaps his fan shut and swims over to me, his eyes as icy as the water that presses down around us. "Tell me, did I force you to come to these depths?" I stare at the orisa, swallowing down more words, my shoulders quivering. "You offered me your service. I did not demand it from you, Mami Wata." His words are soft, winding through the water like ribbons. "The anger and pity that you feel are for yourself. Remember this and show your *respect*."

His last word catches at me. Olokun stood by his promise to help bind Esu, thereby saving those I care about. That deserves my deference, even if his past actions do not.

"Besides . . ." Olokun swims close enough for me to make out the twists of his short curls. "Do I not show compassion now?"

My shoulders slump, and my spine curves over once again. I think of what is expected of me next, and I nod. It doesn't matter how I feel—we must do what needs to be done. *I* must do what needs to be done.

"We will put your outburst down to tiredness and the cold," says Olokun, flicking the chain behind him. His eyes are shuttered now, any displeasure consumed by the silver and black. "Come."

The last shreds of my anger dissipate as Olokun turns to leave, his tail a sinuous slink of purple. Behind the throne is another tunnel, and with a flick of his fin, Olokun disappears within it. Quickly, I follow.

The passageway splits off into a dozen others, some to areas I have never seen. Before long, we are outside and swimming into lighter water, the frigid depths bringing a numbness that seeps inside me. Olokun soars upward out of the black blue, skimming along the reef, golden chain trailing in his wake, seemingly infinite but never long enough for him to reach the surface. I track the glints of metal, swimming faster, chest tightening with every stroke I make.

We are close.

Olokun doesn't look back at me, so he won't see the glaze of tears, but as I move nearer to him, I can see his lips are pulled tight, chin held up.

"There are . . . more. This much I know from what the squid have told me." Olokun's words are cushioned in the indigo satin of the water.

I close my eyes and nod once, and then I am propelling myself up, drawing level with the orisa as we crest the reef.

Before us stretch the burial sands. The half-moon curve of pale silt spreads out as far as I can see, its surface littered with mounds that range from whale-sized to smaller than me. I swallow, heart beating faster as I make out the new bodies.

All who die in the sea end up here in Olokun's kingdom.

"Another òyìnbó ship?" I ask quietly, squeezing my words around the lump in my throat.

Olokun keeps his eyes on the people who have come to rest in his realm. Slowly he nods his great head, caudal fin waving in the water. Together, we scoop the silt from the bottom of the sea, covering each hand, each foot, smoothing sand over open mouths and sightless eyes. Burying the people who were taken, who could not be saved. I tuck wrappers over chests, touching a hand to scarred cheeks and tangled hair. I cry as we create new graves. Every time, it tears at me, and every time the pain grows until I think I can't take any more.

Once we are finished, we return to the reef, silent as our gazes sweep over the dead. My hands form fists, nails digging in, breaking the skin of my palms. Small crescent wounds and bursts of blood are spawned, only to dissolve instantly.

"Before, you and your sisters gathered their souls, and I prayed over the bodies I buried." Olokun's eyes fix on the blue of the sapphire hanging around my neck, his words quiet. "Now *we* bury them and pray together." He holds out his hand to me. "Keeping their remains safe and blessing them. I know it is a hard burden to bear, but your service and added prayers are an honor to the dead, Mami Wata. Something special. I am glad to be able to offer them that, not just the actions and words of an orisa who seeks redemption."

I look down at his large palm, with its faded brown lines. My anger is gone, replaced with the melancholy that now accompanies me everywhere. I slide my fingers over his, intertwining bones and flesh, letting him pull me next to him. I am grateful that I can offer the last words over these stolen people, that we give them more dignity.

"A ṣe ẹrí nípa pé a rí ibi à ti sùn yín, a dẹ ṣe ìwúre pé kí ìrìn àjò yín sí ọdọ Olódùmarè jẹ ìrìn àjò ìbùkún." We look down together as the prayer streams from our lips. "Ara yín á tún áyé wá; ẹmi yín á sì jẹ ọkan pẹlú àwọn alálẹ. Pẹlú àwọn ọrọ wọn yí, a gbée yín pọn. A ò sì ní gbàgbé ìgbésí aiyé yín."

I don't cry anymore. Instead, I try to think of the lives they lived and the peace they have now.

"We witness your final resting place, and we add our blessings to your journey home to Olodumare," I murmur again as Olokun releases my hand. "Your body will rejoin the world, while your spirit will be at one with the ancestors. With these words we honor you and your life. Your death will not be forgotten."

The orisa gazes at the mounds, large and small, before he turns away, his tail propelling him through the dark. I do not follow—I know by now that he will not speak. He will meditate on the loss of life that the tides bring to his realm.

I shut my eyes and try to calm the tremble in my hands. Still, I can't stop the darkness that pulses against my closed lids. I've helped bury them, have spoken the prayer, but if I do not feel this pain, then who will? I think of how I could have been in one of these graves if Yemoja had not remade me. Despite yearning to be human, I was given another chance at a different kind of life. One that I should still be thankful for.

I slide my arms around my waist, but I am too cold to offer myself any comfort. Instead, I clutch at the jewel of my necklace and think about the souls of the people I gathered. Those golden and silver threads of life, their memories, echoes of their joy. I imagine their ghosts rising up from the silt, brushing sand from remnants of patterned wrappers, out of the whorls of their ears and the blackness of their hair. They will look around them, at the heavy layers of the water above and the maw of the deep just outside Olokun's kingdom, and they will wonder what happened, where they are. And then realization will crash down on them— their life, their death—and just when they think they cannot stand it, the ghosts will regard the bodies we have buried. Some will crumple in despair, while others will make fists of their vague fingers, smashing them against chests that no longer rise and fall, pressing against hearts that no longer beat. A fury felt even beyond life.

My lips flatten into a line. I will the ghosts in my mind to follow their souls and return home, to welcome the embrace of Olodumare. I send my apologies to them, clasping a hand to my own breast, fingers splayed over a heart that still beats, even though it feels shattered and cracked by loss.

Then the water rushes in a sudden current. Fear, as quick and vivid as a sea snake, darts in. I sway, bursts of ghosts still blooming on my eyelids, as small icy fingers slide around my wrist.

CHAPTER TWO

I OPEN MY eyes to a hand clutching my arm, skin pinched between slim brown fingers. My first thought is that the ghosts have somehow made their claim on the living, have come to warn me that they are still here. My heart skips at the hard grip, and then I look up and see not a wraith but a halo of black hair and full cheeks.

Folasade. The sapphire in her necklace glows an icy blue, matching the one at my throat, a sign that I am one of seven.

My breath loosens, but my chest is still taut. Pulling her to me, I wrap my arm around her, my own hand now clutching at chilled flesh, the soft tips of her tight black curls sliding against my forehead.

"Folasade," I gasp, squeezing her tighter so that I can feel the beat of her heart against mine. I hold her, keeping her anchored to me, mind still working over the fact that she is here. And then my joy is slit by a sudden flood of anxiousness.

Folasade should not be this deep.

After Yemoja left the river Ogun to follow the first stolen people across the ocean, she made a truce with Olokun—she would gather their souls to return home and he would honor their bodies, saying the last prayers over their flesh and bone and showing respect at their final resting place. Each orisa carved out their territory, with Yemoja's being the top part of the sea and Olokun's being the very bottom. Since Olokun had no choice in this, being bound to the dark depths, he was adamant that Yemoja—and, by extension, Mami Wata—not intrude on the Land of the Dead.

I risked Olokun's wrath when I sought his help in defeating Esu. Now I am paying the price in the cold dark, and Folasade has followed me here.

"Simidele, I'm glad I've found you." She pulls away and manages to aim her smile at me. Uneasiness creases the corners of her mouth as she takes me in. "Are you well? You seem . . ."

But Folasade doesn't finish, doesn't need to. I know what the weeks and months have done to me. My skin is dull and my spine curves over, weighted with longing for the surface. For the light, warm air, and white-tipped waves. For Yemoja and the other Mami Wata.

For Kola.

My heart stutters at the thought of him, recalling the scent of black soap and the brownish pink of his bottom lip. It has been so long, but I can still bring Kola's face to mind, the cut of his cheekbones and the slide of his smooth skin under the palms of my hands. An ache stretches through me when I remember the pureness in the golden twists of his soul, spiraling back into his body after my prayers and the twins' powers took hold.

At times like these, it feels as if there is no room inside me for anything else but him. Memories of the crinkle of his eyes when he would smile, the frown that would crease his forehead if he thought my feet hurt. Imaginings of what could have been.

But these are cruel ways of punishing myself. Even if I hadn't bartered my freedom for Olokun's realm, Mami Wata can never be with a human. I bring my hands to my face, pressing cold fingertips to my cheeks.

"Simi?" Folasade peers at me intently, worry lines forming between her eyebrows.

Focus on the present, I tell myself, lowering my hands and shoving the memories of Kola away, knowing that they will crowd back in. They always do.

"Why are you here, Folasade?" I whisper. I look around us, searching for the bobbing lights of anglerfish or the giant squid whose limbs seem long enough to reach the surface if they wished. Either would slink back to Olokun to tell him of the intruder.

Folasade squeezes my hand, a small smile trembling on her lips. I think of how she would lecture me about the ways of Mami Wata, so pious in her manner of serving Yemoja. She should not be here, I think again. Not just because it's dangerous for her, but also because it would have been easier if she hadn't come, reminding me of what I am. What I had before. It would have been easier if I didn't have to see any Mami Wata at all.

"I came to see how you are." Folasade moves closer, but her words waver, and I know there is something else. Fear is sown in the tense quick glances she takes, in the hunched set of her shoulders and the small groove between her eyebrows. "Yemoja has been worried. We all have."

I try to smile but only end up baring my teeth. I should tell Folasade to leave now, but the selfish part of me, the lonely part of me, doesn't want to. Instead, I take her hand, drawing her along behind me, moving quickly over the ridge of the reef.

"Come," I say. Folasade's fingers clutch at mine as she sees the tombs of silt and sand, and I can feel the bend of her body, the turn of her head as she keeps the dead in view until we swim down, heading deeper into the water.

The hue of the sea changes as the current reaches for us, its freezing swirl yanking us down to the darker part of the water. I relax into its pull, holding on to Folasade as we land on chilled sand with a gentle bump.

"Olokun will be resting after prayers," I say. Black tides all but consume the shipwreck, but I know where its rotting timbers rest and I lead us toward it, using the dip of the seabed and familiar shapes of rocks to guide our way. "And even if he weren't, this is the last place he would come."

There are certain reminders of humankind that Olokun doesn't like, and any evidence of their presumptuousness in try-ing to claim even a part of the sea turns his mood darker than the deep. The òyìnbó vessels he hates most of all, curses spilling from lips twisted with rage whenever there are new ones. Ships of strangers that come from other lands to pillage ours, sowing discord and stealing people, whom they treat worse than animals. There have been more and more wrecks recently. If there are any of the stolen people inside, the orisa retrieves their bodies and takes them to the burial sands. But Olokun enjoys leaving the òyìnbó to rot, their bones slowly turning white in the scouring tides of the sea. For this, I rejoice. It is all they deserve.

The wreck lies on its side, one mast leaning into the dark-ness, the other missing, carried by currents into other realms. The tatter of one long-ago white sail undulates in the water, and a ragged hole in the hull is a darker shade of black, an obsidian maw. Anger bubbles back up within me, the only thing of heat in such cold depths. How can they treat people in such a way? To deny them their humanity, treat them as if they are the same as spices and fabrics, and then cast aside their bodies as if they are nothing more than unwanted possessions? Even when our kingdoms war, any prisoners captured are still . . . *people.*

I sink down to the seabed, level with the gaping hole in the ship. The first time I came to the hold, the heavy manacles and cramped quarters reminded me not only of the pain and fear the people have felt but of my own on board such a vessel. A bleak fury wound its way through me, and I ripped the iron restraints from the rotting wood.

The hold is now empty of anything but barrels, the kola nuts, pepper, and turmeric they stored long dissolved. A touch on my wrist lets me know Folasade is still following me, and together we swim inside, taking care not to let the splintered edges snag our skin. We skim through the absent deck and head toward the only door that remains, its brass hinges dull now, a patina of green replacing their shine. My fingers curl around the cold handle, pulling until the rotting door opens, allowing us to slip through.

The same luminous sea moss clings to the slats of the floor and walls, giving enough of a glow for us to see the opulence of the captain's cabin. Dark brocade curtains wave gently in the water. The back end is a long shattered window, once open to the horizon, now wedged tightly against the sand and bedrock. I move past a desk tipped on its side, carved legs exposed, floating next to the chair. My fingers brush its back, disturbing the disintegrating shreds of silk.

There are no bones here, no reminders of the òyìnbó who

once commanded this ship. I always wonder who the captain was, how his conscience allowed him to pack people in among spices and ivory.

Folasade glances about her, taking in the bedchamber, a small niche in the side of the cabin. Pale slivers of curtains obscure the lumpy pallet, but the twist of sheets can just about be seen, weighed down by a pair of long leather boots, now covered in lichen. Folasade shudders and spins around so that we are face to face.

"It's the only place Olokun will not find you," I say, my voice strained.

Folasade doesn't answer, but her eyes flick over me as she reaches out, taking a small pearl from my hair. She examines the gleaming orb before closing her hand around it. "Yemoja worries for you. I came to see how you are."

"I am . . . fine." I have to be, I think as I push away the curls that float across my face. "Tell her she doesn't need to worry. This was my choice and I will honor it." Pausing, I tear off a strip of fabric from the chair, thinking of Yemoja's fierce embrace, of the curve of her smile.

"How did you come to such an . . . agreement with Olokun?" Folasade's head leans on one side as she examines me.

"How could I have bound Esu? I'm not powerful enough to do that. It's all I could think about as we headed to his island." I swim toward the back of the cabin. "I saw from the map on the babala-wo's walls where Olokun could be found."

"And you asked him to help?"

"Olokun was furious at being left in the deep. Esu had not passed on any of his messages of regret to Olodumare." I stare out the broken window and imagine the sights it once held. Dawn.

That first flush of delicate light that dusts your skin and gilds the world. The time of day I miss the most. I sigh and turn away. My life is not marked by the rise and fall of the sun here; all I have is the tides to measure the days and weeks. "He agreed to help me if I shared his burden in burying the dead."

"And you accepted." Folasade frowns at me, thick eyebrows slashed above her brown eyes. "Olokun tried to drown humanity. And now you are down here with him."

I think of the darkness and the icy bite of cold. I don't want Folasade or any of the other Mami Wata to worry even more about me. Pushing back my shoulders, I hold Folasade's gaze.

"Olokun is honoring his truce with Yemoja, and I am honoring my bargain with him," I say. "We bury the dead and deliver their final prayers."

"Of course." Folasade grips the chair in front of her, staring back at me. "But if it's redemption that he's seeking, only Obatala can absolve him."

"I know."

Folasade watches me still, but I look away. There's no use in going over what has been agreed. When I promised Olokun I would serve him in return for his help in defeating Esu, it was the right thing to do.

It *is* the right thing.

If Olokun hadn't helped me bind Esu, then the trickster would have gained more power, using it to control orisas and all humankind, bending them to his will.

"What does Mother Yemoja think? Of me being here?" These are questions I have asked myself, and my stomach roils as I say them out loud. Does the orisa think I've betrayed her once again?

Folasade tucks the pearl back into my curls, letting her fingers trail down my cheek. "She mourns you." I nod, sorrow darting through me. "You know that she admires your bravery and sacrifice. She just wishes . . ."

"What?" I say. I try to ignore the pulse of my heart as it rises in my throat. "What does she wish?"

"That things could have been different." Folasade's fingertips brush against my collarbone, her eyes holding mine. "She worries over the pain of your choice. The darkness that you live in. And so do I."

I pull back, taking a moment to blink away my tears, thinking of the determined metallic gaze of Yemoja. The ferocity of her love in creating Mami Wata, and the devotion and care she shows to humankind.

"She says that she understands your choice. That you will always be her daughter. No matter what." Folasade moves closer to me, her scales violet blue. "She asked me to tell you that she hopes one day you will be able to come back to us."

"I thought she might be angry," I whisper. I hold a hand to my heart, relief flooding through me.

Folasade shakes her head. "Mother Yemoja is furious only over the loss of you." She peers out the empty window, shuddering. "But this is not where you belong. You were not made for burials and prayers over bodies." Folasade purses her lips as she faces me again, leaning forward, cupping the sapphire around my throat, the one that matches hers, the one that all seven Mami Wata wear. "You should be with us, gathering souls."

I snatch my necklace away from her touch. "Don't you think I know this? That I wish I could still see the sun, Mother Yemoja—" My voice cracks and I pause for a moment, the shiver of my chest shaking more words free. "I had no choice but to seek Olokun's help, Folasade. Kola would have died. Bem, the twins, all of Oko—"

"Just as you had no choice when you saved Kola from the sea?"

I draw back, hissing as if she has burned me. She might as well have. "I would never have left anybody to die! Not if they could be saved."

Silence grows between us. My outburst is swallowed by the gloom of the wreck, but I still can't look at Folasade.

"I know you wanted to help," says Folasade finally, her voice softer now. "I know you did what you thought was best, but—"

"No!" I say. "I'm sorry that I'm not able to do what Yemoja created me for, but she has six others still. I won't be made to feel guilty. Not after everything I've done and all I've given up. It's a shame that Yemoja understands but you don't." Pushing past her, I yank open the door, shaking with the grief I normally keep carefully tucked away. "If you've come here just to tell me everything I have done wrong, then you should leave."

As I swim back through the ragged hole, the splintered edges catch against my shoulder. I wince but the scratch only takes seconds to heal, and then I am rushing through the water, pushing my way toward the reef.

"Simidele! Wait!" calls Folasade behind me. "I'm sorry. I came to give voice to Yemoja. . . ."

But I don't listen. The months of being this deep crush against me and I press a palm against the thump of my heart. Seeing Folasade was a welcome relief, but now her presence and her criticism shape the ache that stretches across my chest. I need to get away. From the deep and the reminders of my failures. I swim hard against a sudden current, upward, cresting the rock barrier in one smooth motion. I push away thoughts of Olokun and the repercussions of nearing the limits of his realm and I go farther than I have before, leaving the cold and darkness behind. If I can just see the brighter blue, even an illusion of sun . . .

I need to see light.

I soar through the sea feeling as if my chest will burst. The tops of the waves are in sight, spires of sun fractured by the sea, just as Folasade grabs my arm. She yanks me to a stop, spinning me to face her, my curls clouding the water between us. I swipe at them, jerking my hair out of the way, turning my head to where the water is lighter, warmer. It is so close.

"Simidele, please. I was sent to ask you—"

A boom interrupts her, and Folasade's hand slides from my skin as we look up through the layers of water above us. The surface has been split open and shapes both large and small pierce the waves. Shards of wood plunge into the deeper water, followed by the curl of bodies and trails of blood. Men, their hands clawed and limbs slack in death, sink slowly, cradled by the current. The sea swirls around them, dragging them down, welcoming their corpses.

I swim forward, stomach lurching at the sight of stained wrappers that did not protect the men they draped, at crimson-soaked wounds and unseeing eyes.

The cloud of blood spreads in the sea. Blackened edges of wood continue to rain down, leaving a broken hold above, the remnants of a ship that has seen war and death.

I look up as the vessel begins its inevitable descent, my heart tightening at the memory it brings. The flood of life lost and the flare of death in its pinkish smear. Reaching a hand upward, I pause.

They are all dead. But it is no longer my task to gather their souls, to take them to be blessed by Yemoja before releasing them to the Supreme Creator. I look to Folasade, at the lines and twist of her mouth, which echo the horror on mine. She starts forward, hands outstretched, eyes fastened on the nearest man. The slice of an arrow wound in his throat shows how he lost his life. His hair waves in the water, tight curls loose from rows of braids that follow the curve of his skull.

Folasade turns to me, eyes wide, hands trembling. "There are too many."

As the man sinks closer, I pull her away, closer to me. "Wait, look."

His breastplate gleams in the muted light, but we can still make out the symbols stamped into the leather. Eight slash marks with concentric circles on top, each whorl representing a different warlord, the emblem of the only warriors who can rival orisas.

Iku, Arun, Ofo, Egba, Oran, Epe, Ewon, and Ese.

"The ajogun," I whisper.

CHAPTER THREE

FOLASADE SHRINKS AWAY from the dead, allowing me to pull her backward, putting space between the men who so clearly pledged their allegiance to the eight demon warlords. From loss, disease, and torment, the anti-gods are responsible for different afflictions, all bringing disharmony to earth and all intent on the ruination of humankind. Iku, as Death, roams freely, but the others are kept in their dark realm lest they bring about the end of the world.

Folasade tries to wriggle away from me as I clutch at her, fingertips digging into her skin. I have never seen someone who worships the ajogun up close, and my heartbeat thunders in my ears. To see such a pledge, marked so openly, scares me more than the thought of spending the rest of my life in the black cold. Some people choose darkness, but they do not often flaunt it. Those who submit to the ajogun can't be blessed, their withered souls left uncollected. I shudder when I think of a soul not returning home.

"Who has killed them?" I ask. Looking up at the sea above us, we watch as splinters of their ship slip beneath the waves, following the bodies down to the murkier part of the water. With a push of my tail, I surge upward, only to be yanked back by Folasade.

"Simidele, don't. It's too dangerous."

I look down at her hand wrapped around my arm and shrug her off. The presence of men supporting the ajogun . . . it twists in my guts. It doesn't feel right. Besides, I think as I scan the water hurriedly for the slink of squid, if I am quick, no one will know. I am bound to Olokun only on my word. I'll go back.

"You can stay here," I say. With shaking fingers, I reach for the light that filters through the waves above. The slip of water is like warm satin as I swim upward, and when I break through the waves, it is to an endless sky that mirrors the sea in its shade of azure. All at once the sun and the air hit me and I gasp, drinking in the smell of salt and the scorch and char of seared wood. The sea lifts me up as giant waves weave into one another, a watery blanket of heaving blues. As I'm lowered and then raised once more, I blink slowly, taking it all in, forgetting for a few seconds the death below me.

The sun is hot on my face, bright orange behind my eyelids. It is all I have been craving and more. A snatch of light and sky before I return to the Land of the Dead.

Folasade surfaces beside me, gulping the warm air in shallow breaths. She jerks her head from side to side and stops. I follow her panicked gaze to the waves filled with the shattered remains of a ship. The cracked mast floats on the swells, timber bobbing about in ugly shards, the scent of burning thick on the breeze.

Smoke coils up into the twilight sky, heavy on the still, warm air. The crackle of the fire and its leaping red-and-yellow flames make me sleepy. I lean back against bàbá as the people of Oyo-Ile chatter around us, my stomach growling at the scent of fried plantain. I turn to ask my father if we can buy some, and then I see her. Ìyá pauses at the mouth of the marketplace, her black wrapper camouflaging her against the night, its scarlet swirls mimicking the central fire. My mother always matches her outfits to her stories, and red and black can only mean one thing. I eye her wrapper, my mouth going dry. Tonight, ìyá is not smiling. I pull my father's arms around me, burrowing back against him.

"There are, and have always been, forces in opposition." The crowd falls silent at the sound of my mother's voice as she makes her entrance. "This has always been the way. This is life. We keep the balance through ebo—what we give. This manifests in many forms, be it a choice, a prized animal, part of our crops, the offerings we place on our altars." Her arms are held stiffly by her sides, eyes hooded as she comes to a stop in the center of the clearing. "We give these things up, say these prayers, to keep peace in our world, such is their importance."

Murmurs ripple through the people gathered; nods come from the elders who sit on small stools, their children and grandchildren gathered close. I feel bàbá shift, his grip tightening on me.

"If we do not, then the ajogun will draw nearer, always thirsting to be set free from their realm, hungry to wreak havoc on ours. While we earn our blessings, it is equally important for us to remember the dangers, the reasons we make such sacrifices. What comes with the good is also the bad." My mother pauses. Shouts of agreement echo among the crowd as she lifts her hands into the air and waits for silence. "Esu keeps this balance, and so, even though we have to bear the burden of his trickery, his actions are what counts. We all know

24

what is at stake if Esu does not placate the ajogun, but just in case, tonight's story will help us to remember that. It is not a tale of what has been, but of what could be."

A thick quiet blankets the people now as my mother stalks closer to her listeners, her eyes black with the night.

"Here is a story. Story it is." I watch as she looks up at the glitter of stars strewn across the sky. "In years from now, this land will have new leaders. They will choose to forget that their ancestors and orisas are still there to guide them. The leaders will take on a new belief and most people will shun their ancestral orisas, even changing their names to distance themselves. New influences will push out the old, until one day, they will scoff at the ways of Ifá and any that give orisas respect and thus power." My mother sweeps her gaze over the crowd before her. "Esu will lose patience when people do not give him the honor he deserves for keeping the ajogun at bay, and he will withdraw, letting the warlords creep closer to our realm." I shiver at her words as gasps spread among the listeners. "The ajogun, using this neglect, will trick the weak into worshipping their malevolence, and finally into releasing them."

"I don't like this story," I whisper, my voice quivering.

"I know, but it is an important one," murmurs my father as a breeze rushes through the clearing, licking at the fire, pushing the flames higher.

"Iku already roams freely, claiming souls naturally with Olodumare's blessing, but when this happens he will be joined by Arun, Ofo, Egba, Oran, Epe, Ewon, and Ese." As my mother speaks each name, shadows leap up, carving her face into a mask of cold foreboding. "They will ravage the world, destroying each part in their own way, claiming the souls of all they kill. Disease, affliction, wars.

Brother will turn on brother, sister on sister, as they fight for what is left."

"Bàbá, I want to go home," I say, turning to burrow into my father's chest.

"You must listen, ọmọbìnrin ìn mi, it is important. The story will be done soon. . . ."

I twist one of my plaits tight around my finger, tugging it gently.

"The leaders will curse their stupidity when the land and people fall," my mother continues, "but it will be too late. No one will be safe, not even orisas." My mother lowers her head, standing in the center of the clearing. "The ajogun's entry to our world means its end." There is silence as she slowly raises her hands, palms held out to the moon above. "I tell this to you now to help you keep faith in Ifá, in our lands and in orisas. In us." Her gaze rakes over the crowd, falling on me. I know she can see the fear that stains my face in the firelight when she straightens up and pastes a smile onto her lips. But it doesn't show her dimples, and her warning has nestled deep inside me like a thin splinter.

"Remember this has not come to pass, and will not, if we stay strong and do not forsake our ancestors or ourselves." She claps once, as if to break the spell, and aims her smile around the market-place. "Let us remember our resilience and loyalty. Our strength is in our convictions and in our faith."

The mood is tight, a stretched-out tension that holds us all. Ìyá sways to the edges of the crowd and plucks a skewer of spicy beef from a young boy, taking a bite and grinning, her lips shining with grease. "We take nothing for granted and we praise all that we have. And now, let me tell you another story to end our evening. One of abundance and joy."

Her action seems to release the people from their fearful stupor, and they cheer at her radiance, the story of the ajogun filed away at the back of their minds.

But not mine. It squats there, ugly and heavy.

With narrowed eyes and my hair cloaking my shoulders in heavy, wet curls, I look about me, shuddering at the memory of my mother's story. Sea gulls swoop down, cawing at one another and then soaring back behind low clouds. Light spills over gentle swells that belie the violence I have seen beneath the surface. It seems that after so long below the sea, just the air can now bring on one of my visions. The recollection fills me with a flood of disquiet. I twist, my tail flaring, searching for those who killed the men pledged to the ajogun.

The only remains of the destroyed ship are scraps of sails that drape the waves, catching on occasional blackened timbers. A fin slices through the debris, a shark accompanied by others searching for an easy meal. They lurk, tails thrashing, as I turn my back on their shadowy forms, not wanting to know if they find anyone.

And then I see it.

Another ship. The victor, I think.

It's near enough for me to make out the solid wood of the hull, and the large sails that are being hoisted, ready to catch the eastward wind. Figures scurry among the rigging and I squint, swimming closer just as Folasade catches up to me.

"Simidele!" she hisses, moving alongside me. "We need to swim back down now. You know this!"

I do, but I can't bring myself to look away, watching the ship prepare to set sail. Something pulls at me, my stomach twisting in a spasm as the hull cleaves through the waves. My tail curls beneath me as I clutch at my waist, skin hot in the chill of the water. The ship, I think. I need to get closer.

Folasade gasps in panic as I start toward the vessel, but before she can grab me, I dive under the waves, knifing through the swells, just deep enough that I can't be seen. The crack of the sail is loud when I surface, and a call breaks through the constant murmur of waves as two people move into view.

The slither of nerves and something else, something like excitement, tug at me, spurring me on as I float closer still. Seconds slide by as I press my palms down on the weight of the water, trying to push myself up to see better. Both have their backs to me. One of them is impossibly tall with the sun gleaming on a bald head, and next to him is someone who makes my chest tighten. Even if I didn't recognize the set of his shoulders, I can see the twist of scars that line his back. Permanent reminders of the injuries he received on the òyìnbó's ship before he was thrown overboard.

Kola.

The sea ripples, a wave raising me higher just as I feel as if I have swallowed the sun and the moon. For a moment, I think I am dreaming, that coming from the deep so quickly has disoriented me in the way it does humans.

The slink in my gut spreads throughout my body, lighting up every nerve, my heart thrumming. As Kola turns and faces the sea, large hand shielding his face from the sun, I drag in another breath, trying to calm myself. Kola leans forward over the side of the ship, and then he reels back and places one hand against his stomach. As he bends over, I wonder if he's feeling the same intensity that I am. If he knows that I am close by. How else would we be in the same part of the sea at the same time? And then his eyes rake over the water and for a moment, I swear he sees me.

Feeling as if my throat is closing up, I swim closer. Folasade calls something to me, but I am only focused on Kola, and soon I am close enough to see that his hair is longer now, a tiny cloud of black curls that I know would smell of coconut oil and sunlight.

Just as the wake of the ship buffets me about, spinning me in the water, Kola turns away and begins speaking to Bem, gesturing with a sharp jab at the sea. "I don't care . . . something . . . knew I . . . come here."

I strain, trying to catch the rest of his words, but they are caught and swallowed by the slap of the waves and the constant cawing of the sea gulls. My shoulders slump beneath the waterline as Folasade's hand encircles my arm.

"Come," she whispers, the word gentle.

But I don't move. I want to see Kola's face properly. Just once. If I can see him one more time, then I will return to the deep with that image if nothing else. I wait, bobbing on the new crest of a cold wave as Folasade's grip tightens.

Please, just turn.

Bem throws his hands up and stomps off, disappearing. But Kola, as if hearing my thoughts, spins around.

All at once my chest feels as if it has been cleaved open. Even from this distance I can see the curve of Kola's cheekbones, his muscled arms as he clenches the rail and peers down at the water. A frown thickens Kola's brow, and his lips are pressed tight, no softness there now. I remember the fit of his body against mine as his soul sparkled between us, the wounds Esu had inflicted on him too severe for him to live. The slip of his hot skin as I chanted ragged prayers and pleas, anything that I thought might bring him back from death.

Might bring him back to me.

My hands pushed against his chest, the rings shining bright circles of gold on the twins' fingers. As Ibeji incarnate, Kola's brother and sister had healing powers that rejuvenated his body, and my pleas and prayers helped guide his soul back to him.

I could show myself to him, I think. Speak to him again. It would give me something to hold on to when I go back. Something to make the sunless depths easier. I open my mouth, Kola's name forming on the roll of my tongue, but then I close it. What good would it do? It would change nothing.

I watch as Kola turns, his face drawn slack with disappointment, shoulders slumped. This is for the best, I tell myself as he calls out to those on board and the ship bears east, pulling away fast.

• • •

"Come quickly, before Olokun finds out you have gone."

I know Folasade is right, but I let myself crest a wave as Kola sails away, a sharp numbness spreading through me. The ship grows smaller, cutting through the sea. I watch until it is just a speck in the blue, blinking until I can no longer see even that.

Folasade sighs and takes my hand. Overhead, a slice of translucent moon can be seen, a pale crescent that shares the sky with the sun. In the distance, the horizon is a stretch of darker water, flattening ahead, luring me with its promise of land beyond it. Oko and the Oyo Kingdom. Something other than the glacial ebony depths that wait beneath me. I am glad that Kola will live a full life, even if the thought of him living it without me hurts.

"Come, Simi," whispers Folasade, her voice softer than I've ever heard it before. She tugs me again and we dip down, the water swallowing us in one draft. Sinking, I let myself fall through the gradients of blue, from light to dark. Herring and mackerel and sea scallops dart around us, flashes of silver scales and flat eyes watching me as I descend far deeper than they ever will. When the blue turns to black, I close my eyes against the shadows.

"Simidele." At my name, I open my eyes and try to smile as Folasade takes my face in her hands, fingers cold on the slip of my skin. "I can't come any farther."

Below us the darkness seems to pulse. It is now that I let myself think of Olokun. Of what he will say if he finds out I have left, even fleetingly. I tip my chin and squeeze my fingers so that they don't tremble, knowing what I will tell him. That I didn't leave, not really. That I made my choice and I do not break my promises. But Folasade is right. If Olokun finds her in the deep, there is no telling what he will do.

"Thank you," I say. "For coming this far. For reminding me."

"I would do it again." Folasade's lips curve downward in a sad smile. "When you asked about Mother Yemoja before, I was about to tell you the other reason for my visit." She takes my hands, our fingers entwined. "There is something that she wanted me to ask."

I tighten my hold, my curls floating around us like black clouds in the water. There is an edge to her voice, a waver of panic. "What is it?"

"The remains of the battle earlier. These are not the first.

Yemoja is deeply troubled. Oya has told her of more fighting on land. There is great unrest between the Nupe and Oyo kingdoms."

"People will always create wars," I answer, even as nerves spark inside me. "It is part of humanity."

"We know. But these have intensified. With their sudden increase in unusual violence, Yemoja is concerned that, somehow, the ajogun are involved." Folasade looks toward the surface, her eyes flickering. "And now, after what we have seen . . ."

I think of the men who sank around us. Of their insignia and their obvious pledge to the ajogun.

"Esu keeps the ajogun in check," I say, pushing a firmness into my words. "He stops their influence and prevents anyone from freeing them."

Folasade moves closer to me. "He does. But Esu has not been seen since you entered the Land of the Dead. Yemoja wanted me to ask you if the trickster is still imprisoned by Olokun."

My mind fills with seething waves and the stark jut of rocks, with Esu's palace on a splinter of land, its topmost chamber walls open to the sea. With the riddle I used to distract him and my lunge, which led to our plummet. The cold burst of current that welcomed us and the way I dragged the trickster deeper. Deep enough for Olokun to surge from the raven water, his golden chain no longer hidden by the gloom. I watched while he wrapped the thick links around Esu, speaking words in the orisa's ear so that he might breathe in the sea, binding him until he turned him over to the Supreme Creator to face justice.

"But Olokun gave Esu to Olodumare. That was what was agreed." My voice rises as I twist my fingers together, knuckles a pale brown. "He told me that the Supreme Creator would set Esu on the right path again. Remind him of his duty and place."

"It may be what you agreed," says Folasade; her words are needle-thin and I feel their sting. "But can you be certain that this is what happened?"

"Olokun promised," I answer. But my words are thick with an unease that even I can hear.

"Think, Simidele. Did you see Esu released?"

I shake my head, remembering my first days in Olokun's realm. The icy murk that sank into my very bones and the uncertainty about my role in such a dark place. *Why would he keep Esu?* And then I think of Olokun's messages of penitence that the trickster did not pass on to the Supreme Creator. *Would Olokun keep Esu imprisoned out of spite? To punish him?*

"Did you see him released?" repeats Folasade, gripping the tops of my arms now, her nails pressing into my flesh. "Because if Esu is still bound beneath the sea, then the ajogun's power could be harnessed and the anti-gods are at risk of breaking loose. And then . . ."

I know, I want to say. I know what will happen. I shiver, thinking of Arun, Ofo, Epe, and the other warriors. If they break free, they will destroy everything and everyone.

"I'll find out," I say, pushing my rising panic down. "I'll ask Olokun."

"No. If Olokun has misled you, then he is unlikely to admit it." Folasade pauses, eyes darting down to the blackness spread beneath us. "I worry that you have forgotten all he is capable of. Why he wears the chain he does, and everything he might do in order to escape the confines of the bottom of the seas and oceans."

"I haven't," I say. *Have I been foolish to trust such an orisa?* "I know what he is capable of, the same as you."

Folasade twists her lips to the side, a fold of lines between her eyebrows. "Look for Esu," she urges. "But if you find him, do not act rashly. I will be back, this time with Yemoja. If Olokun has Esu, she will know what to do."

"But what about the accord?"

"I'll find you." She peers about us in small, panicked movements. "The others will wait at the halfway point between the top and the bottom of the sea, where the water goes from blue to black."

I nod my agreement as I clasp Folasade to me one last time. *What if I am wrong?* I stare over the curve of Folasade's shoulder and into the blackness beyond. *What if I have bound myself for lies?* When I promised Olokun my servitude, I believed that I was saving the lives of Kola, my friends, and all those in Oko, but if Esu has not been able to fulfill his duty, if he has not been overseeing the offerings to the ajogun, then none of it matters.

The ajogun could break free.

And it will be all my fault.

CHAPTER FOUR

WHEN THE ARCHWAY of bones rises from the silt, I think about Esu being imprisoned in the Land of the Dead, and I swallow evenly. The anglerfish watch me pass, their huge jaws full of thin teeth as long as my arm. Trying not to flinch, I use the light they provide to stop myself from scraping against the rocks draped with silt on the ocean floor.

I swim through the thickening gloom, drawn by the ominous glow of Olokun's palace. The temperature falls as I plunge back into a world I have forced myself to adapt to, hating every dark moment of it. Before, I knew that my sacrifice was worth it. And now . . . Now the thought that I may have done all this, and only made things worse, won't leave my mind.

I enter the twist of murky tunnels, hands shaking. I've been gone longer than I thought, and the pull of a slow cold current tells me I am late in serving Olokun his meal. The orisa remembers overhearing fishermen speak of how the rulers of kingdoms on land are treated, feasts served with every spiced meat and any fruit that the Aláàfin desires. Since I arrived, Olokun has had me perform some semblance of this; while I serve his favorite delicacies, he sits on his throne, plucking whatever I have to offer from thin stone trays.

I hurry to the small hollow that connects to the main chamber, glad that I have already spent time gathering what the orisa deems edible. The space is filled with stone jars of various sizes, salvaged from tributes to Olokun and used to store food. I pull out the ones I know are full and reach inside another, larger container for the swordfish I caught yesterday. Holding them all precariously, I hurry to the throne room. The quicker I get this done, the sooner I can search for Esu.

Olokun is looking down at his tail, caudal fin swishing gently, his purple scales flashing in the glow of the moss and squid. As I swim toward him, I look for signs of anger, or knowledge of my absence. Carefully, I offer the lidded stone bowl to the orisa, retreating a small distance as Olokun grasps it easily in one hand. He doesn't say a word.

While his silence is nothing new, I feel a different type of unease. Does he know I have been to the surface? I don't touch my own bowl, waiting until he lifts the lid on his, revealing the small black and red fish eggs nestled inside. They glisten as Olokun scoops them out, quickly guiding them to his mouth before they disperse in the water. I pluck out a few of my own. He will want to see me eating, to have company in consuming a meal.

Olokun finishes the fish roe, watching his sea horses dart around him, their tiny translucent wings and fragile bodies decorating the water. The creatures are always within reach, a myriad of colors ranging from red to yellow to the black-and-white stripes of the zebra sea horse. They settle on the edges of his coral throne, even resting lightly on his shoulders before moving away, faint palpitations in the water small signs of their presence. Some glide down to the arms of his throne, snatching at the tiny shreds of shrimp the orisa leaves for them, before soaring away, small tails curled delicately.

"Tell me." Olokun's voice booms and I suck in a breath. "Will there be more than scraps to eat, or would you have me starve today? This is not how the Aláàfins and Obas are treated on land."

We are not on land, I want to say, but I choke it down and set my own pot aside. Sliding the golden dagger from the braids at my crown, I chop the swordfish into chunks, skewering them on its own razor-sharp bill before arranging them on a flat slice of rock. Reaching into another jar, I pull out brownish-green kelp, samphire, and red dulse. Edging the fish with the seaweed, I weigh them down with heavy oysters and purplish-black mussels, my mind whirring.

If Esu is imprisoned somewhere, surely it would be in a place close to Olokun. The circular hollow of the hall is familiar to me, but as I peer around the orisa, examining a tunnel entrance, I realize that the labyrinthine twists and turns of the rest of the palace are not.

Olokun watches his tiny sea horses flit about him, only looking at me as I present the food to him. With large hands, he grasps the swordfish's bill and clamps his teeth on the fillets. He gestures to the oysters and I lift one, taking the shell in my hands and cracking it against the rock. I pry open the curved seam and pass Olokun the oyster before doing the same with a mussel, extracting the orange meat from its hard casing. As the orisa tips the food into his mouth, the thick column of his throat flexing, I chew mine, the faint tang of mushrooms reminding me of forests and moist black earth. Olokun regards me, eyebrows knit tightly.

"What is it, Simidele?" He pauses, using the swordfish bill to pick between his teeth. "You seem . . . not yourself."

I lower my eyes. "I'm fine."

"Then eat." Olokun gestures to the food.

I pick up a strip of samphire and bite into the crisp green stalk. The food sticks to the roof of my mouth and I have to swallow several times before it goes down. Folasade's words still ricochet in my mind and I watch the orisa as he selects the dulse seaweed and pushes its redness between his lips. Would Olokun put the lives he mourns at risk? Would he hold me to a bargain that he himself has not kept?

"Do you hope . . ." I trail off, unsure how to form my words in a way that will cause less offense.

Silver flares in the black of Olokun's pupils. He leans back against his throne, the swordfish bill still in his hand. "Do I hope what, Simidele?" The orisa's rumble reverberates around the hall. A flurry of sea horses scatter at his sudden movement, colored tails bright.

It feels as if some of the samphire is stuck in my throat and I cough lightly, a hand to my neck. I should leave the conversation there, feign forgetfulness and help myself to more cold morsels of food. But the words leave my mouth before I can stop myself. "Do you hope that by burying the dead, the act will spur Obatala on to absolve you of what you did? That the more you bury, the more you pray over, you will be forgiven and unchained?"

Olokun leans forward, his eyes on me. "I am adhering to my agreement with Yemoja." The orisa's cape of pearls shifts around his giant shoulders, glittering in the near gloom, but his posture is easy, loose. "Besides, I would see the bodies of whoever dies in the sea buried. Their remains given proper respect." Olokun shifts, holding out the swordfish bill and spearing more kelp from the stone tray. "And if Obatala sees this and . . . recognizes the change in me, then so be it." The orisa smiles as a tiny golden sea horse floats toward him. It perches on his hand, tail coiled around his forefinger. "But do not worry for me. I will be free. One way or another. And then, so shall you."

One way or another. My stomach churns. Keeping Esu from binding the ajogun and then using him to bargain with would be a definite way for Olokun to gain his freedom. The more I think of the trickster imprisoned, the more it begins to make sense.

Olokun rises from his throne in a quick fluid motion. His large hands snatch at my wrist and he pulls me closer, bending over me, nostrils suddenly flaring. I stifle a gasp of pain, heart slamming against my rib cage as I lower my gaze.

"I know that it must take its toll. All of this. I . . ." Olokun's voice is firm but without anger, and when the orisa loosens his grip on me, I dare to slide a look up at him. He moves away, taking his hand from my arm, revealing delicate bruises on my skin before they heal at once. "I thought that perhaps you could widen your search for tributes. Not as deep, perhaps? I am grateful for the honor you show your promise, but I know that you often miss your world from before." Olokun doesn't look at me, reaching instead for a few sea horses that glide toward him. "It has not escaped me that you have found it hard to adjust to being so deep, to the task I have taken. I would not see you completely unhappy."

I hold my fingers to the soft skin of my wrist, still feeling the sharp dig of his grip. *He doesn't know what Folasade told me about Esu.* I try to keep this in mind even as his words prickle at me. *I will be free. One way or another.*

"I would like that," I answer, reaching for the tray once more, dipping my head to shield my determined expression. If Esu is hidden down here, then I will find him.

. . .

I lean on the moss in the small scooped-out hollow of my resting space, fingers looped around a rock that casts a bright yellow light on my surroundings. Olokun gave the sunstone to me when I first arrived; having spent a thousand years here, he knew his way in the darkness, whereas I struggled to navigate my way around his palace.

I think of Olokun's sudden generosity, offering me a little more freedom. Was that born of guilt? What if he has kept the trickster locked away down here, waiting for the right time to use him to bargain with? I curl my fingers tighter around the sunstone and rise, heading toward the main tunnel.

The slinking lengths of passageway are a warren of cooled lava and coral, their coldness enough to make me shiver. As I dip into the first of them, I hold up the sunstone. I haven't explored most of the tunnels that make up Olokun's palace. When I first arrived, the orisa advised against it, citing the unpredictability of navigating them, hinting that they were not quite empty. Imagining deadly currents and strange creatures, I always turned away from the misshapen entranceways, not wanting to know what I would find in them.

Now I run my free hand over the rippled walls, their sides reminding me of dried honey, steadying myself as the blackness all but swallows me. I should be used to the lack of light, but the thought of what it might hide still scares me.

These lower levels are more tangled than those above. And

much darker. This far down, the cold has a taste to it. A frigid tang of salt laced with rot. I hold a hand to the dagger in my hair, checking that the golden blade is still there. I've not had cause to use it for anything other than preparing fish for Olokun, but I still know its weight and how to wield it.

I move slowly, then pause at a rush of water just in front of the gaping maw of a tunnel entrance bigger than most. Something slithers within the thick darkness as I lean forward, and tendrils of fear tighten around my spine. Obsidian shadows shift as my heart stutters. *Something is there,* I think as I pluck the golden dagger from my plaits, just as two tentacles shoot from the midnight blackness. One wraps around my arm, squeezing tight, as I open my mouth to scream. The other limb slides against the skin and scales of my waist.

Small hooks graze my side as I push the rising terror down, remembering my commands. *Let go!* I think, my blade beneath the tentacle as I steady myself, trying to ignore the bursts of pain. I still can't see the main body of the squid, but its beak glimmers in the weak light of the sunstone. Razor-sharp and ready. This squid is smaller than the giant ones I sometimes see crouched over the archway of bones, but it's still large enough to be a problem if it doesn't heed my commands.

Let go, I repeat. The limb around my waist remains tight for several seconds before loosening, but I keep my dagger there, pressed against the orange skin. *Let me go now, or you'll lose your flesh,* I add, and increase the pressure, the keen-edged blade cutting into the squid's tentacle. I don't want to kill it if I can help it.

After a moment, it retracts, sinking into the darkness. I back away, my torn skin healing as I grip the sunstone tighter and turn into the lower tunnels. The temperature plummets as I swim deeper, and I shiver even harder, causing the light to shake. The tunnel I come across next is narrower and more brightly illuminated than the others. I can just make out a pulsing glow in a shade of green that reminds me of polished jade.

Something scuttles beneath me and I jerk, causing shadows to leap up the rippled walls, their fractured outlines matching my heartbeat. I move the sunstone wildly until I see a small red crab. I lean against the passageway, taking a moment to calm myself. *It's not Olokun, and you've dealt with the squid,* I tell myself. *Which means that the light is something else.*

Or someone else.

I swim forward cautiously, moving through the gloom and murk, which slowly dissolve with a combination of the sunstone I brandish and the greenish light that grows brighter.

The tunnel twists once more until it reveals a phosphorescent dead end. Small bumps pepper my flesh as I peer ahead. Stalactites and hardened lava have created an almost-room. Green seaweed grows along small fissures, pulsing with a strange lime-colored light. I draw closer, my other hand clutching my dagger. The natural rock formations have formed bars so that the space resembles a cage.

And then a body slams against the thick lengths of rock, and an angry scream is released. The noise creates a wave of sound that forces me backward and I tumble, bashing into the wall, dropping the sunstone. The rage-filled roar swirls in the water as I scramble about, snatching up the stone light with trembling fingers.

As I straighten up, the scream stops, and I lift my head slowly to meet the pure silver gaze of Esu.

CHAPTER FIVE

LONG FINGERS WRAP around the bars as Esu opens his mouth, bellowing again. My stomach roils at the sight of the trickster thrashing his head from side to side, plaits whipping through the water. Esu pauses only to ram his face against the stalactites, metallic eyes on mine.

Yemoja was right.

I press my palms against my chest, breath and voice caught tight.

"So shocked, little fish?" The orisa's face ripples into a cold smile of sharp teeth and full lips.

"You should . . ." My voice is faint and weak, pathetic even to my own ears. I gather myself, realizing that I am gripping my dagger so tightly that my nails dig into the meat of my hand. "You shouldn't be here."

Olokun hasn't kept his side of the bargain. All these months I have spent in the glacial darkness have been for nothing. How could I have been so naïve? I choke down the hot shame that rises in my throat as I draw back, not taking my eyes off the orisa.

Esu raises his eyebrows, perfect arcs of black, before he throws his head back, releasing swells of wild laughter.

"And yet I am." The orisa pushes his face harder against the bars. "Whose fault is that?"

"Olokun said he would return you to Olodumare," I whisper. "That the Supreme Creator would judge you, remind you of your duties."

"That Olodumare would punish me? You know that this would only be fleeting. I am *needed*." Esu chuckles and lifts his face from the mineral rock. "Besides, look where I am. Olokun gave me over to no one."

"But he promised." I can hear bewilderment and shame in the cracking of my voice.

"Olokun knows better than to give away his only bargaining tool," says Esu. "For over a thousand years he has been chained far beneath the sea. Do not think that he truly believes that his duties of burying the dead and praying over their remains will absolve him."

"But—"

"Olokun knows the punishment he endures will never end. Unless . . ." Esu's hands wrap around the stalactites. The large ruby of his necklace, flanked by smaller spheres of onyx, bumps and sways against his chest. "Well, unless he has something to bargain with."

I approach slowly, cautious of the orisa's long reach and the ire he most likely still has for me, for what I've done to him.

"You?"

"What else?" Esu backs farther away now and I drift closer still. His eyes gleam from the murk of his cell. "If I am not there to keep the anti-gods at bay? My worth increases beyond measure and Olokun has leverage."

"Wouldn't Olodumare know this? That you are missing . . ."

"The Supreme Creator knows what I tell them. That is all. They do not need to concern themselves with anything else." Esu puffs out his chest. "I am trusted to be the mouthpiece for all they need to know."

I think of the ajogun, of their gloating over sickness and pain and death. My mother's words echo in my mind. *They will ravage the world, destroying each part in their own way. Disease, affliction, wars. Brother will turn on brother, sister on sister, as they fight for what is left.* I swim closer still as Esu slides backward, stooping and dipping his head so that it doesn't scrape the top of the cavern. "What do you think has been happening?" I hate the waver in my tone, but I can't keep my voice even. "On land."

"What do you think, little fish?" hisses Esu before folding his arms across his chest. "How about this? I will answer your question and you will release me."

I shake my head, thinking about how angry Olokun will be once he knows I have found Esu. But if he hasn't held up his side of the bargain . . . why should I? "I . . ."

Esu sighs, annoyance flashing in his eyes, but he beckons me closer anyway. "Here," he says, impatience in his crooked gesture. "Come. If you want the answer to your question."

The orisa watches me carefully, holding out the ruby of his necklace through the bars. I glide forward as he points to the jewel that spins between us, turned burgundy in the gloom. I stay as far away as possible, stretched fingers reaching for the gem, and when they graze the ruby the dark waters around me fall away.

The earth is scorched. Swathes of dust are spun in a giant whirlwind, spiraling up into a sky that presses hungrily against the land. There is nothing living as far as I can see, only dead lands draped with the ash of those who have fallen. I swallow, tongue thick, as eight silhouettes appear in the distance. Even though I can't make out their faces, their elongated limbs and the tilt of their heads fill me with a creeping fear. The largest pulls away from the rest and lopes toward me. Iku, the only one able to traverse both realms at whim. I shudder at the black pits of his eyes, turning away and trying to run, but the ground sucks at my feet, pulling me down into the hold of a dying land.

"This can't have happened already," I gasp, jerking away, still feeling the terror at the approaching warlords.

"Not yet," admits Esu. "But it will. Unless I am free to bind the ajogun. Only I can placate them, cajole them into remaining in their realm. You know this." Esu's voice is quiet, his words firm. "And if I do not, and they are released? Then anarchy will reign. For orisas and humans, the ajogun do not care. They will not be content until all is ruined. Until all is dead."

I sag against the stalactites, nearly dropping both my weapon and the sunstone. "Olokun is going to wait until there is chaos on earth before revealing he has you."

"Exactly. And then Obatala will have no choice but to accede to his demands." Esu watches me, letting the ruby fall back against his chest. "Olokun does not care about anything other than being free. So the question is, what will you do now, little fish? Considering that this is all your fault."

I flinch from the bars and the silver black of Esu's gaze. "I was only doing what I needed to. To save Yemoja and Kola. And the others."

Esu laughs again, this time softer but still as insidious. He leans back against the far wall, the green glow from the seaweed creeping over his cell, highlighting the broad planes of his face.

"That may well be, but it doesn't change the fact that here we are." He lifts both hands palm up and gazes around him in mock surprise. "And I am imprisoned rather than offering what it takes to keep the ajogun placid. To keep them from destroying us all."

"That's not what I wanted." I shove myself against the bars, a sudden hot anger flaring in my chest. The thought of what will happen, caused by my actions, burrows deep. "You know this!"

Esu is quicker than I can see. A blur and swirl of the water and he appears in front of me. With one powerful hand, he snakes his fingers around my throat, clasping the skin and muscles and veins tightly. I struggle in his viselike grip as the orisa tilts his head closer.

"It does not matter if that was what you wanted," he growls. "If that was what you intended. It is what has happened, and why we are both here right now."

I open my mouth in a shallow gasp, fighting to wriggle free. Just as I fumble for my dagger, Esu releases me and I fall backward, cushioned only by the water.

"What would you have me do?" I rasp, hand flying to the bruises that circle my throat, smoothing the skin that is already beginning to heal. But I know the answer. The dead men I saw in the water are proof that the ajogun have worshippers who would do what it takes to free them. There is only one thing I *can* do, and the thought of it layers on top of my dread of the warlords.

"Release me," answers Esu, holding his arms out, the spread of them so wide that his fingertips touch each side of his cell. "Return me to the land, sky, and sun, and I will do what I have always done to keep the ajogun at bay."

Esu smiles but I still don't speak. We both know that I have no choice, but I think back to all the orisa has done and the way he attacked Kola. Even now I can still remember my terror at the blood that soaked through Kola's wrapper. The red that stained the lines of my palm, clinging and drying in the cracks.

Esu regards me coolly, bringing his hands together, nails pointed at the ceiling of black stone. "You're wondering if I would betray you. What I would truly do. To you. To others."

It is as if he has hooked the thoughts out of my mind. Yemoja did not tell me about the decree with the Supreme Creator; Olokun has not kept his side of the bargain. Why would Esu be any better? "You nearly killed Kola." My words are small yet hard as I narrow my eyes. "Why would I believe you? Trickster orisa, twister of thoughts and words, capable of taking any form, taking from *anyone*."

"You need me." Esu grins now, lips stretched to reveal his large teeth. "Lives will be lost. Have already been lost. You know that unless you help me escape from here, the ajogun will wreak havoc on earth before Olokun even bothers to bargain with Obatala."

Folasade's mention of the Oyo Kingdom and of the neighboring Nupe returns to me. Thousands live in their lands. I feel my expression crumple, anger fading into fear and a crushing guilt.

I tip my chin, ignoring the uncertainty that cuts at me. "You ask me to put my trust in you after everything you've done."

"I do."

"Even though you were willing to forsake lives to gain more power?"

"This is true. I did commit acts I should not have. But I sought power to make the world right." Esu is silent a moment before flexing his shoulders, the tips of his braids scraping the smooth skin. "Think on this also, little fish. I inhabit this world, too. If it falls . . . what is there for me?" The trickster's voice is quieter now, the silver melting from his eyes. "Besides, you cannot escape the fact that unless I am free to bind them, the ajogun can be released. You do not have a choice."

He is right. Tears sting my eyes, but I blink rapidly, trying not to let them spill. "When? How close are the ajogun?"

The trickster pauses, mouth moving as he counts. "If I have the tides correct, then the moon will be full in around two days' time. We have until then."

My eyes widen as I hold a hand to my throat, panic at my decision caught in the flesh and skin as I struggle to swallow.

"Simidele," says Esu, and I start at my name from his mouth. "Little fish, come here." He beckons me closer. "I respect your hesitancy. Only a fool would not be wary of what I say, what I am capable of. But I will give you something. An offering that holds me to my word."

I stay where I am, looking at the curl of Esu's fingers, thinking of the way he grabbed me. He lifts his hand to his neck, unclasping his chain, the ruby glistening even in the murk. "Take it. Keep it. For as long as you have it, I am bound by my word to you." Holding the red stone in his palm, he presents the jewel to me.

I don't move, my mind going over what he has offered, thinking of the vision the ruby gave me.

"This gem is linked to my ability to bind the ajogun. A gesture of trust. Take it. Keep it until it is time for me to use it." Esu dangles the necklace between the bars. His voice lowers even more. "They will not stop. Not until the world is in ruins. Not unless I can strengthen the binds and keep them at bay."

I've been here for half a year now, which means Esu has been imprisoned for just as long. I shudder when I think of how near the ajogun must be, of the malignant energy that may already be harnessed. All because I used one orisa to help me defeat another.

I feel my shoulders slump. There is no choice. I slide the dagger back into the braids at my crown and accept the jewel. Esu smiles, his teeth bone white in the midnight water, and I try not to tremble. I think of putting the chain around my neck, but it doesn't feel right to have it hanging next to Yemoja's sapphire. Instead, I wrap it several times around my left wrist, where the ruby hangs like a bulbous drop of blood.

CHAPTER SIX

THE STALACTITE BARS are hardened mineral deposits that have made a perfect prison. I give them a tug, despite Esu's annoyed gaze. He sighs, twisting his neck from side to side, slouched against the wall.

"I know I am greatly reduced in this water, but if I could not break through them, do you truly think you can?"

I ignore him, running my fingers over the places where the stalactites protrude from the rest of the rock. The surface is rough but without seams, there are no weaknesses, and my frustration grows. I hit one, the water swirling in the green light, my knuckles splitting as they strike stone. Trails of the glowing seaweed float around me like long sinewy limbs. I freeze, an idea forming in my head. I spin away from Esu.

"Where are you going, little fish?"

But I don't answer, swimming hard and fast through the slink of tunnels, holding the sunstone before me to light the way. When I reach the larger passageway, I slow down, peering into the inky gloom. The fear I felt last time is replaced with a cautious respect.

Come. My command is swallowed by the black, but something shifts, shadow on shadow. *Follow me.*

A thick tentacle, dark orange in the light of the sunstone, slithers from the entranceway, curling up in the space between us. The tentacle is lined with hooks and suction cups; it's easy to see why some fishermen call them red devils. The limb is followed by another as the squid propels itself from its hiding place and reaches for me.

You will not hurt me, I order. The squid pauses, the large orb of its eye staring. *And I will not hurt you. This way.* I look back only once to see the squid shooting along behind me in graceful swoops and arcs. Occasionally, the creature's tentacles brush against the slide of my spine, but it minds my commands and doesn't try to harm me.

Esu is still pressed against the bars when I get back. Recoiling, he bends his body into the curve of the wall, wary of the squid, which takes up the width of the passageway.

"Stay there," I tell him, moving to the side.

I point to the stalactites as the creature watches me. *Pull these. Break them.*

The squid shoots close to the bars. It wraps its two feeding tentacles around the closest rocks and then grips the others with all of its limbs.

Pull, I command, forcing my voice inside the creature's mind, showing it images of the cell broken apart.

The squid's eye blinks once, and then the creature is yanking at the stalactites, its body shaking with effort. There is a cracking sound, but nothing breaks.

"Esu! You need to push from your side, too!" I shout, wrapping my own hands around the nearest column of rock.

The orisa eyes the squid before moving forward and heaving

against the stone bars. I strain against them as well, my face so close to the creature's feeding tentacles that I can see the sharpness of its deadly hooks. The large clot of the squid's eye quivers, and I wonder if the creature is thinking of how it would like to dig them into my skin. But it continues to follow my directions and the splintering sounds become louder, jagged webs in the three main bars giving us the impetus to keep pulling and pushing. Esu closes his eyes, face creased as he heaves against the bars, muscles corded and veins bulging. The central stalactite snaps, followed by the two closest to it, and I pause as a cloud of mineral dust blooms between us. The squid continues to yank, its tentacles holding two uneven stalactites.

Esu peers between the holes left but doesn't move, his eyes on the large creature in front of him. The squid releases its grip, but its tentacles lunge for the orisa pressed against the rock.

Go, I command with a flick of my head. *Return to your lair.*

The squid hesitates for a moment, its beak opening and snapping once, body trembling with a violent want.

Go. I push my thoughts at the squid, willing it to listen. The creature swivels, its giant eye staring at me for half a second. And then it is gone, propelling itself back into the tunnels.

"Well done, little fish." Esu turns sideways, angling his broad shoulders through the gap and slipping free.

As he brings his other leg through and stands in the tunnel before me, I do not recoil, although my heart slams against my rib cage. Instead, I try to compose my face into a calm blankness, one that doesn't give anything away.

"Do not look so worried," he says. "I said I would not go against my word and my promise." The orisa gestures to the blood-red ruby at my wrist before nodding at the blackness ahead of us. "Now, please, lead the way."

I'm not sure how much the ruby counts as a binding agreement, but it's too late to go back on what I've started. Feeling the weight of his jewel against the ball of my fist, I begin to swim back through the tunnels, pausing here and there to allow the orisa to catch up. Whenever I look behind me I see his glowing greenish face, his arms cutting through the water in slashes, feet a faint kick behind him. He looks almost as monstrous as the anglerfish. *You had no choice,* I say to myself, *and now you have to get through the rest of this.*

The closer we draw to the larger main tunnels, the more nervous I feel. Am I just expecting to swim out of here with Esu? I pause, stopping at the mouth of the tunnel that links to the main ones.

"What is it, little fish?"

I turn to glare at Esu. "Stop calling me little fish." I peer ahead and lower the sunstone, lessening its light.

"You are worried about Olokun?" Esu bobs in the water, hands against the walls to stop his body from rising.

"Hopefully he'll be out in the depths. He checks the land for more dead and he usually has most of the anglerfish with him." I don't mention how gentle Olokun is with the bodies, how he folds them in the seabed, giving them the respect they deserve. It doesn't change the fact that he has gambled with other lives, and I know that Esu will only remind me of the greater number of dead to come if we don't act now.

I think about the orisa who crouches next to me in the dark. Is it the ruby that keeps him from reaching out to wrap his hands around my neck, to snap the bones as easily as a chicken's? Or did he mean what he said? That he wants to fulfill his duty and bind the ajogun?

"What are you waiting for?" hisses Esu, eyes gleaming in the meager light. "Every moment we spend here is time that we can ill afford."

He's right, but if we're caught by Olokun there will be no one to bind the ajogun at all. I ignore the orisa's harsh whispers and venture slowly out of the tunnel. Shreds of glowing moss stud the sloping walls of the main passageway, filling it with leaping shadows as the warm currents surge gently through. There are no sea creatures, and I can see the very faint glimmer of the hall.

Spinning back to Esu, I beckon him, my heart thumping. "Let's go quickly," I whisper. "Follow me."

I dart left, feeling the whirl of water behind me that tells me the orisa is close. I glance back once to see Esu frowning, lips in a flat line as he swims hard. We move along the tunnel as fast as we can. As the blood thunders in my ears, I keep expecting to see the bobbling light of an anglerfish, its orb highlighting long spikes of teeth. But we see nothing and soon the tunnel has spewed us from its mouth and into the currents outside Olokun's palace. The thermal seeps spread their glittering loops of water, warming our skin but speeding up my pulse.

Esu glares about him, but I lead him toward the whale bones, grateful for the firefly squid that are dotted around, casting small glowing blue pools. Above us, the ivory stretches into domed skeletal archways, each one rushing past as I swim faster than I have in some time.

"Quickly," I urge, scanning the water.

We crest the reef, rising above the dark red coral, and then the sweeping semicircle of the burial sands is before us. Esu gazes down at the rise and fall of the silt. He lowers his eyes and places his right hand on his chest, above the beat of his heart, lips moving in a prayer I can't hear.

I know he's thinking of the dead at the hands of the òyìnbó. The long limbs of children on the cusp of adulthood, the folds and wrinkles of faces that have seen many years. Families left behind and lives ended before the sea swallows them all and joins them with their ancestors. They are home now, I think. I still remember every soul I gathered, their journey home to Olodumare blessed.

"Come." I surge toward the surface. There will be more dead if we don't leave Olokun's realm. Esu's long kicks still don't make him as fast as me, so I clench my teeth and clamp my hand around the thickness of his wrist and pull him upward.

We are still far from the surface, but the sea is shifting now, from midnight black to dark indigo. Soon the water will match the sky, and light will filter into the depths, glittering on the swirls of fish and even on the pink and gold of my tail. I will take a small sip of air and the sun will warm me.

When the water turns brighter still, I feel the beginnings of relief as I spot purple scales sparkling against brown skin.

Folasade.

She dips down, a spear of red coral in her right hand. Her eyes widen when she sees Esu behind me.

"I knew it," she gasps, suspended where the water changes shades. I watch as she casts a nervous look above her.

And then I see them.

From the murky currents, there are flashes of scales. Greens, orange, yellow, red, and a pale iridescent gray reveal themselves with each twist and swoop.

Abeni, Niniola, Morayo, Iyanda, and Omolara.

The other five Mami Wata descend through the water to hover by Folasade, each one gripping a spear with a serrated silver tip. Esu floats behind me, stopping at the sight of the weapons.

"Stay where you are, trickster," hisses Folasade as Abeni and Niniola lunge forward, keeping their spears leveled at his face.

"We need to leave now," I say, scanning the darkness below. "Before Olokun comes."

"Simidele." The voice rings out, rippling through the water. I know its richness, and the black silk tones fill me with comfort as I tip my face up.

Yemoja glides down as the sea shifts around her in hues that match the colors of her tail, her hair a spreading black of kinks and curls that darken the water. In her hand, she carries a golden sword with a curved blade, its hilt set with polished diamonds. The orisa smiles, her pearl veil waving above her pointed teeth. When she reaches me, Yemoja runs long nails down my cheek before cupping my face and pressing her warm lips against my forehead.

My heart races as guilt runs through me, hot and sharp. I didn't ask her permission or even tell her about leaving for the Land of the Dead. Even now, I have Esu, but I am the reason he is down here. The reason that Yemoja and the others have had to break their accord with Olokun. I look up, daring to meet Yemoja's gaze.

"Are you well?" she asks, holding me away so that she can look at me. I nod, unable to speak. Yemoja turns, gesturing to Esu. "Come."

Abeni and Niniola reluctantly lift their spears so that the trickster can swim between them. As he glides from the cold deep, he keeps his right hand on his chest, opening his mouth. Yemoja raises her hand.

"You do not need to speak." Yemoja's eyes narrow, glittering. "I have searched for you only out of necessity."

For a moment, I think Esu will say something anyway. But he nods once and allows Morayo and Iyanda to herd him between them, their single long plaits snaking behind them. As the Mami Wata encircle him, hiding him from view, the water rocks beneath us with a roar.

Yemoja and I are spun in a tumble of bubbles and scales, the sound reverberating through the water. Twisting against the motion of sound waves, I gaze down, stomach clenching. Below us, I spot the glints of a gold chain, obsidian eyes forged with silver, and a mouth wide open in a raw scream.

Olokun.

CHAPTER SEVEN

THE ORISA HOWLS again, surging up from the deep. He swims higher, his cape a spread of undulating black pearls.

"What is this?" sneers Olokun, his eyes flicking over Yemoja and the others. "What happened to our agreement, Mother of Fish?"

I shift anxiously as Yemoja looks down at Olokun, her veil swaying. She inclines her head minutely. "You took one of my Mami Wata."

Olokun does not swim up any farther, hovering in the dusky part of the sea, golden chain spooling behind him. I wonder how long it is, how far he can go. "I cannot take what was given. Simidele made a bargain."

I think of Esu imprisoned and a protest begins to build in my throat.

"And what of ours?" asks Yemoja, putting a hand on my arm. I bite back my words, frustration prickling.

"I have kept mine," hisses Olokun, waving his abede. "It is you who have broken our accord. None of you should be this deep." Olokun glances up at the cluster of Mami Wata. They float in place, curls and tails hiding the brown skin of Esu's body and the kick of his legs.

"If that is the case, then Simidele should not be here, either." Olokun's eyes slide back to Yemoja as she speaks. "Her bargain with you does not override her place with me and the treaty we struck." Yemoja reaches for me, tucking me against the warm skin of her side. "I claim her back."

Olokun surges toward us in a violent rush of water, abede held outstretched. "How dare you question me!" he booms, slashing his fan at us.

Yemoja dips her spine, avoiding the razor-sharp tips of Olokun's abede. Taking advantage of her movement, the orisa seizes my arm. "Simidele made her choice of her own free will."

My chest swells with anger as I try to yank my arm away. "I did make the decision, but you . . . You *lied*!"

"What do you mean?" Olokun doesn't let go but loosens his grip. His eyes burn dangerously. "I have not gone back on my agreement to bury the dead."

"Not that," I say. "You said you would give Esu over to Olodumare." I lean toward Olokun, words crackling past teeth gritted in anger. "But you did not. *Why?*"

"Ah, so that is why you're here." Olokun glares at Yemoja. "To tell tales."

"I saw him," I say quietly. "In the cold belly of your palace."

Olokun lets go of me and turns his face away, aiming it at the surface. "I will not argue with you. You have felt what it is like to be in my realm." Olokun turns back to me and his face ripples, eyes a light silver now. "I settled in the cooled vapors that became the seas and oceans when Olodumare created the world, but I was not trapped here. Not the way I am now. Not the way I have been for more than a thousand years. Forever limited to the dark cold."

"And why is that, Olokun? Would you now tell the story as if you were innocent?" Yemoja asks, her mouth pulled down, her voice stained with sorrow. "You tried to drown humanity."

"And now you've condemned them again by keeping Esu, knowing what might happen." I lean toward him, my hands clenching into fists.

The truths unspool between us, swallowed by the water and the shadows as Olokun turns to me. He has the grace to lower his eyes briefly before he speaks. "I want to see the sun, Simidele. To feel its heat. I want to taste the fire of peppers, to scoop iyán while it is hot." Olokun blinks slowly and snatches a gaze at the surface above us. "I know you, too, have missed all that the rest of the earth has to offer, but even you cannot know what this is like. The eternity of existing in this way."

"So, you would rather bargain with Esu and risk the lives of thousands more. If redemption is what you are seeking, then this is not the right way to go about it."

"Redemption takes too long!" Olokun's eyes harden, his nostrils flaring. "I will have my freedom. I will not wait for another millennium." The orisa comes closer to me, waving the serrated pleats of his abede in the water. A trickle of fear threads its way through my veins. "It is not for you to understand, Mami Wata. That is not your role."

I know now that what Esu told me is true. Olokun would have kept him imprisoned until humanity was threatened, until people died, and then used him to bargain with Obatala for his freedom. I shiver in the dark water, thinking of the lives that would be lost, all for Olokun to see the sun.

"You have broken our agreement," I say, anger roughening each word.

Olokun sweeps his hand through the water, gesturing to the

Mami Wata above him. "If we are speaking about breaking accords," he says, "then Yemoja and her daughters should be held accountable for breaking theirs."

I eye the hulk of Olokun's body as he glides closer to us, his mouth open in a wide smile, teeth glinting like the bones of the dead. The chain that binds him to the bottom of the ocean shimmers like coveted treasure. There is a tautness to him as he lowers his head, muscled shoulders rounded and ready, his tail coiled. I want to look up at Esu, to see if he is still hidden, but I don't dare.

"The accord has officially been broken," Olokun says, his tone deeper now as he points his abede at us. "And you are all in my realm, where you should not be."

"Do not act rashly." Yemoja's voice pours through the sea like molten lava.

But Olokun doesn't heed the orisa's words. He rushes toward her, snapping his fan open to reveal the long sharp points. Bubbles pepper the water as Yemoja pushes me to the side, meeting Olokun's abede with her sword, holding her blade fast against the clash of his metal fan. The two orisa spin in the water, a whirlpool of scales, silver eyes, and bared teeth, until Olokun pulls away, snatching one of the abede's pleats free. With a powerful flick of his wrist, he throws it at Yemoja. The makeshift dagger buries itself in the orisa's side and she cries out, her scream of pain curdling in the currents.

At once, the other Mami Wata break formation, swooping down to take their places by Yemoja, tails glittering against skin in shades of brown, aiming their coral-and-silver spears at Olokun.

"No!" says Yemoja, but it is too late.

I look up, just as Olokun does, to see Esu suspended in the sea, where the dark meets the light. Olokun's eyes widen and then he is snarling with a fury I have never seen before. "You would dare go against me?"

I brace myself for Olokun's attack, seeing the others do the same, their spears gripped fimly. But Olokun doesn't chase after Esu as I expect him to. Instead, he closes his eyes and begins to murmur, his abede shining in the gloom.

Yemoja backs away from him, her face slack with shock at the words she hears. "You need to leave now," she says to me, then whirls to face Esu. The other Mami Wata circle her, eyes sharp and hair soft in the sea, knuckles tight as they hold their weapons ready.

Still I don't move. Something is happening beneath us. I watch the depths behind Olokun as the shades of the black water waver. And grow. The darkness spreads like a cloud filling the sea around us. There's another flex from the deep and it feels as if the ocean and the darkness are peeling themselves apart.

The Omniran.

A quiver of foreboding shivers through Yemoja before she sets her expression and glares downward. Olokun smirks as the shadows beneath him swell until they form a tentacle that is as long as a ship. The blackness writhes beneath us, made solid in growing monstrous form.

"Come, Omniran," calls Olokun. "Like me, you've been caged for too long."

Lightning pierces the waves, illuminating us in fragments that fill the sea with a jagged glow. A boom follows from the surface, the sudden sound filtering even this far down. The water rocks us about, the tides growing violent as a storm born in the sky above spreads to the sea below.

Olokun smiles, his eyes flashing and teeth bared. A shriek

splits the water, echoing all around us as giant tentacles shoot up from the shadowy depths.

I've never seen the Omniran, despite being in the Land of the Dead, and even though I have heard some stories of the creature, none of them are the same as seeing such a monster. The giant squid has been skulking in the deep for a millennium, banished after hunting too many of the water creatures Olodumare created. As the Omniran's limbs unfurl, it fills the sea below us, and I feel a streak of fear.

Olokun whips his abede up, snapping it open with a flick of his wrist. He plucks another of the pleats from the fan's silver folds and throws the shard at Yemoja, who raises her sword to deflect the attack. Abeni, Morayo, and Iyanda surge after her, while the others space themselves out, trying to form a barrier to the trickster.

"Get Esu to safety!" Yemoja calls to me as she dances away from Olokun's abede, her scales a sparkling blur. Beneath the orisas, the mass grows, another monstrously large tentacle joining the other. "I'll do my best to quell the Omniran."

Olokun uses her distraction to land one of his spikes in her left side. Yemoja gasps but plucks it from her skin, hand over the wound. Niniola jabs at Olokun, catching his attention and allowing Yemoja to plunge down, commands spilling from her lips as her wound heals. Twirling in the orisa's blood, Mami Wata flood around Olokun in a loose circle, using their spears to keep him where he is. Esu glances down once and then starts to swim slowly to the faded light above.

Olokun grins; he is twice the size of Mami Wata, and his chest and shoulders gleam with muscle. "Come," he says, waving the remnants of his abede to beckon us. "Let me see how well Yemoja has remade you."

Iyanda lunges forward, spear aimed for the thickness of Olokun's throat. He glides away from the attack, dragging the abede along her arm, its sharp spikes opening the brown of her skin from bicep to wrist. Hissing, Iyanda spins away to heal while Abeni takes her place.

Below us, the behemoth stirs; an elongated tentacle rises, cutting through the water. In one giant swoop, it snatches Morayo just as she is bringing her spear down toward Olokun's chest. She howls as the thick coil tightens around her midriff, hooks piercing her skin, spilling her blood around her.

I blink the burn of tears away. This is my fault. I raise my blade and start forward as the sky releases another angry bolt of light. With the storm battering the sea above, underwater currents react even more, cold water swirling while lightning pierces the waves in blasts of white.

"Mother Yemoja—" I want to tell her that Olokun will not back down, that I've seen the feral want on his face, the stretch of his body, when he looks up at the surface. I should have known that Olokun would not stop at anything. Instead, I took his assumed role as keeper of the dead to mean that compassion was as important to him as it is to me.

Olokun blocks the attacks from the six Mami Wata, his face contorted by a snarl, making him almost unrecognizable as the orisa I thought I knew.

There is another rumble from above, this time felt deeply in the reverberations in the water, but still Yemoja continues to glide down toward the Omniran. Rapid bolts of lightning carve up the sea, highlighting our faces as the orisa moves through the thrown shadows, her face lit up in violent flashes.

A limb whips through the water toward us, but Folasade hacks at the thick orange flesh and giant hooks. She slashes down, and then pauses as lightning lands on the glare on Morayo's face, the fear in Abeni's, the anger in Niniola's. Another roar of thunder echoes in the water.

"Mother—" I cry as Yemoja launches herself at a tentacle that slinks toward her.

The orisa throws a look back up, eyes widening. "I said, go!" And then she is speeding closer to the Omniran, words spilling from her lips in a frantic chant. The creature lashes out, reaching for Abeni, but slows down at Yemoja's commands. She shouts more orders, panicked glances thrown at Morayo until the giant releases her.

"Simidele! You heard Yemoja!" shouts Folasade as she and the others spar with Olokun, taking turns to attack in twos before spinning away to heal. He has only two shards of his abede left and is using them like long daggers clutched in both fists, each one spilling the blood of Mami Wata. "Take Esu to the surface! Olokun can't follow that far."

At her words, Olokun peers down at the Omniran, whose great body is swaying in time to the lulling croon of Yemoja. Only she could control such a huge and ancient beast. Even as I watch, the shadows thin, the monstrous limbs sinking back to the ridges of the bedrock. I swim fast, grabbing Esu's arm and yanking him toward the top of the sea.

With a snarl, Olokun turns away from Yemoja, and when he sees me with Esu, the orisa screams. Slashing out at Omolara, he hacks once at the glitter of her tail, cleaving her iridescent scales.

He doesn't wait to see her sink and heal in the sea before he drives the shards into the stomachs of Abeni and Iyanda, twisting both blades deep. The others scramble to contain him, but it is too late. Olokun breaks the circle and soars after me.

"Go!" I scream at Esu. But his legs are no match for Olokun's tail, even with me pulling him along.

The orisa roars as he reaches up, fingers grasping for Esu's ankle. I push the trickster up, boosting him so that he is not far from the upper layer of the sea. And then Olokun's grip weakens, fingers slipping from Esu's foot as blood seeps into the water.

I look down to see Olokun hanging suspended in the water, Folasade's spear protruding from just under his ribs. His chest heaves as he stares down in disbelief, framed by the blackness of the deep.

CHAPTER EIGHT

LIGHTNING FLASHES IN sporadic bursts as I drag Esu closer to the storm that batters at the surface. A frantic look beneath us shows me Olokun ripping the spear from his chest, his screams choked by a mouthful of blood. Swimming harder, I claw toward the tops of the waves, heart rising in my throat, pulsing with every frantic beat.

A scream makes me look down again. I see Yemoja draw level with Folasade, striking at the orisa's back in a merciless arc. He spins in the cloud of bloody water, whirling to face them, clutching what is left of his abede. All the other Mami Wata have joined Yemoja now and are striking out at Olokun as he roars and slashes with the slivers of his fan. I spin, pulling Esu with me as I aim us toward the surface, just as thunder crashes again. For a moment, we are lit in the shaft of light created by a bolt of silver that has cut through the waves.

"Hurry!" I shout, gripping Esu tighter. "Don't slow down now."

Risking another small glance below us, I see that Olokun has managed to gain on us, having darted away from Yemoja's sword and the other Mami Wata's spears. His golden chain still drips from his waist, and I know that if we can all just swim a little higher, he won't be able to follow.

Yemoja slashes at his stomach with her sword. "Go!" she screams. "All of you!"

Niniola pauses beside Yemoja, her green scales like fallen leaves in the water, but the rest of the Mami Wata drag her with them, all swimming as hard and fast as they can. Shards of light reach down, showing terror in the whites of their eyes. I shove Esu into Folasade's arms.

"Take him." And then I am diving back down.

I am not leaving Yemoja.

Bleeding, her chest heaving and her hair spread out like a trail of dark seaweed, Yemoja doesn't take her eyes from Olokun. She lunges forward with the last of her energy, trying to slice at Olokun's ribs, but he swats her sword away, grabbing her by the tail and yanking her to him. While she fumbles to regain her balance, the orisa brings her closer to him, crushing both her wrists in a tight grip. Yemoja looks so small as Olokun's mouth twists into a sneer.

"Stop!" I shout as I reach them.

"Stay out of this, Simidele," snarls Olokun, but he does not attack me. I think of the time we have spent burying the people who have been stolen, the shared misery at being so far beneath the sea. Olokun said he would let me go to the surface, to see the sun. If he has any small amount of care for me, then I will use it.

"Let her go." I straighten my shoulders and lift my gaze to his. He could snap her neck in seconds, I think, trying to quell the tremor that rips through me. "Let us go. Esu is needed. You know this."

Olokun raises his head to where the light from the storm filters in once again. The brightness gives his face harder edges, the cleft in his chin as deep as carved rock. "I will not be a prisoner anymore."

I think of his desperation, of my own time spent far from land. Olokun will stop at nothing. Yemoja stills and I move closer, dagger held at my side as Olokun watches me.

"I know. And I will make sure Esu takes your petition to the Supreme Creator." I consider my words carefully. "But you need to let us go."

Olokun looks down at me. He blinks slowly and opens his mouth to speak, but before he can do so, Yemoja wrenches herself free, twirling away and raising her sword. Before Olokun can react, she brings the blade down, slicing at his arm, coming to a stop only when it reaches the bone of his shoulder. With a scream, she pulls the blade free and grabs my hand, dragging us both toward the surface. I snatch a look at Olokun, one hand clamped on his wound as he surges after us, rage and pain in the twists of his grimace.

We swim fast, but still I sense Olokun gaining on us. When I look down, he is just a length away, and then he lunges, reaching up. I flinch as his golden chain snaps tight and he is yanked to a halt. His gaze fixes on mine, full of misery and vexation.

And then Yemoja turns me to her, the flashing lights from the storm highlighting our faces. "Keep going, Simidele." She cups my chin and slides her other arm around my waist. "Don't look back."

• • •

We split the surface of the sea and arrive at a dawn that purples the sky like the fading bruises on our skin. The storm is pulling out, but I can still taste the metallic tang of lightning. The other Mami Wata are dotted around me, resting on the waves, cautious and still healing. Folasade traces a hand across a gash on her temple as Omolara swims closer, her gaze skimming over us both, checking that we are whole.

Esu floats a short distance away, his face angled to the clouds that have been left shredded after the storm, white wisps over a hard blue sky. "The air!" he calls. "Can you smell it?" The orisa chuckles to himself and takes another deep breath, chest rising and falling. A broad smile is stretched across his face.

Yemoja swivels her head, curls sending sparkles of water in the air, as she counts us. When her lips tremble with the number seven, her shoulders slump with relief.

"They're all safe," I say. No thanks to me, I think. "I'm sorry, I should have waited for you." There is anxiety in the waver of my tone. "I should have just found Esu and waited."

Yemoja is silent a moment, watching Morayo and Abeni smile at the horizon, where the sun rises in a growing ball of red and orange.

"Those are many 'shoulds' when we both know you do not do . . . what you are supposed to do." She turns, pearl veil swinging, and smiles softly at me. "You should have waited before rescuing Esu, but you were brave enough to take a chance. If you hadn't, we would have lost time trying to determine how to get him out." I stay silent, watching the pinkish light gleam on Yemoja's pearl veil. "You should have gone with the other Mami Wata to the surface when I was battling Olokun, but you didn't. I am here and unharmed because of that. So in this case, keep your 'shoulds.' I do not want to hear them."

I lower my head, lips to the water. But I can't stop thinking about when Olokun drove his blades into the soft bellies of Abeni and Iyanda.

Yemoja moves closer and whispers, "I think we both know that you are a creature unto yourself. One that I created but have been unable to control or contain. I accept and celebrate you, Simidele."

I swallow, the taste of guilt bitter at the back of my throat. Yemoja's compassion knows no bounds, but none of this should have happened. This fight, the trickster imprisoned beneath the sea for far too long. All of it is my fault. I turn away, leaving them to talk quietly as I swim to Esu. The only thing I can do to make amends is to make sure that the ajogun are bound.

When I near the orisa, he turns to smile at me, his eyes alight with a dawn that is slowly changing from pink to yellow, its heat already spreading.

"Can you feel it? The sun?" He tilts his face back to the sky, letting his thin plaits trail on the top of the sea.

"Are you hurt?"

But Esu doesn't answer me. He keeps his eyes closed, a placid smile still in place. I think of the violence we have left below and know that, if anything, it is matched in the orisa before me. Yemoja's veil is a testament to this, to Esu's malicious whims, the swinging pearls hiding the gouges the trickster scored in her cheeks as punishment for creating seven Mami Wata. I lift my wrist, watching as Esu's ruby sparkles in the dawn.

"I asked if you—"

"I am fine, little fish." The orisa flips onto his front and cuts through the water to arrive in front of me. He stops, arms moving in slow shallow arcs, keeping him afloat as Yemoja swims to our side. Water slides from the slope of her shoulders as she regards the trickster. When her lips part, I see the power in the angle of her head, the slight tilt of her chin, and I am proud. Proud of her strength, her lack of fear, and the force of her courage.

"Esu."

The orisa bows his head once, right hand on his heart, before meeting her gaze. "Yemoja." Their names swirl before them in the fresh burst of dawn, an uneasy truce born again.

"I could drag you back down to the deep, give you over to Olokun." Yemoja lifts a hand to her veil, fingers slipping under the pearls to touch the scars beneath. "But I do not hold on to energy that does not benefit me." Yemoja swims around Esu, ripples in her wake encircling him. "You are free because of your role. Nothing more nor less. I know that your nature calls to placate the ajogun; despite your search for more power, this is one of your most important callings."

"It is."

"And so, I am willing to release you, to let Simidele take you to land, to aid you in all that you need to bind the anti-gods. To protect us all."

Esu twists as Yemoja passes behind him, trying to keep her in his sights. She doesn't stop, coming full circle to face him. The emerging sun spills onto the glimmer of her crown, bathing her face in gold, sparkling on the pearls across her face and in her hair.

"I have never shirked my role," answers Esu, wiping a hand over his face, pushing back his plaits, which skim the waves. "And I will not now. Besides, how will I have my fun if the world is laid to ruin?"

Yemoja ignores his last words and turns to me, her hands finding mine under the line of the water. "Simidele, will you see this done?"

I nod, thinking of the part I have played in what is at stake. "I will," I answer.

"As will I."

Folasade appears at my side. Her mouth is twisted in determination, her shoulders set in hard angles.

"No," I say firmly. "I won't put anyone else at risk. Please." I turn to Yemoja. "Don't ask that of me, too."

"I will be fine," Folasade declares, narrowing her eyes at me before facing Yemoja. "Besides, I think Simidele needs to be . . . tempered."

I open my mouth to argue but am silenced as Yemoja raises her hand, raw diamonds and citrine set into rings that glitter on her long fingers.

"And this way," continues Folasade, "there will be two of us to oversee Esu. I would not want Simidele to deal with this burden on her own."

I watch Esu, who has returned to floating on his back. Even though he has given me his ruby, I still feel uneasy. Folasade snakes her hand into mine under the water. Releasing a sigh, I squeeze her fingers once. I would be lying if I denied finding some relief, some comfort, in the thought of having her with me.

"Are you sure of this, Folasade?" asks Yemoja, placing a hand on our shoulders, her palms warm.

"I am," answers Folasade. "I would risk more if it means safety for us all."

"Then so be it." The orisa gathers us to her, pressing her lips to our curls. "I do not like it, but I also know that it is what is needed." She flicks a look at Esu. "Without him, the world is already descending into chaos."

"I won't let you down," I say. How fitting, I think, that the orisa who causes so much discord is now the only one who can stop it all.

"Simidele," says Yemoja, her voice as soft as the gray-and-pink clouds above. "I know this."

I duck my head to hide the hint of a smile. And with those words she releases us, then calls to the other Mami Wata, ignoring their expressions of confusion when Folasade and I stay where we are. We murmur our good-byes, bobbing on small waves. Yemoja inclines her head, gesturing to the deep, and watches as each Mami Wata dives beneath the sea, shimmers of green and yellow and red, until only the orisa is left. Yemoja turns to us, lit up in the glow of fresh morning sun, hair and shoulders drenched in golden light.

"Take care; may Olodumare guide you and the world find its balance with your help."

I press my hand to my heart, and Folasade does the same. Yemoja smiles at us, teeth sharp against the fullness of her top lip. And then she is gone.

"Which one of you will be helping me to shore, then?" Esu's snort pulls us from the absence of Yemoja. I turn to see the orisa swiveling his head sideways. He lifts his hands up, treading water. "Since there is no doubt that we would get there sooner."

I inhale deeply as Folasade sighs and swims to his side. I follow more slowly, my eyes caught by the ruby that dangles from my wrist. Despite his vow to me, I am wary. I don't think I will ever be anything but, and I tell myself that this is a good thing. Orisas hold their own secrets. Shame burns in me at the thought of Olokun manipulating me when I should have been more cautious. Faith is something I've given too freely. There will be no assumptions and blind trust this time.

Together, Folasade and I hold Esu's arms tightly, propelling him in the direction of the shore. The air grows warmer as the sun burns across the cloudless sky. Just beyond the rise and fall of the waves, we see a thin slip of land, the beach layered with green as it gives way to forest. My stomach flips in the water when I think of the shifting sand and the warmth of damp earth between my toes. Of Oko, hot swallows of pepper soup, the stars as they scar the sky.

Of Kola.

I envision the reddish brown of his skin and his wide smile. The velvet touch of his fingertips as he cradled my feet when they were sore, hands wrapped around my soles as if they were the most precious thing he had ever held. Kola had looked at me then as if I were both the sun and the moon, his night and day. I squeeze my eyes shut.

Esu shifts in my grip, bringing me back to the sea and the whip of fresh air. Stop, I tell myself, opening my eyes to the brightness of the new day. I am not in the deep. I must focus on the now—getting Esu to shore so that we can work out what needs to be done next.

The slice of land grows, and I find myself swimming for it, the pull of what feels like home tugging at me, making my strokes faster. Esu crows at the sight of the beach and paddles away from us, riding the waves until he can crawl from the water. He heaves his body onto the hot sand and sighs with relief. Folasade pauses in the brown-and-cream frill of the shallows, her eyes wide, taking in the shoreline.

"Come," I say gently, letting the sea roll me onto the beach, the air skimming along my tail.

The draw I felt when I spotted land fades now, dissolving with the scales that the sun and air touch. Folasade chooses not to change unless she has a soul to bless with Yemoja, sticking to her form as Mami Wata, shunning the land. Now she watches as my scales turn to brown skin, their pinkish gold transforming into a wrapper that fits snug about my chest and hips. I stand, listening to the bones in my ankles click into place, feeling the burn of the sun on my bare shoulders. With my toes sinking into the wet sand, I close my eyes, the shiver of leaves in the breeze a gentle rustle. This is nothing like the cold deep, its sunless dark that felt as if it were seeping into every part of me, even my spirit.

I smooth the folds of my wrapper tight against my skin, allowing a small smile to form as I beckon to Folasade. She hesitates before letting the gentle waves of the shallows push her closer. As she emerges from the sea, her scales transform into a purple wrapper that swirls around her body. She takes the hand I offer, eyes cast down at the length of her legs.

"Are you sure you want to do this?" I ask. "I can manage."

"I know." Folasade stands up straighter, slipping her hand from mine and running her fingers over the broad swell of her hips. "But I promised Yemoja. Besides, who will keep an eye on you?"

Folasade smirks as we turn to watch Esu uncurling from the beach, raising both hands to the sky. When he flinches, I think it's from the hot sand, but then there are short whistles of air as arrows pepper the ground next to my freshly formed feet.

CHAPTER NINE

THE FIRST PEACH-AND-GOLD light of the day shines down on our compound as a nearby rooster crows. I yawn, rubbing my eyes as my stomach rumbles loudly, and pull my wrapper tighter.

"But bàbá, why do I have to learn this?" I ask as he holds out the dagger. It's heavy in my grip, the ivory handle carved in the shape of a fish tail, each small scale picked out perfectly. My father squints, holding a hand up against the rising sun. I can feel the frown wrinkle my brow. No one else I know has to get up at the first part of the day. Why should I?

Bàbá sighs and lowers his body into a squat beside me so that his gaze is level with mine.

"I know you'd rather be asleep, but this is important."

I look down, tracing a toe in the red dirt. It's been a few months now, this practice that my father insists I do. I know it's because he is worried about me. The Tapa, who have been attacking the Oyo Kingdom for decades now, have become bolder. Raiding villages and burning them down, taking people back to the Nupe Kingdom. I've overheard his late-night conversations with the other scholars, about whether war should be declared. Their voices often grow thin with fear, rising with the smoke from their carved-leopard pipes.

Even ìyá's stories have become filled with lessons of courage, of battles fought decades ago, telling the tales of kingdoms formed and broken and remade.

"We're in Oyo-Ile, bàbá," I say. "The walls will keep us safe. Besides, Ara doesn't have to learn to fight."

"Walls can be torn down, ọmọbìnrin ìn mi." Bàbá places a finger under my chin, tipping my face to his. "We should not count on them. I'm teaching you how to defend yourself so that you will never have to rely on anyone."

I bite down a sigh and climb to my feet, slapping the dust from my wrapper as bàbá's eyes flicker over my face, the corners of his mouth creasing. I don't want to add to his worries. Holding the dagger tight enough that the carved scales dig into my palm, I drop into a crouch.

"Like this?"

Bàbá stands up, too, smiling now. Reaching behind him, he retrieves his shield, scarred wood that still shines. He beckons me with the flutter of long fingers, eyes brighter now. "That's right. Hold it firmly."

I adjust my grip, dancing forward, letting the cool air and the movement wake me up. Despite my complaints, I enjoy the grace it takes to attack, to defend.

"Now, come at me." He lowers his shield to peer at me over the top, grin cracked wide. "And don't hold back."

The Tapa are all I can think of as more arrows thud into the sand around us. My father trained me to fight, always aware of the danger they posed. Folasade trembles next to me as Esu hunches low, eyes a hard silver as he scans the tree line. There is nothing for a moment, only the caw of sea gulls and the rush of the sea behind us. And then I spot movement in the edges of the forest. Our attackers slide from behind the trees, bows held ready, although the taller one who leads them holds a sword. He moves across the beach toward us, feet sinking into the sand, his stride sure and firm. The light flashes on the long blade he wields, his face shaded by a hand that stops the glare from the sun.

I feel that same yank in me, the one that led me to this beach. It rises in my gut as I brandish my dagger, the tip shaking.

"Don't move or you will be cut down." The leader's words ring out loud, but he falters when he's close enough to see us, stopping short of where we stand, half a dozen men behind him in a blaze of sunlight.

My stomach clenches again, this time like a closed fist, and the world slides sideways as I try to take another breath.

"Simi?" asks Kola, the sword falling from his grasp, sinking into the sand. He reaches out a hand toward me.

My newly transformed legs shake, and I think for a moment that I might fall, crumple into the sand, but Folasade is by my side, keeping me upright. I open my mouth, but nothing comes out.

Breathe.

Just focus on trying to breathe.

The small glimpse of Kola at sea was a cruel kind of pleasure, but having him in front of me now almost feels worse. Leaving him on Esu's island broke a part of me that remained crooked and unhealed even in the sea. At times, I had to push thoughts of him aside, or face a type of madness where you can think of nothing but what you want, even though you can't have it.

Especially when you can't have it.

"Simi," repeats Kola, and the shape his mouth makes when he says my name is exactly as I remember it.

I finally suck in more salty air. He moves toward me, and I take a step, too, caught in the shimmer of Kola's light brown eyes. We walk over the hot sand, the sea crashing behind us, but even that fades. How is it that he is here? I stare up at him, close enough that I can smell the familiar coco scent of black soap. A faint beard grazes his chin now, and his arms are thicker, shoulders broader.

"Kola—"

He stiffens, looking over my shoulder. His back straightens, jaw tight as he glares behind me. Kola's soft mouth hardens into a snarl as I spin to see Esu unfold himself from his squat. He pushes me to the side and snatches his sword from the ground. I stagger in the shifting sand, heart quickening at what I know is coming next.

"Wait!" I say, but Kola is already lunging for Esu, knuckles tight as he grasps the hilt of his sword. The orisa jumps backward, spine curved, stomach sucked in so that the blade just misses his gut. But Kola moves forward, faster than I've ever seen him, catching Esu's arm. A thick line of blood flows down his skin as the orisa yelps in surprise. Either Esu's time below the sea has dulled him or Kola's skill has sharpened.

The boy stalks forward now, using Esu's surprise to gain ground, lifting his weapon high. I move before I can really think, lurching between them. The sword flashes in the bright sun.

"Stop!" I say, squeezing my eyes shut, waiting for the blow that doesn't come. When I open them, it is to Kola's face creased with confusion.

"Simi, what is this? You would defend him?" Kola moves closer, eyes flicking over to Esu with venom. "After all he did to us?"

"I know." I lift my hands, edging forward so that Kola is forced to lower his sword and back away. "But . . . please, just listen to me."

Behind me, Folasade is at Esu's side, palms pressed against his shallow wound to stop the bleeding. The trickster says nothing, but his glare is aimed at Kola. I pray that he doesn't smile or say something to tip the situation into chaos.

Kola paces from side to side, nostrils flared. The warriors behind him edge forward. Arrows are still nocked and more blades glint in the growing sunlight.

"Kola, please," I say, my voice sounding pathetic even to my own ears. "Trust me. You know you can." He looks down at me, blood lining his sword, already drying to a deep burgundy in the hot sun. "I can explain. But we need to gather ourselves and work out what needs to be done. Give us that at least."

Kola takes a step away from me, free hand twitching, and I want to reach out to him. But I wait until he finally nods at me, walking backward to speak with the men who have accompanied him. They talk for a few moments, hard glares and a few raised voices.

"Let me speak," says Esu. The bleeding has stopped and now he stands tall, pride in his eyes mixed with a dark glint. "I will explain."

"No." My answer is quick. I don't trust him not to antagonize Kola. "I know that you're needed, but all he has is thoughts of what you did." All *I* have is thoughts of what you did, I think but don't say.

Esu sighs and takes a step back in the sand, Folasade hovering next to him. "As you wish."

When Kola returns, it is with an uneasy look sliding across his face. He gestures toward a large palm tree and I follow him.

The knot of tension in his back is plain to see, the scars from the lashes still crisscrossed in raised ridges. I think of the òyìnbó ships and shiver.

"What's happening, Simi? Why are you with him?"

I snatch a look over my shoulder at Esu. How can I tell Kola that my alliance with Olokun was a mistake? That I left him only to be lied to?

"What is it?" Kola asks. He stands apart from me. His distance hurts, but the look on his face is worse. Suspicion is woven through the folds of his frown, and every time his eyes meet mine, they skate away again. "Why would you defend the orisa who took my brother and sister? The same one who . . ." Kola stops, lips tightening.

I take a deep breath and steel myself. "Olokun didn't honor his promise to me. He kept Esu." My shame-filled whisper floats on a long exhale. Twisting my fingers, I focus on my toes sinking into the sand.

"And this is bad?" Kola scoffs in the direction of the trickster. I look over at Esu, who stands tall, feet planted wide apart, talking to Folasade. "I would see him buried deep beneath the sea for all eternity for what he did."

"I would, too, but remember his roles?"

"Yes, but—"

"The ajogun, Kola." I dare to look up at him now, waiting for what I have said to sink in.

His sneer fades, eyes widening as the realization hits him. "So who will appease them . . . ?"

"No one." My reply is heavy.

Kola watches me carefully as I explain everything. When I finish, silence stretches between us as sweat gathers at my hairline, sliding down my neck. There is no breeze, and the day is growing warmer. Above us, a gray dove coos before taking flight, shattering the stillness.

"I'll take you all to Oko." Kola shakes his head, mouth creased. "I'd rather have Esu where I can keep an eye on him. We can plan what we will do from there."

"We?" I look up at Kola, and this time he meets my gaze full-on. He doesn't smile, but there is something other than anger there.

"Did you think I would let you do this on your own?"

• • •

The journey to Oko is filled with the constant comments of Esu, from joy at a yellow-striped butterfly to disgust at the stones beneath his soles. Kola hasn't spoken since we left the beach, barely glancing at me. Instead, he and his men keep Esu in their sights, their bows with arrows still nocked.

As the orisa begins to gripe about the growing heat, Folasade looks over at me with a grimace. She keeps pace with the trickster, but I notice a very slight limp when she walks. I gesture to her feet, wondering if they are hurting her since the dull ache has begun in mine, but Folasade shakes her head, raising her chin.

"How do you bear it, little fish?" Esu asks, closing the gap between us, his skinny plaits grazing his jaw. I check to see if Kola has noticed the orisa speaking to me and feel a silly rush of relief when he doesn't look over. Esu lifts a foot and removes a stone from between his toes. At first I think that he means my feet, but then I see him fanning himself with a large leaf.

"The sun?"

"Yes, I forgot the sheer intensity of it. The heat almost feels too much after the deep chill of the sea."

"You'll adjust," I murmur, walking faster, trying to catch up with Kola. He has only looked back at me once, but it was enough to see worry in the set of his face.

As the sun climbs the sky, I draw level with Kola, focusing on putting one foot in front of the other, the scent of the salt slowly fading as the sand beneath our feet changes to grass. I want to ask him how he is, how his family and Bem are. I want to talk about Yinka, about Issa and his sweet face.

I look sideways at Kola. "Have you been well?" The question is plain, and I wince at its simplicity.

Kola shows no sign of hearing me as he turns to his men. "Wait," he commands. "Let's stop for water."

Behind us I hear Esu exclaim his pleasure and Folasade's quiet, terse reply. My face burns at Kola ignoring me. But what should I have expected? I left him without much explanation. I'm about to turn away when he hands me his waterskin, directing his men to share with Folasade and Esu.

Kola is careful not to let our fingers touch, snatching his hand away the moment I grasp the container. I take a big gulp, water trickling down my chin.

"They respect you." I wipe my mouth and gesture to the men, who circle Esu and Folasade loosely.

"They're pledged to me." Kola secures his waterskin, still not looking at me. "I'm the captain of the Oko guard now. Bàbá says it is good practice for when . . ."

"When what?" I ask. Kola glances at me quickly and I see a flash of sorrow. I know how much his family means to him, the things he did to get back to them.

"For when he eventually dies and I take his place." Kola's voice is soft. His jaw flexes as he composes himself. "I'm learning all I can, while I can."

"That is—"

"Simi, why did you leave the way you did?" I close my mouth on words that die in my throat. Does he really mean, why did I leave him?

"I had to," I say eventually. I've asked myself this same question time and time again, all the while knowing that it was the right decision. But now, for some reason, I am the one who can't look Kola in the face. "It was easier the way it was."

"I looked for you, Simi," says Kola, his eyes meeting mine, bright and intense. "Every chance I got."

I want to step forward, to cup his face and tell him that he has been all I can think about since I left. That deep in the dark and cold waters, the thought of him has burned through me.

I take a breath and look down, away from the heat of Kola's gaze. His search for me doesn't mean that things are different. Mami Wata can never act on their love for a human. We still can't be together, and now his responsibilities mean his life will always be Oko. Still, I want to offer him something.

"I saw you. Just the other day." I think of when I spotted him on his ship. When we saw the dead who had pledged themselves to the ajogun. "There was another ship . . . ," I say, remembering the debris that layered the waves in charred wood and bodies.

"Yesterday? We hunted down a Tapa ship." Kola's eyebrows rise. I watch a bead of sweat slide from his hairline and settle into the thick twist of a new frown. "After, I thought I could . . . sense you. That you were there."

I think about the pull I, too, felt. Was that coincidence? Kola moves closer and my pulse spikes and stutters.

"I wanted to stay, to search more, but Bem argued that it was best we leave, in case there were more ships," he explains. "The Tapa have increased their attacks, striking along the length of the Oyo Kingdom. Even against Oyo-Ile."

"The capital?" *My home* is what I want to say, my mind going straightaway to my mother and father. I wonder if they are done mourning me or if they still believe I am alive. Either way they will be grieving my loss. Perhaps I can get word to them, I think, twisting my fingers together.

"People are saying that soon the Aláàfin will declare war." Kola's face shows a seriousness in the hollows of his cheekbones. "The Nupe Kingdom has killed many."

I flinch, small bumps rising on the backs of my arms even in the heat of the day. "I saw the men's armor, from the ship you attacked."

"We were able to intercept them before they raided the coast." Kola smiles but it doesn't reach his eyes. "When I think of them coming so close to Oko . . ." He sucks in a breath and twists his head from side to side, stretching his neck.

"I saw their leathers. The marks on them." I picture the eight slash marks and the circles that represent each warrior, and I swallow the thickness in my throat. "I don't know if you were close enough to see, but they were pledged to the ajogun."

Kola runs a hand over his black curls and looks back at Esu and Folasade. "Then it's true." His gaze meets the orisa's, and I see his eyes harden as he fully accepts what I told him earlier.

"Now you see why Esu is needed."

CHAPTER TEN

WE APPROACH OKO through mahogany trees so dense that they ring most of the village with natural protection. The air is filled with the trill of forest robins, flashes of their orange breasts breaking up the green foliage. Esu follows the flight of one of the small birds, pleasure shining in his eyes, oblivious to the daggered looks that Kola gives him. Needing the orisa now doesn't change what he did, and, feeling wary of what both might do, I slide between Esu and Kola, avoiding the latter's stare.

"We won't enter via the main gate. Everyone is even more on guard with the Tapa attacks," explains Kola. "The last thing I want to do is turn up with Esu and watch the villagers riot. Not after what he did to Taiwo and Kehinde."

"How are they?" I ask at the mention of his younger brother and sister. I smile at the thought of Kehinde's fierce glare and Taiwo's bright grin.

"Well," says Kola, and even though his tone is curt, I can see the warmth that their names bring to his eyes. "They ask after you. A lot."

"Perhaps I can see them?"

"They'd like that," answers Kola, staring at my mouth for a

beat too long. He turns away when I notice, and I blink, pushing down the glimmer of pleasure.

The men uncover the discreet gateway, barely distinguishable from the tall wall that wraps around Oko. Kola warns them not to speak of Esu, but to let Bem know to meet him at his family compound. Half of them leave while the others secure the entrance behind us. Holding a finger to his lips, Kola ushers us along. We slide past, Esu and Folasade behind me. I turn, wary of Esu and Kola so close together, but the boy merely cuts a glance at the trickster with narrowed eyes.

We stand in a loose group on an empty dirt path running behind what looks like the Oko guard barracks, just next to Kola's compound. It is midmorning, but hidden from the rest of the village, we can only hear the shouts of market traders, the shrieks of children, and the occasional calls of chastisement after raucous laughter. A waft of something sweet frying is carried on the breeze and I inhale it greedily.

Kola leads us along, small puffs of dirt clouding his ankles as he hurries toward a door painted the same tan as the wall. When he cracks the panels open, a rush of roasting meat and the fiery kick of peppers meets us. Esu groans loudly, holding his stomach, and Folasade shushes him. Kola beckons and we slip into what turns out to be the cooking quarters of his family compound.

"We have until twilight. Oyo representatives of the Aláàfin are here. Everyone is with the council, discussing the Tapa. Let's find out what needs to be done." Kola gestures to Esu, but the orisa has his eyes on the cooking pots.

"I will need to eat first," he says, wetting his lips.

Kola frowns, taking time to calm himself before he answers.

"We will eat while we discuss the situation." He freezes at the sudden patter of footsteps.

"You're back already . . . ?" The voice reaches us before the girl does. When she steps into the doorway, her gaze goes straight to Kola. She lifts a hand to her forehead, shading her eyes, and for a minute I think my heart may have stopped its beat. She takes another step inside and I remember again the set and curve of her shoulders, her round face and full cheeks. *There will be a dimple in her left cheek,* I think.

Ara.

The sour burst of pears floods my memory. Fingers sectioning my hair, weaving the curls into neat lines of braids. A laugh as deep as the river we sometimes swam in. A gap between her two front teeth, but the bottom as straight as the walls around Oyo-Ile.

My closest friend from home.

The girl who was searching the forest for wild fruit with me when the òyìnbó attacked. When they took us. The girl I haven't seen since I was dragged to the sea, bundled on a boat, and taken to the larger ship that skulked in the deeper water.

"Simi?"

I don't speak, not capable of doing more than nodding as I stumble toward her. Ara cries out, but I don't catch the words. Instead, I'm flinging myself into the arms she holds open. And then we are squeezing, wrapped around each other, tears sliding into smiles. I sniff and Ara moves as if to pull back, but I don't let her. She is warm and smells of shea butter and home. I press my lips to her cheek and then against her ear.

"You are alive," I whisper. Those words alone feel like a miracle.

Grinning, I let her peel away from me, holding my hands, our fingers intertwined as we look at each other.

"And you're here," Ara says, dimple in her cheek, her hair braided neatly in the korobá style she has always favored.

"I am." I want to hug her again. "How are you in Oko? What happened to you?"

Ara shakes her head, smile fading as her arms go slack, the tips of her fingers still captured in mine. She looks around me at the others and then down at the ground.

Esu is lifting the lids of pots, scooping out hot rice even though Folasade scolds him and Kola's face fills with thunder.

"We'll be outside," murmurs Folasade behind me, pulling Esu by the arm as he crams some rice into his mouth. Once Folasade and Kola have led Esu through to the courtyard, Ara looks back up at me. She smiles, but it is a shadow of what it used to be, and I am left with thoughts of what has happened to us both. They crowd in, stealing some of the joy at seeing Ara again.

"After they separated us, where did they take you?" I ask quietly, thinking of when we were forced to walk to the coast. I thought the river Ogun was powerful, but seeing the giant waves and water stretching to the horizon for the very first time made me feel so small.

Ara sucks in a breath, her lips trembling as she twists her fingers. "The òyìnbó traded me." There are faint scars on her wrists, but those are only the ones I can see. I know that, just as with me, there are more, unseen and deeper.

"Where? Who with?"

"The Tapa."

The Nupe Kingdom. I can't help my sharp intake of breath. "But . . . why?"

"The òyìnbó wanted their gold and ivory, and the Tapa wanted the òyìnbó's weapons." Ara tries to lift her chin, but I see her shoulders tremble. "And people like me to serve in their city."

I'm scared of asking her more. Now is not the time. Drawing Ara to me again, I clasp her tightly as if I can squeeze the pain and the memories from her.

"It's all right, Simi," Ara whispers in my ear before pulling back. "I was taken to the temple in Rabah. I did whatever the Oba's iyalawo needed. I managed to escape a few months ago. Kola found me in the forest when he was patrolling with the guard. They help anyone who is trying to escape the Tapa." Ara's eyes are round and shining.

"I'm sorry." I lower my head as guilt eats away at me. Soon, I think, there will be nothing left.

"Sorry for what, Simi?" A small line forms between Ara's eyebrows. "What happened was neither of our faults."

"If I hadn't made you come to the forest that day—"

"No one *made* me do anything." Ara's fingers dig into the soft flesh of my arms as she seizes me, pulling me to her. "What happened was the òyìnbó's fault, and then the Tapa after them."

"But—"

Ara shakes her head, her mouth curled at the edges. "I think it was better than what you had to endure."

I pull back at her words. "What do you mean?"

Now it is Ara's turn to hold on to me, her glare softening. "Kola has been looking for you ever since you pledged yourself to Olokun. He told me what happened to you." She looks down at my legs and then up to the emerald that adorns the dagger stashed in my hair.

I don't know if I want her to see that part of me yet. The things I have had to do. How changed I am. I want to be the girl she grew up with, the one she laughed with late at night, who ran through the streets of Oyo-Ile, escaping from our chores.

"I've been helping Kola. The iyalawo knew certain things, had knowledge that he hoped would help when he becomes the village leader."

"What kind of knowledge?" My tongue feels thick as I stumble over the words. Kola told Ara about me, I think as I see him return with the others. What else did he say?

"Let's eat." Kola's voice is gentle as he calls to us, holding out some wooden bowls with concentric circles carved on them. "There will be more time after for you two."

"Why didn't you tell me when you first saw me?" My eyes narrow. "About Ara."

Kola avoids looking at me, but I see him pause. "There were . . . other things that were more of a shock." He glances at Esu. "Even if we hadn't agreed on all of you coming back here, I would have made sure that you were reunited."

His answer annoys me, as if it was a punishment for being with Esu. But at least Ara is safe, I think, gazing at her in awe. She is here. And that is enough for me, for now.

"We can speak later." Ara hugs me again and whispers into my ear. "There is hope."

Hope? Hope for what? Whatever she means, there is no hope unless the ajogun are bound. Together, we head into the bright light of the compound's rectangular courtyard.

I pass the rest of the bowls out as Folasade grabs the calabash of water and hands it to Esu, who looks down in disgust at having to carry anything. Ara offers a platter of charred beef to Kola first, its spiced scent heavy in the air. Folasade lowers bowls of mangoes and rice. The freshness of the food reminds me of the disease and death that began to blight Oko after the twins were taken. The memory only increases my gratitude for the simple meal in front of us, and I murmur a small prayer of thanks to Yemoja.

The others settle on woven mats of orange and red, and as I sit down, I must remember how to bend and twist my limbs, enabling me to sit cross-legged. Folasade does the same, frowning in concentration at the position that was once so natural but is now almost alien to her. Esu reaches for the beef, and I feel a flash of annoyance that he is getting to eat what he nearly destroyed.

"Simidele!" The voice is low and rumbles across the courtyard and in one moment I have unfolded myself, jumping to my feet and whirling to see Bem. He breaks into a run, crossing the space between us in seconds and lifting me up so that he can spin me around. The deep bass of Bem's laugh vibrates between us and I squeeze him back, my arms wrapped around his neck. Bem sets me down gently, eyes going to Kola.

"The guards told me you were back . . . with guests. But never did I imagine!"

Kola nods, and the simple gesture causes the smile to slip from Bem's face. "What is it?" He turns back to me now, running his gaze over me. "Are you well?"

I nod, shoulders drawing up, tense for the moment I know is coming. I open my mouth to warn him, but Bem is scanning the compound now, confusion creasing his face when he notices Folasade and Esu. And then his expression hardens and he lunges toward the trickster, fists bunched.

Kola rises quickly, placing a hand on his friend's broad chest. "It's all right. Sit down." Bem strains for a moment more, but Kola mutters something that only he can hear, and then he lowers himself slowly, lips pressed into a thin line. "All will be explained."

Kola and Bem sit opposite Esu, platters of chicken, beef, hot rice, and fruit between them. Neither can seem to help the glowering looks they give the orisa, and I find myself whispering prayers of patience to Yemoja as we take turns rinsing our fingers in the calabash.

Hoping to distract them, if only temporarily, I spoon beef onto everyone's rice. Esu smacks his lips together, mouth shining with grease from the chicken he has already helped himself to. Ara sits next to Bem, murmuring to him, keeping him calm as he continues to glare at Esu. Eventually, he succumbs, scooping up the rice and beef spiced with peanuts, chilies, and ginger that she puts in his bowl.

"Simi, can you tell the others what you told me?" begins Kola. His words are polite, but he still doesn't look at me and he doesn't touch any of his food.

I try to swallow, a ball of rice stuck in my throat, mouth drying at the thought of explaining my mistake. But Folasade saves me.

"Esu was bound beneath the sea by Olokun. Confined to the Land of the Dead."

Bem puts his bowl down with a loud thud. "That sounds about right to me." His lips twist, and I know he's thinking of Yinka, lost in the volcano on Esu's island. Of Issa and his death in the jaws of the sasabonsam.

Esu pauses, a sliver of meat halfway to his mouth. "I will admit that I was not . . . at my best."

"Your *best*?" Kola splutters, eyes bulging as he jumps to his feet. "You took my brother and sister. Left our lands to rot." His voice cracks. "We lost friends because of you."

"Come, Kola," says Ara softly, rising. She places a hand on his shoulder briefly. "Let's see what Simi says."

Shame snakes inside me and tears prick at the backs of my eyes. He's right. We lost so much, and a lot of it was my fault. Taking a sip of water, I force the rice down my throat, then push my bowl away.

Esu scoops up more meat, shoving it between his lips and chewing, ignoring Kola. Once he finishes, he wipes the grease from his lips. "I am what I am. My actions reflect me, and this I cannot help. I am the trickster, messenger, Lord of the Cross-roads. To count on anything else would be like expecting to swim unharmed with crocodiles." He tilts his head to the sky. "Olodumare knows this. All know this."

Bem's expression is still thunderous, and Kola's face is like stone. "But what matters now is keeping the balance of this world. Our world," I say. I glance at the ruby dangling from my wrist as it spins in the sun, scattering red light on my skin.

Esu pauses for a moment, his eyes flicking down to the crimson jewel. "Simidele speaks the truth."

"And how do we know that you won't trick us again?" Kola asks, a muscle twitching in his jaw. He smacks a hand against his thigh. "How do we know that you will bind the ajogun but not leave us in some other worse position?"

"You do not." Esu stares back at Kola, the silver in his eyes flaring like icy shooting stars. "But this is my purpose. Even though you may not like it, this world is mine, too. I would not see it destroyed." He lifts his hands up in the air, fingers shining with grease, and grins sharply. "After all, as I said before, what fun would I be able to have then?"

"We have no other choice," I add, ignoring Esu's last jibe and trying to keep my voice steady. A trickle of sweat runs between my shoulder blades. "It seems as if the Tapa have already made use of the thinning veil between us and the ajogun."

"What do you mean?" asks Ara, her eyes wide.

"The Nupe ship that we attacked a few days ago," Kola explains. "Simi and Folasade saw their dead. They had symbols of the ajogun."

"They had pledged themselves to the ajogun?" asks Bem, fear curling the ends of his words.

"Yes. If they are siphoning their power somehow, those attacks reported from Oyo-Ile make more sense."

"And if they are using the influence of the ajogun while waiting for them to be released, then they could be harnessing that power to control creatures of a different kind." I swallow hard at the thought of the Ninki Nanka and the sasabonsam.

"Idera did say . . ." Ara sits down, fingers twisted together in her lap. When she looks up, her eyes are round. ". . . that for every village the Tapa conquer, in the ajogun's name, for every . . . life . . . they take, the warlords are fed, if you will. And then they are drawn that much closer to the veil."

"Idera?" I ask.

"She is the Nupe Oba's spiritual adviser. Her power is . . . immense," says Kola. "And growing."

"The more they kill, the easier summoning the ajogun will be?" I ask.

"That's what Idera believes," says Ara. "It's why she has been encouraging the Oba of the Nupe Kingdom to attack as many villages and cities of the Oyo as possible. Idera claims to be able to influence the victories of the Tapa. She blesses the soldiers. To give them strength and cunning in battle."

This would mean she has made a bargain with them, I think as Esu nods his head coolly. "With every death in their name, she is bringing the ajogun closer, harnessing their energy in order to

97

make it easier to release them." The trickster picks a sliver of beef from his teeth before looking around at all of us. My stomach dips when I think of the wars, the famine, and the pestilence that the ajogun will unleash.

"Why can Olodumare not do something about this?" asks Kola.

"Perhaps they would have been able to," says Esu as he licks his lips free of grease, "if I had been free to pass on what is happening. Otherwise, the Supreme Creator does not concern themselves."

"And now you are." Kola folds his arms, watching the trickster.

Esu waves a large hand lazily in the air before plucking another drumstick from the platter before him. "It has gone too far. By the time I request their audience, the moon will have fattened and then Idera will have released the ajogun. There is no time."

"They have to be bound by the full moon?" Kola's voice rises, and I sense a panic that mirrors my own when Esu first told me.

The orisa chews his chicken slowly, his eyes on me. After he swallows, he sucks each finger before answering. "That . . . or released."

I place my bowl on the floor, unable to take another bite. "So then, tell us, what needs to be done to stop this?"

Esu sits up straighter, plaits skating the tops of his shoulders. "The binding of the ajogun would usually involve rituals with the aje. The Mothers would help me in placating and catering to the anti-gods' darker nature." He pauses, wiping his hands on his wrapper and sighing. "But I have been away too long. Too many rituals have been missed."

"So, what does this mean?" I hate how thin my voice is, stretched with the strain of relying on such an orisa.

"There is only one way left to prevent the ajogun from obtaining their freedom." Esu leans toward me, tapping the side of his nose with his thumb. "We need to seal whatever gateway has been prepared for their entry into the world. This will stop them from escaping and their power from being used. Once this is done, I can go back to keeping the balance between them and this realm."

"Tell us exactly what is needed," urges Kola as he looms over Esu.

The orisa closes his eyes in a long blink before continuing. "If we don't act by the next full moon, the ajogun will ruin the earth and the blood of the land will flow. The world as we know it will cease to exist." The trickster looks up at Kola, his eyes a careful black. "To put a stop to this, we need the soul and song of a creature long feared. 'He who stops the flow of rivers.' The Mokele-mbembe."

"Mokele-mbembe?" I ask.

"That is what I said." Esu beckons to me, gesturing to the ruby. "Hold it up."

Slowly, I lift the jewel, thumb and forefinger framing it.

"Now, stay still." Esu stares at the gem. "The Mokele-mbembe's power is tremendous." Light twists up from the jewel and I gasp, my hand shaking. "Hold it still, I said." Esu frowns at me as the red glow twists and spins before us. "Some think it is a monster or a demon or both. Either way, it is a creature that wreaks terror, the way it rises from the depths, cracking boats with its long neck and its ironclad back. Snapping the bodies of men in its jaws." Esu pauses as the red glow begins to transform, solidifying and creating a squat body and then a long neck. With fiery eyes, the small monster opens its mouth and roars silently, spikes of teeth lining its jaws.

"Legends say that the Mokele-mbembe sings each time it takes a life, and that if it is killed, the songs it sang while consuming souls will be released as one, twining with its own essence, creating an anima full of great power. A sound that the ajogun crave. One that will pacify them or release them, depending on the ritual."

The tiny conjured Mokele-mbembe snaps at me. I flinch just as Esu clicks his fingers and the creature disappears.

Ara sits back, her mouth open. "You need its soul song?" She lowers her eyes as we all look at her and dips her fingers in the calabash of water, shaking the droplets in the air. "I have overheard stories of this monster from the iyalawo in Rabah. Idera was certain it held the power to summon the ajogun."

"What did you see in your time at the temple?" I ask gently. I don't want Ara to have to relive anything that hurts her, but the more we know, the better prepared we'll be.

"She has a great interest in the ajogun and there are rumors that they are the source of her power." Ara's voice is soft, eyes on her lap. "The Oba has built her a temple that worships the eight warlords."

"How long has she been in the Nupe Kingdom?" Kola paces before us, hands in curled fists.

"She arrived one winter a few years ago," answers Ara. "No one knows where she came from, but she once mentioned an island off the southeast coast. The Oba treated her with respect straightaway, even though some of his advisers didn't approve."

"Why would the Oba trust her straightaway?" Folasade asks, her voice sharp.

"He said he had a dream of the Nupe Kingdom's victory through a power brought by a stranger." Ara's hands shake as she adjusts the folds of her wrapper. "And Idera showed her strength from the beginning. On the night of the Oba's birthday, days after she arrived, all those who opposed her died."

"How?" I ask, chilled at the thought of a ruler impressed with death.

Ara opens her mouth but then stops, shaking her head as tears film her gaze. "It's all right," I say quickly, reaching for her hand and squeezing her fingers. "You don't have to speak of it right now."

Esu examines Ara, his eyes sweeping from her braids to the feet tucked neatly under her. "This iyalawo is correct about the Mokele-mbembe. As I said, what is needed to bind will also set free, depending on the ritual and the intent."

"And how do we get this soul song?" asks Bem.

"Death, obviously." Esu picks up yet another drumstick, biting into the meat with large white teeth. "The only way to glean the Mokele-mbembe's soul song is to kill it. And then Simidele can use her sapphire to contain its essence until I can use it in the ritual, in which I bind the ajogun and seal the gateway."

Esu takes the chicken leg, now stripped of meat, from his mouth and cracks open the bone, cheeks hollow as he sucks the marrow from it, eyes fluttering in pleasure.

"You say this as if it's an easy feat." I force down the hunch of my shoulders and reach for a cup of water.

"Oh, it will certainly not be," says Esu, laying the pieces of bone at the edge of his bowl. "But it is the only way."

Kola finally sits as silence folds over us. Bem looks to him, worry pulling at the corners of his mouth.

"Where is the Mokele-mbembe?" I ask, my voice cutting through the quiet.

"The creature can be found in the water spaces between land and sea." Esu leans back and stretches, his fingernails shining in the air. "Is there anything to drink?"

Folasade hands the orisa some water, but he only peers at it in disgust. "I meant a proper drink." Looking around the courtyard, he jumps to his feet and saunters to the entranceway. Bem and Kola rise, watching the trickster.

Esu laughs and throws a look over his shoulder, eyes flashing. "Do not worry, I am not going anywhere." He reaches the corner and bends down to the altar, which is fresh with offerings. Ignoring the kola nuts, yam, and carcass of a rooster, he reaches for the flask of palm wine, holding it up to admire the images of Ogun that decorate its curved sides.

"That is for Ogun," hisses Bem, hands on the hilt of the sword strapped on his back. "How dare you take his offering."

Kola inhales deeply, lips thin with displeasure. "We can offer Ogun more palm wine. A better one." But he eyes Esu with open animosity as the orisa returns to us and sprawls on the cushions.

Esu takes a large swig from the flask before smiling widely, the drink cocooned in the folds of his wrapper. "Ogun does not need it in the way that I do. He would understand, trust me." The trickster takes another gulp and grins. "Besides, where is your Ogun now?" He peers around us. "I do not see him coming to your aid. Too busy judging people and playing with his weapons. Better that I drink this, then, yes?"

Kola and Bem sit back down, their glares dark in the light of the day.

"Where is this creature?" asks Kola, pushing patience into his tone. "You said the spaces between the land and the sea."

"It can be found in a chasm that is part of the sea but cuts into the earth," answers Esu, selecting the largest plum. He holds it in the air, admiring the succulent fruit before biting into it.

"And what does that mean, exactly?" asks Kola, his voice tight.

I quickly lean toward the orisa, cutting off anything else Kola might say. "You mean channels. The water between two lands?"

Esu finishes the plum, taking his time to savor every chew. "That is what I said," he answers finally, taking another lazy swig of palm wine.

Beside him, Folasade clears her throat and bends toward me across the emptying plates. "There is only one like that, the one between the Oyo and the Nupe kingdoms. It takes no more than an hour or so to sail across it, but it is still connected to the sea."

"You know of it?"

Folasade nods. "There was a great storm once, and I was washed inland to the chasm. I can take us there." She scrambles to her feet, glancing at the sky.

Two days left, I think. "Then we need to leave now," I say, holding out a hand to Folasade, who tugs me to my feet. "We'll go and return before the morning. Esu will stay here." Where he can be watched, I think.

"Good," remarks Esu. He burps loudly and stretches out on his back, skin gleaming a dark brown in the sun. "I need to get some heat in these bones."

"You can't go on your own," says Kola, but I don't look at him, smoothing the pleats of my wrapper instead.

"And you can't breathe under the sea, so I don't see what help you can be." I don't want to keep involving him. The fewer people at risk, the better.

Kola lifts his hands, mouth in a displeased line. "Simi, it would be silly to—" But he doesn't get to finish.

A loud shriek splits the air, quickly followed by more screams, all laced with terror.

CHAPTER ELEVEN

THE SKY IS full of a white-hot sun, but fear slides down my spine, ice-cold and clawed. Bem whirls toward the doorway, already unsheathing his sword. Another cry can be heard, disturbing the blanket of sudden silence. Ara clasps a hand to her mouth, moving closer to Folasade as my hand flies to the dagger in my hair.

"Stay here," says Kola, taking one last look at me before he follows Bem, sprinting to the entranceway of the compound.

I don't know what is causing the screams, but I'm not waiting to find out. "Look after Ara and keep an eye on Esu," I say, before spinning away from Folasade.

"Simidele!" she calls, but I ignore her strangled shout and close the door firmly behind me.

I take a breath, steadying myself before I start down the steps of Kola's compound, dagger held at my side. The wide central street is emptying rapidly as people scatter. One villager tries to push his cart, but it gets caught on a stone and tips, corn spilling onto the bare earth. The man scoops some of the crop into his arms before abandoning the rest, running for a doorway to his left. I descend quickly, feet scuffing on the broad steps as the villagers of Oko scramble home. Guards pour from the side streets, black wrappers and shining swords catching a sun that hovers above the fields.

There are more screams now and as a woman rushes past me, her child bound firmly to her in an expertly tied orange cloth, she clutches at me. "You must go home," she urges as her baby begins to cry. The woman's eyes are round, the whites bright as she reaches a hand backward, patting the soft curve of her child's spine. "It's not safe."

I open my mouth to answer but she reels away, feet kicking up dust as she disappears from the main street. I squeeze the hilt of my dagger tighter, running toward the gates of Oko, where I can make out Bem and Kola joining the throng of guards.

"What is it?" I gasp, coming to a stop next to them. "What's going on?"

Kola turns his wild gaze on me before looking back at the narrow opening. "The Tapa have attacked Oko guards on patrol. There are still some of our people out there."

"They're at the forest! We need to close the gates," says a tall man, his beard striped with white. "We need to protect your father and the council."

Kola shakes his head, his chest rising and falling with each quickened breath. "Don't shut the gates yet. The guards are coming, Adewale!" He points at the sliver of land beyond the entrance to Oko. "Look!"

Over his shoulder I can see a few people making their way back to the walls of the village. They're moving as fast as they can, carrying one between two of them, their progress hampered by the wounded.

"I have my orders," says Adewale, eyes a flat black as he begins to heave at the gates, another guard helping him. "We can't afford a breach of Oko. You know this."

"And you know that I'm in charge of the guard now. Keep the gates open unless you see the Tapa coming." Kola darts past the older man and slips through the gap. As he runs down the path toward the group, Bem follows, shouldering his way through the men. I sprint after them, arms pumping, ignoring the beginnings of pain in my feet.

Kola is the first to reach the Oko guards, scanning the path behind them for signs of danger.

"The Tapa," confirms a woman who is limping toward us, a bow dangling from her fingers as she grimaces in pain. "We were patrolling when we came across them. They attacked us but they've stopped at the tree line."

"How many?" asks Kola, his face drawn.

"Too many," is the woman's quiet reply. "At least a hundred, maybe more. Our best chance is to get back to Oko and hope the gates and walls hold. And even then . . ."

I peer around the group, studying the path behind them, wondering why the Tapa aren't following and attacking. The sun hits the tree canopy, creating slashes of light on an empty pass. The warrior's fear mixes with the smell of sweat and the copper tang of blood, strong in the heat. Bem doesn't wait any longer, taking the injured man from the other two guards and placing him gently on his huge shoulder before turning back to the gates.

"Let's go. Hurry," says Kola as he offers his help to another man with a ragged wound in his thigh, bound with a strip of ripped cloth. "Simi, quickly."

But I don't listen to him, watching the forest. The blur of green blends with the brown earth and branches of cream flowers. All is still in the last parts of the afternoon. And then I see them. A shift in the dark bushes, the shadow against a tree trunk, the glimmer of a blade. The Tapa line the forest, weapons ready. I edge my way backward, not taking my eyes off them. Kola shouts, but still I don't turn. There's a flash of bronze fabric through the trees.

Arms grab me from behind and I am lifted off my feet, carried before I can complain. The gates of Oko loom until I am dragged through the closing gap, deposited on the floor as they shut with a heavy thud.

"What did you think you were doing?" Kola glares down at me as I scramble to my feet. "I told you to stay here!"

"Why would you do that?" I splutter. "I'm capable of making my own decisions." I dust down my wrapper and slide the dagger back among the plaits at my crown.

"And look how they turn out," Kola snarls, stepping even closer to me. Behind him the guards blockade the gate.

I freeze, glaring up at him through a veil of sudden tears. Anger rushes in now, mixing with the truth of his words. Kola shuts his eyes and rubs a hand over his face.

"I didn't mean—"

"You did," I snap, and turn on my heel, stomping back along the main street, heading for the compound. How dare he? I did what was best for *everyone*. Everyone apart from me.

There are footsteps behind me, but I don't even slow.

"You need to stop doing this."

Kola's terse words bring me to a halt and I swing around. "Doing what?"

"Rushing into things!" His teeth are bared and his eyes are hard. "You could have been killed."

"And so could you!" I retort, chest swelling with fury.

"The Tapa are dangerous." His voice is low. "And I don't want you to keep . . . sacrificing yourself for everyone else."

"I know." I keep my reply even. "But—"

"Simi, just . . . let me finish." Kola rolls his shoulders and takes a few deep breaths, forcing himself to be patient, measuring his words. "You would have heard of them before, when you lived in Oyo-Ile, but since you've been gone it's gotten much worse. If I told you about the state we found the last village in . . ."

My fingers uncurl at the pain in his tone, my anger seeping away.

"There was no witness apart from a very small boy. He said something that scares me more than the warriors waiting in the forest."

I wait, a chill sweeping over me. "What?"

"He said that they came at night."

"The Tapa?"

"I don't know." Kola shakes his head. "But whatever attacked them, it sounds much worse."

• • •

I pluck at the emerald in the hilt of my dagger, sliding it free from my braids and keeping it in my right hand. Warriors line the walls of Oko, and the gates have been fortified with blocks of wood. Kola has ordered the guard to make sure everyone is inside their compounds with the doors secured. His parents and the council are still in the meeting quarters, protected with constant patrols.

"Where are Kehinde and Taiwo?" I ask, watching as the men

and women at the walls adjust their grips and stance. There is exhaustion in their faces, the waiting and trepidation taking their toll.

"With my parents. They've barely let them out of their sight since we got back."

I exhale, glad they're somewhere safe. But if the gates and the walls don't hold, then no one will be safe.

Guards are stationed at sections of the walls, with the larger groups by the gates. Patrols check on each contingent, all movements coordinated, obviously well practiced. I hover nearby, trying to calm the churn in my stomach, fiddling with the hilt of my dagger. When a tall youth tried to direct me to the safety of a compound, Kola waved him off, giving me a brief nod.

A scout confirmed that the Tapa were still in the forest. Waiting. A few whispers reach us now and again, questions about why they haven't yet attacked, about what the night will bring. Bem and Kola exchange glances before they both begin to stalk along the lines of guards, speaking words of calm, but even I can see the tightness of their grips, all knuckles and slipping fingers, their eyes darting about with apprehension.

The sun burns its last, blazing through the forest and taking the stifling heat of the day with it. Above us the light leaches from the sky, the moon a smudge behind flat clouds as the stars begin to make their appearance. The guards lining the walls are silent now, their faces tipped toward the stars, gleaming in the growing night. They have faced attacks before, but there is an edge to their fear in the set of shoulders.

Kola slips from group to group, continuing to reassure his people. His demeanor has changed so much in the past six months.

Commanding and in control, he clasps the shoulder of a young man, leaning forward to speak with him, leaving the boy with a face set with courage.

I wait at the blockade, running possible attacks through my mind until all I can think about is blood and screams and the smashing of wooden gates. *Stop,* I tell myself. *Oko is strong and so are its defenses.*

Kola returns to my side and I offer him a forced smile. He hands me a waterskin, and as I lift my lips to drink, a call comes from the dark forest. Long and low, it is answered by another. And another and another, until the shouts fill the air, carried to us on a gentle breeze.

"Simi, stay close to us," says Bem as he grips his sword, flexing his shoulders. "No matter what."

The high walls of Oko seem impenetrable, but I know that nothing can be taken for granted. And as the hoots grow closer, all the muscles in my body tense.

Kola calls out commands and the guards take defensive positions, spears pointed to the tops of the walls, with archers lining the edges of the streets. Another formation steps back, men and women ready with their swords, blades glittering in the moonlight.

The first blow to the gates rattles the hinges. I flinch, moving closer to Kola as the impact turns into a great pounding upon the wooden panels. The guards ready their weapons, snarls of determination in place.

And then the sound stops.

All our faces are turned to the gates as we wait, swallowing the dread that swells in our throats. I hold my dagger out, the trickster's ruby dangling from my wrist, a dark cherry red.

Esu should be here, fighting with the people of Oko, after all he did. I glare down at the gem and then suck in a breath when the jewel flares brightly, emitting a heat that sears the delicate skin of my wrist. Gasping into the darkness, I clamp a hand over the ruby, its glow seeping between my fingers. The pain is bright and immediate as everything else around me fades.

I spin in a slow circle. Oko is gone and I am surrounded by the streets of Oyo-Ile. In the distance is the fifteenth gate and when I look left, I see the main road that leads to the palace. It's dark, with a swirling charcoal mist that clings to my legs like smoke.

Stumbling once, I begin to walk, feet heading automatically in the direction of my home. The light of a crescent moon guides me, its rind a blackened yellow in the sky.

With each step I take, terror rises as I examine every compound gate I pass. The wooden panels gleam in the meager light, but there is enough illumination for me to see the marks. A slash and a circle, the sign of contagion.

Plague. And then I see him, just off the main road, slinking closer to the curved walls of a home. Elongated limbs and crooked fingers that reach for the wood, with ebony nails that spark red fire as he scorches his sign into each carved panel.

Epe. Warlord of curses.

I run. Past the palace guards' section, heading toward the mouth of the marketplace, small puffs of dirt rising with each step. The smell reaches me first. That sweet scent of rot that comes with fresh death. I skid to a stop, stumbling at the sight before me.

The market square, which I can only ever remember being full of spices, fruit, and fabrics or, later on at night, filled with people waiting for my mother's stories, is now an open grave. Bodies are stacked on one another in the center of the space. Ofo, lord of loss, stands in front of the dead, a body in his arms and more at his feet. He turns his head slowly, his mouth opening wide in a smile filled with long spines of teeth. I hold a hand to my nose, gagging on the stench of the decomposing dead, heels in the dirt as I frantically back up.

"No, no, no, no." I push myself up, stumbling around the edges now, desperate to get home.

Just as I reach the walls of my compound, tears running down my chin, the ruby at my wrist glows hotter, rising in temperature until I think it will melt my skin and eat away at my bones. I collapse against the wall, a scream ripping its way out, and claw at the jewel until it begins to cool and the faces around me fade.

Panting, the thump of my heart loud, I open my eyes to a twilight that envelops Oko. "Not real," I whisper, but I'm shaking as I try to rid myself of the premonition of Epe and Ofo. The pounding is still there, but it's coming from the gates. Sliding the ruby away from my skin, I remove my hand, examining the flesh underneath the gem, but there is no mark. "It's not real," I say again, repeating it until gradually my pulse stops racing.

Snatches of voices can be heard, carried on the evening wind. I strain forward, trying to make out the words as they weave in and out among the hammering on the gates. Gradually they grow into shouts that rise in the clear beginnings of night. A cacophony of yells echo in stillness.

"Death to all in the Oyo Kingdom!"

CHAPTER TWELVE

THE GATES OF Oko shake as they are struck again. Cracks rend the air, and this time the wood splinters as something huge batters them from the outside.

"Keep your formation!" calls Kola, but there is fear in his eyes as he surveys the Oko guard scrambling into defensive positions along the perimeter of the village.

I tremble, thinking of my vision, just as there is another hit on the gate, this one even stronger. The wooden panels shudder before a fissure appears, a black jagged line that, with another batter, breaks them apart. As the hinges give way, the dagger in my fist wavers, my breath caught deep in my chest. Through the fragments of the gates, I can see the shadowy forms of the Tapa swinging thick tree boughs against the panels. Clouds scud across the moon, leaving us in near darkness for several seconds as more pounding comes from the entrance of Oko. When the moon fights free, the gates hang in ruins and the first of the Nupe warriors tear their way through the wreckage.

Seeing their swords gleaming in the night light and their eyes flashing, I try hard not to take a step back. Kola shouts, directing the guard to meet the invaders in black-and-yellow wrappers. The

Tapa charge toward us, and I catch the concentric circles slashed through with eight lines on thick leather breastplates. Terror crystallizes into something sharp that sticks under my ribs. Bem rushes forward with his long sword, sweeping the sharp edge over the chests of two Tapa. The Oko guard fan out, formations tight to keep the Nupe warriors from running to the rest of the village.

We are surrounded by the clash of steel and the metallic scent of wet blood. Blades and curses shatter the night air. To my left, an Oko archer is cut down by a Tapa spear that finds her shoulder. All around me souls spiral, glittering gold and silver, rising into a black sky. A lump fills my throat as tears burn at the loss of lives.

I stay close to Kola as he spins through the oncoming fighters, sword cutting through them in deadly arcs. Three men rush at him, but Kola kicks one from his side while slashing at the other two, sending one to his knees. The Oko guard are fighting just as valiantly, but more of the Nupe fighters stream through the broken gates and my stomach sinks as I realize how badly outnumbered we truly are.

Screams echo around us, and Bem and Kola struggle to keep up our defense. Dodging a jab from a wicked-looking dagger, I bring my fist up, hitting out. The girl who attacked me reels backward, stumbling in the cool dirt. I look past the fighting, watching as the darkness shifts and a woman steps through the hanging remains of the gates. Thick locs of hair tumble past broad shoulders and down to the waist of a shining bronze wrapper. Power emanates from this statuesque woman, and there's no doubt in my mind who this is.

"Idera," I whisper, my fingers tightening on my dagger.

The iyalawo swings her head, observing the battle with a detached look. She calls out, a short ululation that alerts the Tapa. They draw back, forming lines around us, waiting.

Idera is almost as tall as the largest Nupe men who watch us, with long legs and muscled arms bound with strips of leather. As she steps into the moonlight, I see shining copper strands wound around her locs, each one rippling with every roll of her hips. I look around nervously. So few of the Oko guard are left standing as they try to pull the injured back into the safety of the village's inner streets. Idera comes to a stop just ahead of us and smiles, revealing small teeth as glossy as seed pearls.

"Not much of a defense," Idera says, gazing around her, her voice a deep rasp against the soft breeze of night. "I heard tales of how this village held its own against the Tapa for years. And now look."

"We will never fold, Idera," says Kola through clenched teeth. He straightens up next to me, his chest rising and falling heavily. Some of the remaining fighters gather around us, a cluster of the last vestiges of strength and determination.

"Ah, so you do know who I am, then." The iyalawo smiles as she replies.

"We know who you are." Kola grimaces. Blood drips from his sword, pattering onto the earth, spotting his feet. "The Oyo Kingdom has heard of you. Of how the Oba of the Tapa would never be making his current moves unless you were by his side."

Idera pauses to grin and I see that her right eye is scarred, its milkiness suggesting loss of sight. "This is true. Real knowledge takes time and skill to use to your advantage."

She moves closer to Kola, pointing at the injured warriors just beyond us. Many are slumped on the bare earth, blood pooling around them. "Oko is spent. Surrender to Tapa rule now and we will think about sparing your children."

Kola grinds his teeth as Bem puts a hand on his arm, keeping him in place. Idera cocks her head to one side, waiting for his reply.

"I won't give Oko up to you," Kola says, his voice low, a lift to his chin. He grips his sword tighter and I know that we will fight. "My people are strong enough, no matter what."

Idera regards us coolly before she laughs. She lifts both hands, her bronze wrapper shimmering. "Then so be it." The Tapa behind her begin to advance, snarls on their faces as they raise their bloodied weapons.

"Be ready!" growls Kola as he takes a step forward, eyes darting over the advancing fighters. Two identical Tapa women with braids that snake down to their shoulders eye him, their spears held high.

I swallow and move beside Kola. A flicker of movement behind Idera catches my eye and I pause, peering forward. The space between Oko's gates is caught in a moonbeam as the clouds part, revealing a cluster of silhouettes in the entranceway. Idera stiffens as the Tapa gather around her, only the slightly crooked set of her shoulders giving away the fact that all is not as it seems. The night sky shifts again, clouds taking the light just as the people move, surging down the street. Idera roars and raises her hands, directing her warriors to the newcomers.

I strain, trying to make out whether they are Oko guards returning from patrol or, better yet, reinforcements from Oyo-Ile. As they run down the central path, they are lit again by the moon. Silver light gleams on a shaved head and high cheekbones. The girl raises her axes and calls out a command to those around her, scanning past the Tapa until her eyes fall on us.

"Yinka," I whisper, my dagger almost slipping from my grip.

CHAPTER THIRTEEN

SHE'S ALIVE.

My legs weaken with the realization as Yinka grins, teeth and mouth arranged with a wild edge. She comes to a halt on the path, the pack behind her, and it is then that I see Aissa. Standing taller than the others with her hair in buns over each ear, she looks to Yinka, who nods once.

The bultungin.

Hope bubbles up within me as I transfer my dagger to my left hand, wiping the sweat from my fingers. I thought I would never see Yinka again after Esu's island. We left her behind when the passageway through the volcano collapsed, and she held off the attacking bultungin so that we could escape. I think of the volcano and the heat from the thick river of lava. The bultungin, bewitched by Esu to defend his lands from anyone who sets foot on them.

Kola fights a smile, his chest still heaving with exertion, but Bem grins broadly, raising his sword at their childhood friend. Yinka nods once at us. Surrounded by the rest of the pack, gray fur wrappers almost silver in the twilight, she gives a low call. Before Yinka has even finished, skin ripples, fur growing and spreading over bodies that fall to the ground. The moon shines down on us, sliced in an onyx sky, its glow illuminating Oko. My heart beats faster as fingernails lengthen into claws and shoulders widen. The air fills with the sound of bones cracking and the accompanying screams of transformations.

"Yinka!" My call is full of caution as the bultungin form in front of the Tapa, a line of hyenas that stand twice as tall as normal ones.

The iyalawo shouts, glowering at us from the center of her warriors. Her voice is edged with ferocity as she commands the Tapa to attack. Yinka remains as she is, axes held in both hands as she adjusts her stance, muscles bunched. Howls echo around the empty streets as the bultungin lower their heads, jaws snapping.

With a snarl, the creature that is Aissa looks to Yinka, and when Yinka releases another command, the bultungin turn and surge toward the Tapa.

Yinka drops her axes and launches herself down the path after them with a grace and speed I remember well. And then she is leaping, soaring through the air as the fur of her wrapper spreads over her skin, shoulders widening and fingers turning into claws. Delicate spots are littered over her flank as she transforms in a ripple of flesh and bone and moonlight. A howl splits her lips and then she is no longer the girl I remember, but a deadly and beautiful creature.

"Follow me!" shouts Kola to the remaining guards behind us. Some are slack-jawed at the sight of the bultungin, but Yinka's presence seems to galvanize them, and they follow, heading toward the bultungin.

I run forward, soft soles hurting in the scuff of the earth. My heart rises in my throat as I try to keep up with Kola. And then

I am knocked off my feet, landing on my side, my breath gone. Above me, the midnight sky bristles with stars as I fight to fill my lungs. I clutch at my stomach, dagger loose in my grip as a face fills my vision. Slivers of white eyes in a vicious glare and bared bright teeth. I open my mouth to scream as the woman above me pushes down, her arm horizontally on my chest, pinning the hand that holds my dagger. She wields a knife, grinning as she brings it close to my neck. I buck beneath her, trying to throw her off. The woman snickers as she presses her blade against my throat. I gasp as a trickle of blood flows down my neck, my breath cut off. And then, a blur and a grunt from above and I can see the stars again.

Kola bends over me. Breathing heavily, he offers me his hand. I let him lift me to my feet, only allowing myself a quick glance at the crumpled figure of the woman.

"Where's the iyalawo?" I ask, turning away and craning my head around, searching for a flash of bronze. The fighting has stopped, with only a clump of Oko guards and Tapa warriors in a final scuffle amid the ruins of the gates.

"She's gone," says Kola as I straighten up by his side, watching the last of the Nupe warriors escape.

• • •

The gate hangs in tatters. I stand back, exhausted, as the guards attempt to blockade the entrance with wooden slats.

Yinka lopes over to me, her cheekbones giving her the regal beauty that so intimidated me when we first met. Now the sight of her fills me with a lightness that I desperately need, and we clasp hands.

119

"Are you all right? What happened to you?" The questions tumble from my mouth. "I thought I'd never see you again."

"What Aissa said was true. I am kin." Yinka squeezes my fingers, throwing a look at the tall bultungin girl. "Which meant that they couldn't attack me." She smiles again, joy creasing her lips.

I think of all my own memories, reclaimed and mine. To know where you came from holds so much power over how you feel about yourself. This I know very well. Yinka tips her chin toward the pack, a calmness settling over her features.

"I'll tell you everything." She turns to me, eyes flashing with a luminous glaze that looks more than human. "I promise."

I nod, squeezing her hand as we watch the Oko guard tending to their injured.

"So many lost," I whisper as cloths are laid over the dead, the murmur of prayers faint as each person is blessed.

Aissa comes to Yinka's side, her skin gleaming in the moonlight. "You were right," she says with admiration. The girl faces me and gestures to Yinka. "She heard of attacks in the Oyo Kingdom."

"We came across people fleeing their villages," Yinka says, her stare hardening. "They spoke of the òyìnbó. There have been more sightings, more stolen. But they also told us of the Tapa attacking, their stories including things I'd never heard before."

"Like what?" I ask, but something about the expression that slides over Yinka's face makes me almost regret it. A flash of pain and suffering.

"The refugees spoke of deaths that were . . . unnatural."

I think of Kola's recounting of the decimated village they found. "Go on."

"Some of the people who were left had been drained of their blood, their bodies ripped apart. There were no children. Not even their remains." Yinka swallows, placing a hand on her stomach as if to steady herself. "The villages attacked were all in the Oyo Kingdom. The attacks were spreading to the coast."

"And getting closer to Oko," finishes Aissa, rubbing Yinka's shoulder. "She insisted we make our way here as quickly as possible."

"I didn't want this village to share the same fate," says Yinka. She rolls her neck, as if to stretch out her uneasiness. I watch her, thinking about what could have happened if the bultungin had not arrived. "Besides, Oko is my home. I would always return."

Home. I think of Oyo-Ile and my parents. If the Tapa are attacking the Oyo Kingdom, they'll eventually get to the capital.

"I just checked on my father and the council," says Kola as he joins us, running a hand over his head and squeezing the back of his neck. "The Oyo Kingdom's representatives are there with them. The Aláàfin has declared war. He's agreed with the council that the Tapa attacks are out of control. The assault begins with the full moon."

"Two days," I say, my voice shaking. I turn to face him. My nerves flutter, building to a tightness that spreads inside me. "The same as the ritual needed to bind the ajogun."

I think of Ara, Folasade, and Esu. "Has anyone seen—"

"No need," comes a deep voice from behind me. I spin around to see the trickster walking down a side pathway, a wide smirk on his face. Folasade and Ara trail in his wake, almost running to keep up. "We are well."

"You were supposed to stay put," says Kola. He rushes to meet the orisa, stopping him before he can step into the main street.

"A shame you didn't come sooner and help defend," mutters Bem as we gather in the sheltered pathway.

"But what if something had happened to me?" asks Esu, hands outspread, black eyes wide. "Who would save us all then?"

His snide question is answered with a growl as Yinka pushes past me, her skin rippling and eyes glowing.

"Yinka, no!"

But it's too late. Yinka runs, leaping through the air to land in front of Esu. With a ragged howl she begins to change, canines already as long as a lion's as she lunges for the trickster's throat.

Kola moves fast, darting in front of the bultungin and grabbing Yinka around her waist. He whispers in her ear as she strains in his arms, and when the changing lines of her body stiffen, I know he's speaking of the ajogun and what has happened. She sags briefly, her eyes still lit with murder, but then her limbs ripple, fur receding and growing as she fights the change. Her teeth are still bared, but now they are shorter, less sharp. Aissa snarls beside her.

"This is hardly the time to bring up the past," drawls the trickster, mouth wry with amusement. "What is done is done."

Aissa reaches for Yinka, pulling her back to her side, glaring at Esu. "Now is not the time," I hear her hiss, her eyes never once leaving the orisa. Yinka's body is tense, but she lets herself be led away, shoulders rising with each breath, all her effort put into keeping her human form.

"Esu, you need to go back to the compound," says Kola through gritted teeth. "Yinka is not the only one with grudges against you."

The trickster opens his mouth to speak, but Folasade grabs his arm and steers the orisa in the direction they came from. Her gaze skates over the dead guards and she presses her lips together, grief in the set of her face.

Kola stands in the middle of the path, his head down. I can

only imagine the restraint it took for him to stop Yinka from attacking Esu.

"Well done," I say quietly as Ara follows Bem, heading to help with the injured Oko guard.

The boy lifts his head and looks at me. "I'm doing what I can to be the leader Oko needs when the time comes." And then Kola is stalking back to the carnage of the Tapa attack, and I am left wondering if he will ever forgive me for leaving him.

CHAPTER FOURTEEN

I MAKE MY way to the main gates, hoping to help, thinking of all the souls that have begun their journey back to Olodumare. The injured are settled onto sleeping mats. I see Ara bent over a woman with her leg a mess of shredded skin and a glint of bone. Ara has a small calabash of water and strips of cotton, which she uses to gently wash and bind the wound. Next to her is a basket of herbs and a small bowl of a light green salve. With patient movements, she tends to the injury, her touch gentle. Once she is finished, she cleans her hands and stands up, then moves to my side.

"Come with me to get some more water," says Ara. "And then let's eat with the others." She begins the walk back to the compound, calabash balanced on the braids that crown her head. "We all need some rest."

I nod and we veer left, turning toward the center of Oko and the well that serves the village. The moon is strong, blurring the edges of shadows and lighting our way. A small carved leopard lies on its side, abandoned, and I pick it up and set it against the wall of a compound. I hope the child who dropped it will find it.

"Kola told me what happened to him. What you sacrificed." Ara's voice is soft, her gaze flickering to my legs.

So he told her the truth about me after all. "Everything?" My stomach clenches at the thought of her knowing that I am not the same.

Ara nods. I think of Kola telling her about how I saved him, that I am Yemoja's creation. What does she think?

Ara sets the calabash aside and moves closer, looping her arms around me. "Simi, you are the same person. Remember Jenrola, my neighbor?" I nod against the warmth of her skin, breathing in the scent of shea butter. "Remember the golden clip?"

Ara had been given a present by her parents for her sixteenth year, a small hair ornament that shone like the sun. She wore it every day, lodged against the tight rows of her braids. One afternoon I was neatening her hair and the clip fell out. We didn't see, but Jenrola did and claimed it for her own.

"She refused to give it back to you and you burst into tears."

Ara laughs a little, her forehead pressed against mine. "I did. And you . . ." She pulls away, a grin shaping her wide mouth. "You demanded it from her. Wouldn't take no for an answer."

I shrug, but a warmth fills me at the memory. "Jenrola had no right to lie like that."

Ara squeezes my shoulders. "But you wouldn't let her get away with it. That is the Simi I know. The Simi you still are." I watch as she hoists the calabash onto her head and turns to the path. "You are just as I remember."

I study her neat hair, the ends of her plaits small puffs of black clouds that frame her smooth face. "And you?" I can sense something changed about her. You can't go through all she has, all we have, and not be different in some way. This I know.

"I take what good I can from any situation." Ara blinks, her eyes a careful blank. "Being in Rabah taught me how to treat and heal the ill and wounded. I kept my head down and listened." Ara raises a hand to the calabash, steadying it with the tips of her fingers. "Make no mistake that this will spur Idera on."

"What do you mean?" I ask, but I think I already know what Ara will say, and my mouth goes dry at the thought.

"I mean that Idera is not someone who likes to lose. She has one . . . damaged eye. It's said that she was punished for looking at one of the Oba's wives in the wrong way. The woman had Idera accosted when rumors of her power were spreading, jealous of the attention the Nupe Oba was giving the iyalawo. She paid a mercenary to warn Idera." Ara looks worried, her lips a thin line. "Idera gained a scar, but the woman lost more."

"How much more?" I ask, even though half of me doesn't want to know.

"She was found with both her eyes put out and her tongue cut off." We stop at the well, its tall brick walls shining a red-brown. Ara lowers the calabash, turns from me to haul up the rope and copper bucket. "Idera is not someone to anger."

I can't imagine how it must have been for her in Rabah. At least she's not there anymore, I think. I tip my face to the sky, breathing in the cool night air, allowing myself to feel grateful despite the Tapa's attack. Grateful for being reunited with so many and for the lives that can never be taken for granted.

Small groups of the Oko guard sit under the stars with bowls of red stew and rice in their hands. Ara leads me over to Bem and Kola, who rest at the edge of the groups. Bem sucks on a whole chicken wing, stripping it clean of flesh in one go, but Kola sits still, staring down at the meat in his hands.

"Are you waiting for that chicken to come back to life . . . grow wings and fly away?" Ara places the calabash of fresh water down in front of them and I pass them a cup each.

When Kola still doesn't look up, Ara folds her hands under each armpit and flaps her arms. "Buck-buck." She leans forward, her head jerking around as if looking for corn, legs bent, eyes wide. Clucking again, Ara scratches at the earth with her bare feet.

There is a moment of silence and then Bem is spluttering, bellowing with laughter. Even Kola smiles.

"What is this?" Yinka strolls toward us, flanked by Aissa, a smile on her lips. "Are we acting out what food we want?"

Kola jumps to his feet as Yinka rushes toward him, throwing her arms around his neck. I grin as I watch them. And then Bem stands up, slinging one arm around them both before grabbing me with the other, pulling me to them. I laugh and close my eyes for a moment, letting myself feel the rush of love I have for them all.

"Come now. I am starving!" We turn to see Aissa looking around her for more food, rubbing at her gray fur wrapper. "Must I act like a chicken to be fed?"

Yinka laughs as we pull away, settling down between Kola and Bem.

"I'll get some more," says Ara, arms still folded, clucking as she makes her way toward the fire. She turns once and grins at us, and my heart feels fuller than it has for a long time.

Kola faces Yinka, his eyes shining. Was he that excited to see me? He still doesn't seem to want to even look at me properly. I hold a sigh in and take a sip of water, then accept the slices of fried plantain Bem passes me.

"What happened?" Kola questions Yinka. "In the volcano."

"And after," I add, nibbling at my food.

We settle down as Ara returns with some ẹ̀fọ́ rírò. Bem slurps happily, ignoring the looks Yinka gives him. She rolls her eyes and continues to tell us how the bultungin revealed themselves as kin.

"With Aissa's help, I traveled to the Dahomey Kingdom, to learn about where my mother was from." Yinka pauses, her eyes shining. She clears her throat and Aissa pats her back gently. "To speak to people who knew her, respected her." A tear runs down her cheek and she swipes it away, nodding to herself. "Despite the . . . difficulties . . . it was everything I needed."

Yinka tells us of the position of general that her mother had held, protecting the Oba in an all-female regiment and overseeing the training of young women as warriors. About the shattered illusions of the other women leaders and their arguments. She speaks of how her mother was ostracized, nearly giving in to death before being nursed back to health when she arrived in Oko. Kola puts his arm around her again, squeezing her to his side.

"What has gotten into you?" Yinka asks Kola, smiling and huffing a little as she shoves him away. "Stop it. I don't remember you being this nice to me before!"

Kola laughs, hand on his chest and eyebrows raised in mock protest. "What? I've missed you!"

"I know. I would, too, if I were you, but all this affection is too much!"

Watching the crinkle of Kola's eyes when he grins makes my heart skip. I remember when he would smile like that at me, and I miss it so much that I ache. I try not to let the tears form, blinking quickly, my appetite gone.

I get up to take my bowl to the giant tub to wash. Cloaked

in shadows, I slink off, heading back toward Kola's family compound. When I ease the door open, it is to the sounds of loud snores. I hurry through to the courtyard, where I find Esu asleep on a pile of sleeping mats and blankets. The orisa's mouth hangs open, legs and arms spilling out on either side. His loud snorts echo around us.

"Folasade!" I hiss, not bothering to keep my voice down. How can the orisa sleep after what has just happened? I feel like kicking him. "Where are you?"

The girl hurries from the cooking quarters, a harsh frown on her face. "All he does is eat!"

"We shouldn't have to pander to him." I suck my teeth as I look down upon his sleeping form.

"He said if he's tired or hungry then he won't be able to plan how we will get to the Mokele-mbembe." Folasade plants her hands on her hips.

I roll my eyes and glare at the trickster. "Pass me the water."

Folasade hands me a full cup, her eyes sparkling as I hold it high over the orisa's head. Slowly, I let the contents fall, the clear water glittering in the orange glow of the lamps just before it splatters on Esu's face. The orisa gasps, sitting upright, eyes flashing silver as he jerks his head around, hands balling into fists.

"What—!"

"Tell us more about how to get the soul song." I look to Folasade, who doesn't bother to smother her wicked grin. "We need to leave as soon as we can." I think of the Tapa and the iyalawo. The devastation they wrought in just a few hours.

Esu climbs to his feet, towering over us both as he shakes the water from his plaits. "Do you know how long it has been since I have slept on a belly full of food and wine?"

I lift my chin and do not turn from his irked gaze, ignoring a flutter of nerves. "You agreed to help us."

The orisa blows air out of his mouth and reaches for the flask of palm wine. When he discovers that it's empty, he lets it roll on the floor, tutting in annoyance. "I told you before. The creature lives in the chasm between both kingdoms, a stretch of water that is also linked to the sea."

"And what of it? What's the best way for us to kill it?"

Esu blinks and smooths back his plaits. "The best way for *you* to kill it is, I imagine, like any other hunt. Stalking and then striking." He plucks a sliver of chicken from between his teeth and regards it solemnly before flicking it away.

"Hold on," I say, narrowing my eyes. "You mean that you're not coming? But you agreed!"

"I said I would bind the ajogun. I did not say I would get the soul song." Esu smiles as he sits back down, his face smug as he selects a chunk of mango from a platter and pops it into his mouth. "Besides, since you have freed me from Olokun, I can no longer breathe beneath the sea. No, it is far better for me to stay here and prepare for the binding." He closes his eyes and flutters his hands at me, pale palms flashing. "And as I told you before, I will need all my energy for the ritual."

I open my mouth to speak, fiery words burning my tongue, but Folasade lays a hand on my elbow, fingers cool against my heat.

"I told you I know where this chasm is." She shoots a dark look at the trickster. "I can take us there."

"You see?" says Esu, not opening his eyes. "She knows." He swallows the mango and smacks his lips together. "If you leave in the morning you should be back by evening. And that gives us one day's grace. I will stay here and ready myself."

Folasade leans closer to me and lowers her voice to a whisper, her eyes hard. "And I would not necessarily trust him if he were there with us anyway."

I bite back my irritation and pull Folasade away from Esu, who merely stretches his arms above his head before folding them over his chest. When we reach the edge of the courtyard, I describe Idera's attack.

"Then Ara is right. The Tapa iyalawo knows about the ajogun." Folasade fiddles with her sapphire, fighting with the expression of fear that lines her face. "Do you think she knows how to release them?"

"It's what Ara says." I think of the dead men in the sea, the ruthlessness Idera is known for and the power she wielded. "I don't want to risk finding out. We need to get the soul song."

While Esu snores loudly, Folasade explains the location of the chasm. "As I said earlier, there's a channel that runs from the sea between the Oyo and Nupe kingdoms. It eventually peters out to a river."

I frown, turning over the details in my head. "Why would the Mokele-mbembe choose this place?"

Folasade shivers and runs her hands down her arms. "Perhaps it is because it's deep, but without the dangers of the sea. Cold and dark enough to hide almost anything."

The waters of Olokun's Land of the Dead spring to mind. Their inky blackness and the chill that creeps inside your bones. "We'll go now. The sooner the better."

"You won't leave until the sun rises at least." Kola steps from the compound entrance, his face wreathed in shadows and his shoulders almost as wide as the doorway. I am struck again by how much he has changed. It's not just his height, but the weight of his words and the expectation that what he says will be heeded. "Not with Idera out there. We still don't know if there are any more of the Tapa waiting."

So, now he is talking to me. I suck in a deep breath, but I know he's right. It would be foolish to go charging into the last parts of the night after what has happened. Folasade wrings her hands.

"We will leave at dawn."

"My parents and the twins are in the meeting quarters," says Kola, his words clipped. He still doesn't look me in the eyes. "The guards have been doubled; you can stay here."

Folasade nods, and I consider her for a moment. I spent time in this village when we were hunting Esu, but it has been much longer since Folasade has been around so many people, and in human form. I reach out and squeeze her hand, managing a small smile, glad that she did not witness the attack.

"I think you should rest. It has been a tiring day," I say.

"I'm fine," answers Folasade, but I see her shift her weight from foot to foot, the strain on her face.

"Please," I say softly, knowing the pain she is feeling. "You're not used to this."

Folasade frowns at me but then her shoulders sag. She knows she can't keep going.

"You can have the twins' room," says Kola as he leads Folasade out of the courtyard.

I walk back to Esu, turning my hand over, examining the golden chain and ruby wrapped around my wrist. As my fingernails click over the gem, I remember how it glowed, remember feeling as if it were scorching my flesh. I think of the eight faces I saw, and I fight a wave of nausea.

"I told you of its power." Esu props himself up on one arm, looking at me. "Have you felt it yet?"

I cup the jewel briefly before facing the orisa. "It felt . . . hot. Just before the Tapa attacked." I don't tell him about the images of a ravaged Oyo-Ile.

"It is linked to me, and therefore to the ajogun." Esu drops his arm, lying back down, and places his hands on his stomach, eyes closed again. "If the iyalawo was using power from the warlords, it will have sensed that."

I peer at the jewel closely, but the ruby is unchanged, still the color of freshly spilled blood. If what Esu is saying is true, then it explains the vision of the ajogun. The bodies of the cursed remain in my mind, and I feel a cold unease snake through me as Kola returns, catching the end of our conversation.

"Was there a warning of some kind?" Kola watches us closely, fingers curled into his palms. Behind him, the moon blazes in a ball of yellow white. "Did you not think to tell us that before the Tapa attacked?"

Esu doesn't move or speak for a moment, and then he opens one eye to grab some more mango. Staring up at us both briefly before closing his eye, he says, "No. That is none of my concern."

I see the switch in Kola's expression at the orisa's answer, the curl of his top lip and the sudden tightening of his fists. He moves forward, knocking over Esu's flask. The air fills with the sweet milky scent of palm wine.

"Kola, stop . . . ," I warn softly. The boy gives me a betrayed look and I try to keep myself from flinching. And then he turns away from me, heading toward the doors just as the clouds scud over the moon, bathing us all in darkness. When the light fights free, all I can see is Kola's scarred back as he disappears through the compound doors.

Esu chews the mango, tipping his face up to the moon. "Aren't you going to go after him, little fish?" he asks, without even opening his eyes.

CHAPTER FIFTEEN

I WHIRL AWAY from Esu and run across to the doors, opening them to the dark night and a path scattered with moonlight. The compound's corners are shrouded in black as the torches gutter out in a sudden breeze.

"Kola!" I call when I spot him at the bottom of the steps. He pauses and I move quickly, despite the growing ache in my soles. The stone is cool beneath my feet as I stop one step above him so that our eyes are level.

"Wait," I say. Kola faces me, his shoulders hunched with anger.

"Is this the way it will be now? You speaking for Esu?" he asks, voice low and tight.

"You know that's unfair. What would you have me do? You don't think I hate having to go along with someone who has hurt the people I care about?" I stop to gulp in some air as my temper ignites. "I have no choice. Not if I'm thinking of others, thinking of more than me."

"And what about me, Simi?" Kola moves closer now, a hard frown rippling across his face. "When you made your decisions before, without even talking to me, did you think of me then?"

I curl my hands into fists. "I thought of you, and I thought of more than you!"

"And that worked out so very well, didn't it?" Kola glares at me now.

I recoil, my stomach dropping as I take a step away from him, tears prickling at the backs of my eyes.

"It wasn't just about you," I say, trying to keep my tone even. "And you know that."

"I know that I needed you," says Kola quietly, and his reply drags me down deeper, making me feel the burst of wanting him, loving him, that is always there waiting. I recognize the shape of his pain because it matches mine.

"All I was trying to do, all I am trying to do, is keep everyone safe." I think of Issa and his senseless death. I think about the choice I made and all I've endured. And now the ajogun and their power could unleash more death and destruction. All of it crashes over me, a wave of bleak and inescapable hurt. "And I can't even seem to do that," I whisper.

All I have ever done is try to help, to save. But all I seem to do is make things worse. And now even Kola thinks I am foolish. The sobs rip from deep inside me and I can't hold them in anymore. I press my palms against my face, trying to cover the tears that fall hot on my cheeks.

The darkest part of the night bears down on us as Kola slides his arms around me, his skin warm against mine. I can feel myself trembling, but I don't move away. I can't.

"Simi, I . . . I'm sorry." I feel him sigh against my hair, his hands slipping to the dip of my spine. "I know you did what was best. I know that."

I shake my head against his chest, wiping at the tears that seep between my fingers. His arms still encircle me as I draw in a deep breath, trying to calm myself.

Kola pulls me tighter to him and I wrap my arms around his back, feeling the twist of scars beneath my palms. "I just . . . I missed you."

I don't say anything for a moment. But then the words are there, pouring out of me before I have a chance to stop them. "I thought about you. Every day." I still can't look up at him. Afraid that if I do, something more will happen. Something that will destroy me.

"We could have tried to find a way. Together." I dare to glance at Kola as he speaks. His eyes are hooded, night shadows wreathing his face.

"You know that what Esu told you in his palace is true." My voice breaks. "Not acting on the way I feel is part of what I am. Who I am. We can never be together. Not properly." I look down at the lines in my palm, their light brown trails dividing my flesh. Portents of life, health . . . love.

Kola sighs as he rubs his hands over his face. "I know." But his voice is small and defeated.

We stand together in the dark, neither of us speaking as the truth settles between us. In a few hours the sun will ignite a new day, and I will leave with Folasade, but for now? I have this at least, I think. Kola near me.

I shift, pressing closer. The boy's sudden intake of breath makes me pause, but the ache of wanting him spreads, working its way up to my heart, forcing the beat of it to speed up, to thunder in my ears as I turn my face so that I can see the shine of his brown eyes. My gaze is drawn to the beauty spot above his eyebrow, and then back down to his lips.

It would be so easy, I think. To fit my mouth against his.

A cold breeze rushes along the pathway, blowing against my legs, lifting my curls. Kola stares at me, his eyes heavy-lidded, lips parted slightly.

"I'm sorry," I whisper, the words rough as I pull away from his grip, his touch. I wipe at my tears with the heel of my hand. Kola swallows, retreating into the shadows. But I see the hurt that I've caused yet again.

This is not fair.

To him or to me.

I stumble away, smoothing the folds of my wrapper, and look up at the thinning moon.

"I need to rest. Folasade and I will leave at dawn." I spin away, back up the steps, before I can do anything else, say anything else. Before words that cannot be unsaid rip their way free and tear us further apart.

CHAPTER SIXTEEN

I WAKE UP to the growing heat of a new day. Folasade is asleep next to me, a blanket draped over her hips and her palms pressed together. Images of black-and-yellow wrappers, and screams that pierce the night, rush through my mind.

I roll onto my side, stretching out my legs and blinking into the faint light that creeps into the room. The walls around me are a riot of bronze and gold and yellow, showing depictions of Ogun and Ibeji, woven and embroidered and drawn. Kehinde and Taiwo have filled their space with light and a reverence that can be felt.

Sitting up, I think of the soul song and the two days we have left, nerves coiling in the pit of my stomach. "Folasade," I say softly, hand on her shoulder as I shake her gently.

She uncurls slowly and I wonder if the memories of her life before are coming back to her in the way they did to me. Folasade puts her hands to her hair, patting the small halo of tight curls.

"Did you dream?" I ask. I hope that if she did, the dreams were of her family, of her friends and home.

"I did," says Folasade, revealing perfect teeth and a smile that reaches her eyes. "I saw my mother. And my little sister." She speaks softly, so different from her sharp words in the water, as if the land has rounded the edges created by being Mami Wata. She tells me of a village deep in the forest, of homes made out of trees and the river that wound through it all. Her eyes shine at the memories and I smile as she finishes, wishing her more of them.

Voices ring out in the courtyard as we walk through the central corridor, our steps stiff as we adjust to legs that crackle with bones unused to the set of limbs. A rose-colored glow bleeds into a dark blue sky, suffusing the compound with a delicate pink. The growing light spreads over the food and drink set out, copper bowls and cups blazing a brilliant bronze. I pause at the entranceway when I see Kola, Yinka, and Ara gathered together, heads bent, talking intently.

"Simi!" says Yinka when she notices me, jumping up and loping over. "You're awake."

"You should have woken me earlier," I grumble, but I lean into her embrace nonetheless. My eyes go to Kola, who nods at me, his gaze cool. I inhale deeply. This is the way it has to be, I tell myself.

"You needed to rest," answers Yinka as she leads us to the food. "Here, sit. Eat."

Ara pours some water and places bowls of fried plantain and àkàrà in front of us. Folasade sits down, arranging her legs carefully, closing her eyes when she bites into the burst of warm sweetness.

"Where's Esu?" I swing my gaze around the courtyard, but the orisa is not reclining on the blankets where I expect to see him.

"Bem has taken him to the babalawo. Esu said the priest can help him prepare." Kola sips his water, his plate of food only half eaten. When he looks up at me, it is with an air of challenge. "Besides, after he took Taiwo and Kehinde, we thought it best that my

140

parents and the other villagers not catch sight of him. We don't want him left on his own in Oko. Bem will keep an eye on him."

I think of the way Kola nearly attacked Esu last night, remembering the orisa's selfish actions. When the trickster snatched the twins, the whole of Oko was blanketed beneath layers of grief and with the fear that the children were already dead. I touch the ruby that hangs from my left wrist. Better Esu is prevented from causing any discord until the ceremony.

"Eat, Simi," urges Folasade. "We will need it. The walk is not easy."

"She's right," says Kola. He hands me a cup of water, careful not to let our fingers touch. "We all need to make sure we're ready."

I accept the drink but don't bring it to my lips. "What do you mean, 'we'?" I look around at them, but only Yinka returns my gaze.

"We're coming with you." She reaches out, plucking the slice of plantain from my hand and popping it into her mouth. "Surely you didn't think we'd let you go on your own?"

"No," I snap, my grip on the cup tightening. "It's just Folasade. We're the only ones who can do this." I place the drink on the ground and fold my arms. "Unless you can all suddenly breathe underwater."

"I told you she'd be difficult." Yinka sucks her teeth and frowns. She swivels to face me. "Come now, Simi. I've already told the pack to stay here, to help with any defense needed. It's not just the Tapa you should worry about. The òyìnbó are creeping farther inland, trying to use the rivers to navigate the forest and central lands. Now is not the time to argue about this."

The brilliance of the sunrise above the compound's roof gives the sky a golden glow, and Kola gets to his feet, standing tall in the light.

"This isn't just about you, Simi." Kola narrows his eyes at me, and I glower back. "There's too much at stake."

Yinka steps between us, hands held up. "What Kola means is that you still need to get there and back, and that is what we will make sure of."

I am silent a moment as their words sink in, and I have to fight not to walk away.

"Simi . . . the Tapa," says Folasade. The slink of fear in her words pushes away some of my stubbornness.

I don't want any of them to risk themselves for us, but I know that they're right, that we could be attacked, and then where would we be? I nod curtly, ignoring Kola's gaze and fixing on Ara. "But Ara doesn't need to come." My friend's face falls open, stripped back in surprise before the hurt seeps in. "We know how to fight and she doesn't."

I don't say that it will break me if any of them get hurt. Even now, Yinka's presence reminds me that we are missing one. Issa. The thought of the yumbo's honey-colored eyes carves a deeper scar in my heart.

"I know how to heal, though," answers Ara, climbing to her feet and adjusting her wrapper. "And I know Idera. I know the way she thinks."

"What else?" I ask. "Will you cluck like a chicken when we're hungry?"

Ara glares at me and I remember the other times I was sharp with her. She pulls the same face now, a squint with her bottom lip slightly stuck out. "I can make sure we're going the right way.

Folasade only knows the chasm from the sea." Ara stands still in front of me, chin jutting out, a familiar stubborn gleam in her eyes. "Besides, I do know how to handle some weapons. I won't be entirely useless."

We eye each other until I sigh loudly. I know Ara well enough not to try to stop her once her mind is set on something. There will be no shaking her off. "All right. We should leave as soon as possible."

"Good!" Ara claps her hands, doing a celebratory dance. She stops when she sees my frown but still grins at me.

"If we're going to make it in time, we can't go by foot. I'll ask my father for the horses." Kola turns to Ara and Yinka. "Gather what you'll need."

Folasade accepts a short sword from Yinka as Ara prepares a small sack of herbs and food she retrieves from the kitchen. Yinka runs her axes over a gray sharpening stone, her teeth glinting as she flashes a quick grin at me. "What? I still like to use them."

When Kola returns, it is with five horses. His face is strained. "The representative from Oyo-Ile has left. Oko is to send contingents to join them tomorrow."

None of us speak as we claim a horse each, silent as we lead the animals down the main path in the first light of the day. The front gates are still being repaired as we slip through them. Hammers and shouts fill the air as metal- and woodworkers labor together to make the village as secure as they can. All I can think about is how the Tapa destroyed the gates so easily. What will they be able to do with more power from the ajogun? The need to get the soul song could not be greater.

We leave Oko and the despair that has muted the village,

cantering through the fields. The forest is a riot of greens and the trills of the red-billed firefinch as we loop through it, heading for the path that we saw the Tapa on last night. Kola and Yinka lead the group, navigating the forest in a way only those who know it well can do. Just as we see the road weaving like a brown ribbon between the trunks of mahagony trees, Kola holds his hand up, pausing in place.

Through the spread of bushes, I catch a glimpse of a small group of homes, their blackened timbers stark against the yellow sunlight.

Ara folds her arms over her chest and waddles ahead of me, swaying her hips from side to side in an exaggerated fashion. Throwing a look over her shoulder, she crosses her eyes and smiles, pulling her top lip high above her teeth, pink-and-brown gums glistening. "Who am I?"

She juts her face toward me and laughs, a honking sound that reminds me of the geese that flew above us just as we left the seventeenth gate. I take a sip from our waterskin and try not to giggle, but when she waggles her head and pats her hair, I spit my drink into the air.

"You shouldn't make fun of your ìyá Tope, Ara," I say, but I can feel the grin that splits my face. Delicately, I pick my way over tree roots and the fallen leaves on the forest floor, watching out for the brown coils of the Gaboon viper. In the last few months, two people in our neighboring compound have died from its venomous bite, and I don't want to be the third.

Ara sighs but drops her hands to her sides. "I know. But she's just always . . . there. Eating all the meat and asking me to cook, making a mess and then saying she's too tired to do anything but sleep." My best friend turns to me, a line between her eyebrows. "I know she's having a difficult time, but why make my life harder, too?"

Ara's ìyá Tope is staying with them after arguing with her husband and has brought her three young daughters with her. Ara has attempted to stay away from home as much as possible, trying to escape the endless plaiting of three messy heads and the work it takes to help cook and clean for all of them.

"I know that she's visiting, but for how long?" Ara groans as she waits for me to catch up.

We keep a steady pace through the forest, wanting to get to the bend of the river where no one really goes, one of the places that will afford us some privacy, to swim and to lie on the sun-warmed earth. As Ara chatters on about how she now has to share her sleeping mat with her youngest cousin, I pause, the smell of smoke strong in the fresh morning.

"She's small, but she has this way of flinging out both her arms and legs—"

I press a finger to my lips as my heart kicks against the bones of my chest. "Shh."

Ara plants her hands on her hips. "I know you may find this boring, but I can barely sleep—"

Lunging forward, I clamp a hand to Ara's mouth and scan the sky. To our east, a thick plume of smoke streaks up to meet the clouds. I point, and my friend's eyes widen when she sees the twist of dark gray. Slowly, she peels my fingers from her face, her mouth slack.

I turn to face the forest in the direction the smoke is coming from. The sun still shines through the canopy, lighting the foliage in shades of green, but now I notice that there is no sound. No birdsong, no calls from the white-faced monkeys that sometimes peer down from above, their beady eyes fixed on us if we have brought dried beef. I swallow and take a step forward.

"Simi!" hisses Ara. "We need to go back."

I shake my head, thinking of the small village and those who call it home. "There might be people who need help."

"There might be people who plan on cutting our throats," trills Ara, plucking nervously at her wrapper.

"Then go," I say. "I wouldn't want to think that I could have helped but didn't."

I set off, stepping on the earth carefully, trying not to stand on any leaves or twigs that may give me away. I look back once to see Ara pursing her lips before following me anyway, as she always does. We won't get too close if there's danger, I think.

As we pick our way through the trees, the smell of smoke curls thick and noxious in the air. Struggling not to cough, I hold a hand to my face, cupping it against my mouth as we near the thinning tree line. I peer ahead anxiously, slices of the village coming into view.

I see the blackened shells of homes first, embers that glow red among the ruined walls, destroyed roofs open to the sky. Not one structure is left standing, and the stench of burning grows stronger. Keeping Ara behind me, I shuffle forward slowly until I see something else in the ruins of the closest home. The outline of a body fallen on the floor, a plait that trails in the ashes.

Bile rises in my throat and I retch, dry heaves wracking my body. Ara wraps her arms around me, her eyes still on the village. When I am done, she turns me to her, her face smooth, eyes hard. "Come. We need to tell your father."

The thought of the Tapa claiming another village makes me shake in both fear and rage. I am yanking the dagger from my hair when Kola places a hand on my arm. He shakes his head and lifts his own weapon, blade glinting.

"Let me check that the way is clear first," he whispers. I open my mouth to argue but then think better of it. I don't want to alert anyone who might still be around. Kola slides from his horse and removes his sword from the strap on his back. Turning to us, he presses a finger against his lips. Sweat runs down the side of his face, glistening in the sun that filters through the sparse canopy as he creeps forward, moving soundlessly through the trees.

My fingers curl tighter around the hilt of my dagger until Kola returns with a calmer expression. He grabs the reins of his horse and beckons to the rest of us. "It's clear. The village has been abandoned, I think. Perhaps one of the settlements that have moved inland to escape the òyìnbó. But be ready to conceal yourselves if I tell you."

"We need to head northwest," says Folasade, tucking her short sword back into the folds of her wrapper. She sits awkwardly atop her horse, flinching each time the animal moves. "Through the plains that border the Nupe and Oyo kingdoms. The chasm follows a small river that widens out just before it reaches the sea."

"I know the route you mean," says Yinka, pointing past Kola. "We passed that way as we traveled back to Oko. Simi and I will lead. Folasade can follow, and Kola can bring up the rear with Ara."

I shift on the back of my horse, trying to get comfortable, almost slipping from the saddle. The animal, a tan-and-white mare, waits patiently as I settle myself. Kola says nothing, mounting his black stallion, which tosses its head impatiently. He positions himself behind Ara and Folasade, checking the way behind us.

"Come, Simi. You're the only one I haven't had a chance to

talk to properly yet." Yinka nudges her horse along as I move beside her.

The path is shaded by the raffia trees that crowd in on either side of us, a narrow strip of land that the forest will always try to possess. Yinka moves gracefully with her horse, and I try to mimic her movements, already feeling the soreness of a position I am completely unused to.

"So what really happened?" I ask. "Back in the volcano?"

"When we entered the volcano passageway, I knew I would do anything to keep you all safe." Yinka stares straight ahead, her profile sharp, chin raised as always. The smooth bareness of her head only adds to her beauty. "I held off Aissa. The rest of the pack managed to get past me, but they were too late. As soon as the boulder was lowered, I felt relief that the bultungin couldn't get to you all."

I remember the snap of teeth and glimmer of eyes as the giant rock crashed back into place, sealing off our escape from the volcano.

"You weren't scared?" I expect Yinka to scoff, but she doesn't.

"A tiny part of me was. But the rest of me knew that something with them felt . . . right."

Sweat pools at the base of my spine and I wipe the sheen from my forehead with the back of my hand. But the heat feels too good to complain about, and it's only now that I feel the chill from the deep truly leave my bones.

"You were family and you felt that." My words lift with the tilt of my smile.

Yinka nods and talks as the sun climbs higher. She speaks of exploring the bultungin transformation, learning about her mother's origins and how to shift.

"How was it?" I ask, thinking of the scales that slice through my own skin. "The change?"

"Oh, it hurt!" Yinka laughs easily, reins gripped loosely. "But it was a clean kind of pain. A sweet affliction that feels as if once started, it can't end. And I wouldn't want to stop it." She turns to me, her eyes shining. "It feels as if I am truly me. Whole."

CHAPTER SEVENTEEN

THE TREES GIVE way to a seemingly endless plain of tall grass, the occasional large bush breaking up the sway of yellowing green. The thought of the full moon tomorrow keeps me going, even though my thighs and back ache in a way I didn't think was possible. At least we're not walking, I think as I turn to check on Folasade again. She tries her best to smile at me, but I see the pain in her expression.

"Let's stop for a rest," I call out.

Kola scans the grassland and nods, dismounting with ease. He helps Folasade, who practically falls from her horse, and he lowers her to the ground as she groans, hands going to her back. I see him glance at me and I slide off my horse quickly.

"I have aches in places I didn't even know I had muscles!" Ara moans dramatically, clutching at her legs. "Does this ever get easier? I feel as if every bone has been rattled and rearranged."

"No," answers Yinka as she leaps from her horse, looking sickeningly invigorated. "But you get used to it."

"I'm sorry," Ara says, turning to her horse as she leads it over to us. "But your back is too bony." She rolls her eyes at the animal as it snorts. "Don't be like that. I honestly don't think my buttocks can take any more."

I laugh as Ara reaches for her pack and brings out some more water. She offers it to Folasade, who gulps greedily. I turn to the horizon where the trees begin again, lining the river that leads to the chasm. I can feel the rush of the water, feel the pull deep in my stomach. The want is there as always, like calling to like. Soon, I think, pushing the need away for now.

We are drawing closer to the chasm and the Mokele-mbembe. I think of the great number of lives it has taken and its insatiable appetite. I wonder what kind of song it emits when it kills. Would it be something dark and low or triumphant and sickly-sweet as it reveled in my death?

Small bumps rise on my skin despite the heat. I rub at them and remind myself of my encounter with the Ninki Nanka. Although the river monster snatched Kola in its giant jaws, intent on drowning and eating him, I freed him. I can do this, I think as I accept the dried papaya Ara holds out to me. But will Folasade be able to? The girl stands now, arching her back to stretch out the ripple of her muscles, taking the fruit she is offered.

"Will you be all right?" I ask.

Folasade nods, chewing delicately and scowling as she scans the land around us. "Yes. But it will be a relief to get to water."

We ride through the hottest part of the day and as the tributary grows closer, I feel it even more. My skin crackles with want, scales prickling beneath.

"How far do we follow the river until we get to the chasm?" I ask Folasade, slowing my horse so that it trots beside hers.

She wipes the sweat from her neck and blows out air in a small attempt to cool herself. "Not long. An hour, I think. What will take the most time is looking for the Mokele-mbembe."

"It'll be deep, though." I shiver when I think of the dark coldness of the chasm. "We know that much."

"True. Although I have heard tales of sightings at the banks when the creature would grab animals or people from the shallow water."

"We shall see," I murmur.

When we reach the ribbon of brown water, I am struck by the swollen swirl of it, no doubt caused by recent rainfall.

"See the bend?" Folasade gestures past a clump of bushes in the distance. "The chasm is just beyond it."

I slide down from my horse and wait for Folasade to do the same. Kola, Yinka, and Ara move to dismount as well, but I stop them. "We'll swim from here." I see Folasade sag with relief at my words. "You can take the horses and meet us there."

Kola jumps down and stalks over to me, his brown eyes lighter in the full afternoon sun, flashing with annoyance and something else that makes me shift my gaze from his. "Why? We agreed we'd see you to the chasm."

"And you will. We'll be in the water and you'll be on land." I gesture to Folasade, who has already drifted to the bank, her feet sinking into the moist black earth. "She has never been in this form for so long. She needs it." I exhale and look back into his eyes. He hasn't spoken to me for the whole journey, and now this questioning of my decision. "I need it."

Kola's mouth flattens into a line as I thrust the reins at him, but he nods once. And then he takes a step toward me and bends down, lips touching my ear, fingertips on my back. I hold my breath, and my heart thumps at the heat of his skin. I still remember the way he pressed the wild lettuce to my aching soles on Esu's island. The gentleness of his grip as he held my feet.

"Be careful. Please."

I shiver at his words. "You got us here safely, and now there's not much else you can do but wait for us." I try to lighten my words, his concern making me softer. "We'll look for the Mokele-mbembe and then meet you at the banks of the chasm." With the soul song, I hope. I force a small smile. "Go. I'll see you there."

Behind us, Ara watches. I beckon her over and hug her quickly before pulling away and reaching up to do the same with Yinka. My heart tightens but I keep my voice light. "Look after them."

Yinka tips her chin at me, staring down from the height of her horse. "I'll see you soon."

"You will," I say. I turn to Folasade as she slips into the river.

The water receives her, swallowing her skin and half of her humanity in one brown gulp. Her wrapper turns to scales, covering her chest in smatters of purple and lilac. Folasade smiles blissfully, her eyes closing briefly before she sinks beneath the surface.

I watch the others as they gallop away, Yinka and Kola leading our horses. It's not good-bye, I tell myself as I step closer to the lip of the bank. I relish the feeling of my scales pushing against the brown of my skin. I don't ease my way in. I dive, entering the river in a neat cut of the water.

My legs fuse together, scales a gold-and-blush shimmer, bright even in the murk. I close my eyes at the relief of the water, then open them, catching a flash of purple as Folasade darts around me, her grin stretched in the river.

"Better?" I ask, dipping toward her, my fin a gilded arc behind me.

"So much." Folasade grins. "I know that you enjoy being in human form, but I would never give this up."

"What about your memories? Did you not enjoy having them back?"

"I did. But, as I always told you, that part of me is past now. I made my vow to Yemoja and that is what counts." Folasade spins in the water, her scales sparkling. "This is what I am."

So sure. So pious, I think, feeling the usual flash of guilt at my own feelings.

"This way." Folasade gestures in the direction the tributary is flowing, her short curls even darker.

The river runs in cooling currents, pulling at us as we swim downstream, where the water becomes cleaner. Soon we can see the brown and gray stones that pepper the riverbed and the tiger-fish that dance beneath us.

"Ara spoke of the Mokele-mbembe on our way here. It is said to resemble the hippopotamus, but its neck is long with a smaller head," says Folasade as she skirts a tiny river snake, its emerald body vivid against the mud. "It often—"

The rest of her words are snatched away by a sudden thunder in the water. The pounding grows, its waves creating a pulse of sound that reverberates around us. We pause, hugging the river-bank, before dipping down to the bottom, seeking depth and safety. With our stomachs sliding on the pebbles and stones beneath us, I try to work out what is happening. The noise grows and gains rhythm, a pattern emerging that speaks to me. Cautiously, I rise through the water, watching the circles and ripples on the surface. I can feel the tempo in my bones as I silently scan the edges of the river. There is a spread of wrappers drying on the earth and the glint of weapons next to them, but it is when I direct my gaze back to the tributary that I see them just beyond the curve.

The women stand in the shallows, backs bent over the beat of the water, white froth rising around them as they stomp their feet underneath. Two small boats are tethered next to them, their hulls in the shade of a tree. Cupped hands dip into the river and smash against it, producing patterns of sound that mesh together. The tallest of the women, shoulders wide and hair shorn close to her scalp, moves in front of the group. She raises her fingers and her voice, rivulets of water sparkling from her brown skin, before bringing both hands down to slap at the river.

"I call you to this new day," she sings, holding a palm out flat and then bringing it down against the water, "when we give thanks to Olodumare and the air we breathe. Let us turn our joy to cunning and strength as we begin the hunt of the day."

She punches down, her fist striking the river in a flurry that the rest of the women copy, their voices powerful, joining with hers. Together, they pound at the water, producing beats met with the stamp of their feet and interspersed with song.

"Feel your courage rising, sisters, as we gather our energy in order to take what we need from the land and water. Keep us safe from the creature that snatches in spite, its fangs and body as large as the space it holds. Keep us safe from the Soul of the Deep."

I strain forward at her words, flicking a look to Folasade, who nods. We are in the right place if what they are speaking of is the Mokele-mbembe.

The women slap at the water again, arcs of clear droplets spraying through the air and soaking the wrappers they wear. Powerful arms alternate strikes with fists open and closed, creating a flow and cadence that hold both beauty and strength. Cold fingers wrap around my arm as Folasade bobs her head, a smile on her lips as she watches the water drummers.

The pulse reaches a crescendo, the river beaten into a frothing submission as it curls at their touch. And then, as one, they stop, raising their eyes to the sun, water slipping down their faces into open grins, their chests heaving.

"Come, show your courage and skill in the hunt," finishes the leader as she wades out of the shallows, heading to the bank. The other women follow her and I sink under the surface again, Folasade at my side.

The beat made by the drummers fades, and I think of the creature they sang of, remembering the Ninki Nanka and its large jaws. "How does the Mokele-mbembe kill?"

"Ara said that stories from fishermen and villagers are varied, but from what she can gather, its bite secretes a type of poison, a bit like the cobra." Folasade frowns, worry in the creases of her mouth. "One bite is enough to both stun and kill."

I say nothing as the river begins to widen out, the current twisting and turning as the brown-and-cream-pebbled riverbed drops away into a black slash. My stomach flips as Folasade grabs my hand, and together we stare down into the abyss below us. A rush of chilled water floods around us as we hover over the chasm.

"It's so dark," murmurs Folasade. "Unless we see it, how will we be able to command and kill it?"

"We'll see it," I say, but even I am unsure of my words, the inky depths below us releasing a fear that slithers through my veins. Glancing up, taking one more look at the blue sky and the tops of the distant raffia trees, I see the small figures of horses as they gallop to the chasm's banks. One rider slides from their animal and presses through bushes that are studded with large purple-and-pink flowers. Kola. The height and shoulders give him away. He raises a hand to shade his eyes as his gaze rakes the surface. I stare back at him for a few seconds, want twisting in me, before turning away and diving beneath the water.

The chill reminds me of Olokun's kingdom as I swim away from the light of the day. Killifish dart around, their neon backs tiny shining beacons in the dark, but even they leave us behind when we plunge through the clear layers of the waters and sink deeper. I pull the golden dagger from my hair as our visibility all but disappears, wishing I had the sunstone.

Folasade is a vague outline next to me as we skim the deepest part of the chasm. Suspended in the glacial water, we wait to see if the Mokele-mbembe will appear, our eyes strained, blood thumping in our ears. After a while, I swim down farther, hoping to entice the creature, twisting in loops and arcs in the water, thrashing my caudal fin. It can't come after us if it doesn't know we are here.

"If we can draw it out, then we can see it and kill it." My plan is not the most complex, but it's the best one I can think of.

Folasade nods, but all I can make out is the bob of her head. I reach out to squeeze her shoulder for reassurance just as the darkness beneath us shifts. We freeze, tails and hands keeping us in place as we peer below. Just when I think I imagined it, there's another movement, and the water fluctuates again as the blackness separates.

A length of murk lashes toward us and we dodge, swimming sideways. I pull Folasade up, hoping to draw the creature closer to the light, as the water rocks us before settling.

"It's not following." I frown into the deep.

"Ara said it has attacked boats, upending them. Sometimes it doesn't even eat them." Folasade glances at me fearfully. "The bodies float to the surface."

"Then it's territorial." I eye the darker swathes of water, my heart pounding. "Stay here, but be ready to attack."

Folasade grips her weapon, its slim blade seeming flimsy even to me, and hovers on the edges of the clear water. I spin, diving back down, my golden dagger held before me, its brilliance dimming the deeper I go. Once the gloom has enveloped me, I pause, shivering.

Come. I press my thoughts through the water, aiming my words where I think the Mokele-mbembe might be. Hoping that I will be able to control such a large creature, or at the very least, draw it out of its hiding place.

Elongated shadows ripple beneath me, but the creature does not appear. With the cold seeping into my bones and unease lodged in my chest, I sink farther.

Come. My eyes rake the deep until I see it. The golden glimmer of large eyes burning red at the center. As if untangling itself from the tangible gloom, the Mokele-mbembe peels away from the blackness and begins to rise. Backing away and upward, my heart pulsing, I snatch a look to make sure Folasade is ready. Beneath me, the giant creature becomes apparent as its long neck snakes toward me, body following behind. With its red-and-gold glare fixed on me, the Mokele-mbembe opens its jaws and roars, revealing large needle-thin teeth and two long canines. I think of the poison secreted by them and shudder, darting away and propelling myself to Folasade.

The feeling of the Mokele-mbembe rising beneath us surges

through me, an awareness that spreads into panic. I don't turn to see the creature coming after me, but I feel it in the shift and roll of the water. Folasade's eyes are wide, her hands shaking as she beckons to me, fingers crooked in a fluttered gesture.

"Move!" she shouts, and I duck to my left instinctively as a muscular tail cuts through the water, swishing just over my head.

Now that the Mokele-mbembe is no longer cloaked in darkness, I can see that its skin is a charcoal gray and its neck is almost twice as long as its torso. The large body speaks of slow ambles, and I have to remind myself of how dangerous it is, and all the people Esu said it has killed.

Stay still, I project. Hoping it will be as simple as me commanding it to let me kill it. The Mokele-mbembe wavers in the water but snaps to the left, chasing after Folasade. Sharks and other smaller creatures are compelled to listen, but I remember the fight that the Ninki Nanka put up. Maybe the Mokele-mbembe is the same. I swallow and grip my dagger tighter.

As the creature rears through the water after Folasade, I nip closer, coming from the side, out of its line of sight. If I can grab its neck, then I can reach its eye and stab through to the brain. At my touch, the Mokele-mbembe tries to jerk away, but I hold on to the ridges of its back, pulling my way up, narrowly avoiding its teeth. It thrashes its head and I am spun through the water, but still I hang on tightly, inching my way closer to its eyes.

We are in a vortex of bubbles as I lift my dagger to strike, only one hand to keep me steady. The Mokele-mbembe bucks, dislodging me from its neck just as I bring my dagger down toward its right eye socket. I miss, tumbling through the water, panic spilling through me as the creature lowers its head, weaving through the water, coming right for me.

Stop.

But the Mokele-mbembe ignores me, and fear winds its way through my veins, causing my heart to stutter. I don't try to control the creature again. Instead I dive down, planning to duck and then swim up, but the monster is quicker, its weight helping it sink faster. It lunges, neck snaking down into the depths after me.

Teeth shine in the fading light as the Mokele-mbembe snaps its jaws, reaching out to clamp its mouth around me. I lash out with my dagger, but I know that it can't stop the attack, not this time. If I am caught, pierced by its venomous teeth, then I will have failed. And then so many will suffer. I force myself not to cower, wielding my dagger as the Mokele-mbembe darts closer, gnashing its fangs.

And then the darkness pulses and a flash of gold, brighter than the Mokele-mbembe's eyes, shines in the black. A chain, its thick links unbreakable, loops around the creature's neck, jerking it backward, forcing its teeth to snap just a hand's width from my face. I look up, peering into the gloom as my heart gallops and my hands shake.

Coils and shining scales and silver-black eyes gradually come into focus as Olokun yanks on the chain that binds him, pulling it tighter and ensnaring the Mokele-mbembe.

CHAPTER EIGHTEEN

BROAD GOLD LINKS glitter in the water as Olokun wraps the chain around both of his forearms, reining the Mokele-mbembe in tighter. I continue to sink into the icy black, staring at the orisa's giant form in shock. What is he doing here? Does he mean to use his chains on me next?

Quickly, Folasade knifes through the water, snatching the dagger from my grip. She reaches the stunned creature and slices across the rough skin of its throat. Blood seeps into the water, tendrils of burgundy that unfurl into the deep.

The Mokele-mbembe opens its mouth, blood flowing from its jaws, gold-and-red eyes rolling in the dusk of water. Tumbling backward, I look from the creature to Olokun to Folasade, swathed in confusion as she pulls my blade free, releasing a clot of blood. Olokun loosens his chains and the Mokele-mbembe begins to sing, a song that echoes through the water.

There are no words but tones and textures of loss and rage and power, twisting together and spiraling into something that pulls at my soul. Sorrow winds its way through me, the sound of the Mokele-mbembe plucking at my guilt and spinning it into something larger. A kind of grief that speaks of lives claimed and taken. I float in the water, watching as the creature's lifeblood empties and its jaws crack open wider. The Mokele-mbembe's song flows in melancholy ribbons that mix with its fading heartbeats, deserting the body that has ruled these strange waters for so many years.

And then I see it. The gold shreds of the creature's soul that leave its broad chest and mix with a red essence from its mouth, the death song it cannot help but sing. Together, they shimmer in the water, weaving among the pulsing resonance to create a maelstrom of soul and sound. My own heart feels as if it is shattering at the creature's end, emotions that I know are controlled by the soul song, spun with the remnants of all those it has killed. Tears slip from my eyes, mingling with blood and water and the harmony of loss and death. I drift, hands placed on the cold skin of my chest as if to cradle my own beating heart. Olokun grips his chains, but even he can't take his eyes off the Mokele-mbembe.

But Folasade does. With her hands to her ears, the gold of my dagger flashing against short curls, she plunges down to the dying beast, her brow furrowed with determination and purpose, her lips moving in a prayer that mingles with the soul song. When she reaches the creature she raises her voice, shouting the words, her prayer cutting through the final melody emitted by the Mokele-mbembe.

"Mo gbà yín! I receive you . . . Mo gbà yín!" Folasade repeats this over and over until the gold-and-red essence glimmers, vibrating and intertwining with the song and streaming toward the sapphire around her neck.

As the body of the Mokele-mbembe begins to sink into the thick darkness it came from, I stare at the jewel of Folasade's necklace. It glows, with a red tint that makes the stone look almost purple. I eye Olokun uneasily as he pulls the chains from the Mokele-mbembe's neck, watching it sink. His black pearl cape all but camouflages him, only the gleam of his large tail standing out in the water.

"Simidele." He turns to me, the golden links flashing, his arms outstretched.

Panic slithers within me as Olokun swims closer. Folasade cradles her sapphire, eyes skating over us both, dagger held out.

"Don't come any closer," I warn, trying to keep the quiver out of my voice. Despite his help, I recall the fury that twisted his face when I left his kingdom with Esu.

The orisa doesn't listen, frowning as he reaches out for me. "Simidele, come here."

I shake my head, swimming away from him, trying to get closer to Folasade. He snakes out a hand, catching my arm. With one sharp tug he draws me to him and I yelp in the water. He grabs my wrist easily, turning me to look at him.

"If you're here to take me back to the Land of the Dead, then you're wasting your time," I hiss, lip curling. "You lied to me!"

"Heed what I say," says Olokun. His face holds a scowl, which he tries to soften. "I know I have done wrong, and I should not have used Esu in that way. It is why I am here now. To make amends."

"Perhaps I'd believe you if you weren't gripping me the way you are."

"There is more to fear than me." Olokun's tone is quieter now, but the undercurrent of urgency makes me pause, his hold still tight on my wrist. The orisa looks up at the surface and we follow his gaze. A boat skims across the water. Olokun turns back to me, his eyes darting from side to side. "I am trying to help you, just as you helped me these past months."

I think of the dead we buried together and find myself hesitating. Despite Olokun looming over me, my pulse no longer quickens. He helped capture the Mokele-mbembe, and it's this that stills me.

"You are aiding Esu, but you need to be careful." Olokun flicks a glance at Folasade, who watches him warily.

There is a crash from above and the surface is cleaved by the arrow of a body. We watch as it shoots down between the layers of water. I can see the dark brown skin of long limbs but not much else. With powerful strokes, whoever it is moves toward us.

"I knew you'd seek the soul song, so I came to warn you. The ajogun can never be truly controlled by a mortal, but there is a mortal who seeks to do this."

"Idera, the Tapa's head iyalawo. She's using the power from them before she sets them free. It's why we had to get the soul song before she did."

"That is right, but another Nupe ship was wrecked. I was able to give one of the men breath to ask him questions. He said that the iyalawo was close to freeing the ajogun but that she—"

"I said, *we know.*" My patience is fraying now, and I think of how he attacked Yemoja and the other Mami Wata. I try to jerk myself free of his iron grip, but his fingers tighten, crushing the small bones of my wrist. "Now, let me go."

"Enough!" Olokun snarls, and grabs my other arm, pulling me to him. "Stop this and listen to me. I—" But the orisa doesn't get to finish. His words are cut off as the chain around his waist snaps tight. He looks down, his mouth slack from shock, and then turns to the dark behind him. I peer past his bulk but can't see what has him.

"What is this?" asks the orisa just before he is hauled backward, golden links bright in the black of the depths as he disappears in a cloud of bubbles.

"Come on, Simidele!" Folasade pulls at me, dragging me with her as she swims frantically upward toward the small boat that still bobs above us.

We split the chasm's water in a gush of breath and energy. I know that Olokun can't come so high, but it doesn't stop me from studying the water beneath us, expecting to see the twists of his hair as he rises after us.

"What was that?" asks Folasade as she hands me back my dagger. "Who took Olokun?"

I open my mouth to answer, but a shadow is shooting up from below, a ripple in the water as something rises. Swallowing, I nod to Folasade, who steadies herself, holding my blade up in the air, the sun glistening on its serrated edge.

The surface splits apart, black curls pushing through, followed by a face that I would know anywhere. Kola opens his eyes, lashes dark and wet as he shakes his head, the droplets glistening in the air. He heaves himself over the side of the boat, limbs slick and shining. As he collapses in the bottom of the vessel, his eyes close and he loses consciousness, chest only just rising and falling with each breath he drags in. *How did he swim so deep?*

My eyes widen. Folasade looks at me and then down at Kola. "We need to get him to the shore," she says, gripping the side of the boat and pushing. I follow her lead, questions whirling all the while in my mind, some as dark as the chasm beneath us.

• • •

The sun stains the sky with burnt orange and streaks of red when we are finally able to get Kola to the shore. He remains unconscious as Yinka and Ara fill me in on what happened. I don't take my eyes from him, grateful that he's still breathing but trying to understand what he was doing in the chasm.

"We were waiting for you to surface, but Kola was restless. It was as if he sensed trouble. He said you were taking too long, that something must have gone wrong." Yinka sits still, Kola's head in her lap, while Ara extracts herbs from her pack, mixing them with water for him to drink. He's weak but awake now, eyes pinned on me. "And then he took a fisherman's boat and insisted on going in after you."

I think of the Mokele-mbembe and its venomous jaws. "Why would you even try to do that?"

Kola tries to get up, but Yinka forces his head back down, her face a fierce blend of concern and displeasure.

"But how did you dive that deep?" I run my gaze over his face, as creased with confusion as my own. "How did you have the strength to pull Olokun back?"

"I don't know!" Kola answers, sitting up. He bats Yinka's hands aside as she tries to get him to lie back down. "I just knew that I needed to get him away from you." He stares at me, eyes hard. "I wasn't going to let him take you again."

"He was trying to tell me something. To help . . ." Those words sound silly even to me, yet I can't help but think about what he was going to say. "And you . . . you could have drowned!" I glower at Kola, wanting to smack him on the side of his head. "This is exactly what I knew would happen . . . why I wanted to come on my own."

Ara rubs my shoulder, calming me somewhat before she takes

the wooden cup from beside her. "Here," she says to Kola. "Stop talking and drink this. You need your strength back."

"What is it?" He shrinks away. "I'm not a child."

Ara rolls her eyes and holds it to the boy's mouth. "Then why are you acting like one? Honestly, must I pinch your nose and pour it down your throat?" She rocks back on her heels and glares. "Because I will if I have to."

"Wha ipf it?" Kola mumbles, keeping his lips firmly together.

"Just some rooibos tea to give you energy." A shadow of annoyance passes over Ara's face. "You want to get back to Oko, yes? It'll be dark soon. Do you want us to waste time waiting for you to gather the strength to ride?"

Kola only hesitates a moment more, and when Ara lifts the cup to his lips again, he opens his mouth and swallows the herbal drink in one gulp. I watch him, the flexing of his throat, the spread of his shoulders and his chest. He's changed since Esu's island, but he shouldn't have been able to swim that deep, shouldn't have had the strength to pull Olokun back like that.

"How did you manage to get away from Olokun?"

Kola shrugs, but I can see confusion in the angles of his expression, the lift of his eyebrows. "I just . . . swam. As fast as I could."

"And that's it?" I picture the size of the orisa and his tail.

"That's it. Olokun couldn't follow when I was high enough." Kola gets to his feet and rolls his shoulders. He eyes the sky. "We need to leave. I want us to be back behind Oko's walls before it's full dark."

He's avoiding the subject, and my unease lingers. None of it makes sense. I raise my eyebrow but he ignores me, turning away toward the horses.

Yinka stretches, her movement lithe and fluid. "Did you get the soul song?"

"Only just." I point to Folasade's sapphire, which pulses in a dark shade of lilac. "Olokun held the Mokele-mbembe back so we could glean it."

"Because he wanted you," says Kola, his tone rough.

"He confirmed that the iyalawo was trying to free the ajogun." I frown, thinking of the rest of the orisa's words, cut off when he was dragged away. I feel a small prickle of worry that I brush off. "Olokun said he had questioned one of the Tapa men."

"But he said Idera was planning on releasing the ajogun?" Ara stares at me, laying a comforting hand on mine when I nod. "Don't worry yourself over Olokun. We have the soul song now." She scrambles to her feet, helping me to mine. "Let's go; we don't want to waste any more time. And the sooner we get back to Oko, the sooner I can rest my behind. I know this trek back is going to be just as painful."

We mount the horses and this time Yinka leads with Kola. I watch them talking, see the girl gesturing, and I know she's asking him about what happened in the chasm.

"Simi?" Ara's voice is soft, and when I turn, the sun blazes around her, lighting the curve of her braids. "You and Kola . . ."

I turn away quickly, shaking my head, my stomach sinking. "There is nothing to it."

"I think there is." Ara's statement is bold. "He told me you can't be together."

I don't speak, trying to move with the horse so that it doesn't jar my spine.

"What if I told you that you could?" Ara's words are still quiet, but this time I jerk to face her. She smiles at me, but sadness clouds her expression. "What if I told you there was a way that you could become human again?"

"Then I wouldn't believe you." I swallow thickly, heart lurching. I don't want to even think of what she's saying. "There is no way. And I want him to be happy. To be with someone he can truly be with." Besides, since we've seen each other again, Kola doesn't even seem to want to look at me, let alone be with me.

"But what if you really could be together?"

The grass plain stretches around us, yellowing in the last light of the day. Beyond the rising ground I can see the beginning of the forest that will take us to Oko. Of course I am drawn to what Ara is asking, but I try to squash down whatever hope is left in me. I don't want to keep yearning for what I can't have.

"Then I would say that you know a lot more than Yemoja."

"Listen, Simi. Idera taught me herbs and healing but also other . . . things. I know she plans to release the ajogun, that she needs the soul song, and I also know the other powers that it holds." I hold my breath, knowing what she is about to say. "What if you commanded the ajogun to make you human again?"

"What?" I snatch another look at her as she shifts in her saddle.

"If you are the one to take the soul song and offer it to the ajogun, then you could control them and ask for all that you want. That includes being human again." She smiles now, eyes glittering. "You could be with Kola."

I gape at her, and then shake my head at the ridiculousness of her suggestion. "As I said, there's no way."

"But if you commanded them, then you could order them

back behind the veil. Banish them and reap the rewards of being with Kola. Why trust Esu when you could be the one to bind them?"

"I'm not going to risk the ajogun. In fact, I can't believe you would even suggest it."

"It's only because I see your pain," Ara says earnestly. "This way, you could get what you want."

The ruby on my wrist hangs heavily, grazing the side of my palm, a reminder of the trickster's abilities. "Ara, you must know some of what these powers will cost a person. They're not straightforward, even I know this from Yemoja and Esu." I shake my head, feeling the familiar disappointment wind through me. "It must be Esu. It is the only way. The right way. We can't risk anything going wrong, and I wouldn't put so much at stake just for something that I want."

Not again, I think. I have meddled enough.

Ara is silent a moment, but then she is turning to me and nodding. "You're right. I was only thinking of you, but it's too dangerous. Idera is not always right. We can't take the chance that it won't work."

I agree, but her words have taken root inside me. This is the problem with wanting something you can't have. The thought of it begins to grow.

We ride over the grass plains as the light bleeds from the sky, and I push away thoughts of being anything other than what I am, what I am meant to be. I hold on to this and try to take comfort.

I urge my horse to go a little faster, catching up with Folasade. The sapphire hangs just below the base of her throat, a tiny glint of red amid the now-purple flush of the stone.

"Are you all right?" She hasn't spoken much since the chasm, but then I think of the weight of what she holds. "Thank you. You did what I couldn't."

Folasade nods and smiles, but her shoulders are drawn up and her face is lined with tension. "I did what needed to be done. I could see the effect the soul song was having on you."

"Still, it's a burden. One I didn't want you to bear."

"I chose to come with you." Folasade's eyebrows rise. She takes a deep breath and lowers her shoulders as she exhales. "It is not something I had to question. Just like you, I'm prepared to do what it takes. It's not only you who cares about what happens."

"I know," I say.

"Well, then. Don't act like this, Simi."

"Like what?"

"As if this is all yours to do alone."

Folasade's words are well-meaning, but they sting a little all the same, and I force myself to nod. "We should be back in Oko just before it gets dark," I murmur, turning away.

When we reach the first trees, Kola and Yinka are there waiting for us. The sun has all but slipped beyond the horizon, and I eye the dense foliage ahead of us uneasily.

"I want us to move fast through this last bit," says Kola, his voice tight. "The plains made it easier to see anything coming, but the forest can conceal too much."

We group together, horses jostling, Folasade in the middle of us, the purple of her jewel shining. The press of the mahogany trees leaches more of the light as Kola picks his way through the spaces between. We follow, weapons drawn, as the moon exchanges places with the sun. There is still light, but its rapid disappearance has Kola speeding up, our horses soon sweaty from a fast canter.

As we enter the path that runs through the forest, I think again of the way Kola pulled Olokun away from me and I shift uneasily. He might be deciding not to give it much thought, but it's clear that something has changed. The way he fought the Tapa soldiers comes back to me. The blur of his body as he twisted and spun, cutting down the enemy with easy strokes, predicting what they would do next. And now this. Diving deep and having the strength to haul Olokun back by his own chains. Although Kola held his own before, there were never any hints of this . . . strength. This power.

But those thoughts are for later. I shake them off, focusing on the shadows and trees that enfold us.

We're not far from Oko when Kola stops his horse. Shifting closer to Folasade, I freeze as he motions for us to stay where we are. Something in the way he holds his body puts me on edge, and I slide the dagger from my hair as Yinka unsheathes her axes silently, body shimmering as she struggles to hold on to her human form.

We scan the spaces between the trees, horses still in the growing cold of the night. Just as I am about to urge Kola to keep going, I catch a glimpse of bronze.

"Did you see that?" I gasp.

"Is it Idera?" whispers Ara, shaking. Her eyes are round with terror as she clutches the leather reins of her horse with hard knuckles.

Pressing my fingers to my lips, I peer forward into the forest. Sweat slides between my shoulder blades, slick on the chill of my skin. I hiss, wincing as a sudden heat at my wrist draws my eyes to Esu's ruby. The gem flares in the dim light, glowing a bright red. I rub at the seared skin as the forest around me fades.

I am standing in blackness, but the dark is punctured with icy stars. The sky unfolds all around me as I hold my chest, the sapphire of my necklace lit up brighter than I've ever seen it, the ruby still burning. It's freezing and I shiver as the moon fights free from clouds and illuminates a stark form in a clearing. Egba, the warlord of paralysis, stands tall, wreathed in a fog that twines around his thin limbs. His head is larger than his body, tilted down as if it is too heavy to hold up. Following his gaze, I stifle a cry. Bodies litter the forest floor, their arms and legs twisted in unnatural shapes. Surrounded as they are by cloth bundles and food, it is clear they have been fleeing something. I watch for the sparkle of their souls, but as I peer closer, I hold a hand to my mouth. They are not dead. Instead, their eyes gleam in the murk, pupils wide. A keening sound starts, joined by others as the people try to call for help.

Egba raises his head, lifting a hand to hold it straight when it lolls back slightly. He reaches out, fingers as long as my arm. The warlord points to the people trapped in their own bodies around him and then I see another figure gliding through the fog. Oran, the warrior who represents inescapable danger. He picks his way around his brother, mouth widening into jaws that drip saliva and blood.

I reach for the closest person, a man who still clutches a knife, knuckles frozen around the carved ivory hilt. There is nothing he can do, and his eyes bulge as a tear slips down his cheek.

"No!" I scream, stumbling forward. But the fog swirls, the stars brightening until all I can see is silver white, so sharp that it slices through my mind.

Despair courses through me as the ruby scorches a fire red, bringing me back. I moan, clasping the skin and bones of my wrist, blinking as the forest comes into focus.

Kola edges his horse forward, moving branches and leaves with his sword. There is still no movement from the dense trees, until I see a pinprick of red weaving through the canopy in the distance.

"What is it?" whispers Folasade as I rub at the sore skin of my wrist, choking on a sob.

Before I can try to answer, a small scarlet glow dips between branches, accompanied by another, and then another, until the sky is scarred with red dots of lights. *Here is a story. Story it is . . .* My breath catches as I remember one of my mother's tales. A glut of monsters and warnings that terrified me every time she told it.

Adzes.

Creatures that transform from fireflies, using their insect form to gain entry to homes, they survive on blood and death, draining the life from those that they attack. People often leave out offerings of coconut milk and palm wine to appease a lone adze, but the creatures are not often sated without tasting blood.

"We need to move," I say as a heavy dread threads through me. I glance around at the others and then I pause.

A shimmer of bronze flashes between the tree trunks. The pulse of my heart fills my throat as I make out bursts of copper. Idera emerges from the gloom, her milky eye shining. She smiles, a crooked arrangement of thin lips and small teeth, and raises her hands. I can't hear what she's murmuring, but my eyes are drawn to the lines of her open palms. As her mouth continues to move, the contours of her hands darken, turning a red that begins to glow and throb. The breeze is thick with a crackle that reminds me of the air just before a thunderstorm. Idera brings her palms up, looking at each hand suffused with crimson light as the adzes swarm toward her.

My horse whinnies nervously, skittish as the iyalawo starts to laugh, a vivid miasma swirling above her. "Go!" I cry. "We need to go *now*."

Kola turns to me, the whites of his eyes gleaming. He doesn't ask questions, acting instantly on my fear. "We're not far from Oko now. Ride after me. Fast."

The sound of the buzzing fills the night as we dig our bare heels into the sides of the horses, spurring them into a gallop. I try to stay close to Folasade, keeping her purple wrapper in my sights, even as my horse leaps over snaking tree roots. Behind us, the cloud of red pinpricks grows, swarming after us. But it is not this form that scares me, but what they will become.

CHAPTER NINETEEN

"QUICKLY!" I SCREAM at Folasade. She hunches forward, her eyes wide with panic, the sapphire glittering against her chest.

She nods, clinging onto the reins of her horse, but as she throws a glance behind us, she doesn't see the branch hanging in front of her. The clawed limb rakes at Folasade's chest and face, knocking her from her horse. My own mare jumps over the girl, narrowly avoiding the soft tumble of her body. I yank on the reins and slide from the sweaty back of my horse, my breaths shallow as I run to Folasade. She rolls over, groaning, a line of blood on her cheek where the branch caught her.

"Come on," I urge, reaching down for her hand, the flush of her sapphire casting her face in a lilac glow. Around us, a dozen blood-red lights descend to the forest floor. They pulse, flickering glimpses of small insect bodies inside. Fireflies. But these are not the ones we are used to, and as we watch, their limbs begin to grow, pale legs and arms elongating. I stumble backward as the adzes change fast, towering over us in their final form.

White limbs and talons and needle-thin teeth in open maws.

The largest plants itself on the path in front of us. With a flat face, two holes for a nose, and a skull that forms a rounded point at the back, it glares at me with crimson eyes and opens its mouth to screech, the fetid stench of death on its breath.

Folasade whimpers beneath me, her eyes fixed on the adzes behind us as they tip their flat faces to the air, sniffing. Our horses prance nervously, hooves drumming on the forest floor, their eyes rolling wildly before they take off. Another spray of words from Idera and the adzes close in, screeching and clicking to one another, the iyalawo behind them, a twisted smile cleaving her face. I don't look away from the creatures as they stalk toward us, eyes flaming in the fresh darkness as clouds hide the moon. Pulling Folasade behind me, I hold my dagger before me, trying to ignore how small it looks compared to the adzes' claws. As the monsters scuttle toward us, I know the only chance we have is to run. But we're not fast enough, and if we both take off at once, they will definitely catch us.

"Go!" I hiss to Folasade. Behind her, Ara rides back to us, staring fearfully at the adzes. "Take her."

Folasade shakes her head at me, but I point to the sapphire glowing around her neck. "You need to." Her hand flies to her necklace and she nods, but tears stream down her cheeks.

"It's all right," I say softly. "But go. Now!" I give her a little push and she slips before righting herself and sprinting toward Ara's horse. Kola and Yinka thread back through the trees, shoulders hunched, eyes flashing. Folasade runs, gasping loudly until she reaches Ara. After scrambling up on the horse, she peers down at me, flinching as the first adze lashes out at me with a long arm, talons raking the air as I stumble backward. And then Ara is yanking on the reins, turning the horse around, and they are gone, galloping through the dark spaces between the trees.

Kola wields his sword as Yinka slips from her horse, snarling

177

at the advancing adze, body trembling, her wrapper of fur growing so that it replaces every inch of her skin. She yowls into the night air as her jaw cracks, teeth sharp, breath steaming. Large pads replace her hands and feet as she paws at the ground, neck lengthening. And then she is loping toward the adze that attacked me, snapping at the creature's long white legs.

"Are you hurt?" asks Kola as he jumps down from his horse, eyes flicking over me. He holds my face in both of his warm hands and I shake my head.

"Take my horse and catch up with Ara," he says.

But there is no chance to flee, and I wouldn't anyway. I'm not leaving either of them. The rest of the adzes pick their way through the trees, all emitting the same high-pitched shrieks, and I take a deep breath, dragging the night air down into my lungs. I will not lose anyone else.

Yinka attacks, locking her jaws around one creature's shoulder, and Kola leaps forward. Following behind him, I slash at an adze that scurries toward us, flinching as its black blood splatters on the bushes. The scream the creature releases pierces my skull, but I don't stop, lashing out again and plunging my blade into its chest. The eyes of the adze sputter out, turning to ashen pits in its pale face.

Yinka bites down hard and twists her head, snapping the neck of the monster she was fighting, and Kola brings his sword down in a silver arc, severing another one's head. An adze moves up behind him, its mouth open wide, teeth shining and sharp. My heart pounds so hard it feels as if it is cracking my ribs as I run forward, lift my dagger up, and slice into its gut. The creature crumples to the ground.

I stand over the dead thing, my chest heaving, waiting for it to rise again. When it doesn't, I wipe my mouth, and Kola turns to face me.

"Idera's controlling them," I manage to say, trying to catch my breath. "We need to get to her."

We face the forest, teeming with the skittering adzes and their searing eyes. The iyalawo stands among them, palms still open to the dark clouds of the sky.

Kola looks at me, his hand grazing my arm, and then he is spinning away, charging through the adzes, a blur of limbs and sword. Yinka lifts her muzzle, eyes gleaming in the moonlight as she releases a howl that spirals into the sky. Together, they tear and hack at each adze, working their way toward the iyalawo.

For a moment, I can only stare at the grace and power of Kola and Yinka as they cut a swathe through the shrieking creatures. Yinka lunges, canines bared, pushing the adzes back as Kola fights his way closer to Idera. When the iyalawo sees his advance, her eyes widen slightly before she narrows them, directing her gaze at me and muttering furiously. Almost as one, the adzes turn and begin to flock in my direction.

I take a step back, raw panic slithering through my veins. I brace myself, blocking the swiping slash of the first adze. The creature moves closer, its talons glinting in the moonlight. As I draw close enough to catch a waft of fetid rot, the adze lunges for me. Spinning at the last moment, I dart left, drawing my dagger along its side. The adze screams, and before it can turn, I ram the blade into its back, twisting the dagger as it cuts through bone and muscle. As I yank my weapon free, I am knocked sideways, a slash to my arm making me hiss.

My head thuds against the ground and a ringing fills my ears as I stare up at the black sky. I hear more chittering as the adzes scuttle toward me. Teeth and red eyes fill my vision and I open my mouth to scream, searching for the dagger that has fallen from my grip. But my fingers find only moist earth and splintered sticks. Two more adzes block the sky and together they lean down, whetted fangs glinting. I look right, hand still groping, until it brushes against the keen gold of my blade. Bringing it up in a quick arc, I don't look to see where it lands, desperate only to get the adzes off me. A squeal lets me know that my dagger landed well, but I know there are more. I lift my blade, the black blood dripping from the tip, seeping into the folds of my wrapper.

Gazing wildly above me, I grit my teeth, the air a blur of night sky, forest, and red eyes as I try to muster the energy to get up. After raising myself on one elbow, I go down again as another adze crashes into me, its talons scraping the skin of my side. The creature presses down on my chest, its rough skin clammy, making my stomach roil. I gasp, trying to breathe properly, my heart thumping as I expect the sharp graze of its teeth. A scream bubbles on my lips until I realize that the adze isn't moving. Pushing against the heavy body, my fingers slipping in its blood, I free myself and sit up.

Kola stands above me, his mouth a grim line, chest splattered with dark gore. He holds a hand out to me and I let him drag me to my feet just as Yinka lopes over to us, her fur receding, wrapping around her emerging human form. Beyond her are the heaped bodies of the other adzes. I'm wondering how they managed to kill so many when I realize that the iyalawo is not there.

"Where's Idera?"

"Gone," answers Kola, running a hand over his face.

She knew they would turn away from her to protect me. I look down, shame flooding through me at holding them back.

"Should we go after her?" Yinka rolls her neck, the bones

cracking delicately. She's fully changed now but her teeth protrude slightly, still a touch too long to be human.

"We need to find Folasade and Ara," I say, worry and fear swirling together as I turn in the direction of Oko.

"The iyalawo used the adzes as a distraction," states Kola as we wind our way through the trees, breath coming in short gasps. The horses have long gone.

"She's after the soul song," says Yinka as she leaps over a fallen tree, not breaking her stride.

We run through the forest as the moon brightens its glow, casting a pale light on us. I feel weak with dread and exhaustion, but I do my best to scan the forest floor, searching for any signs that Folasade and Ara made it this way.

"Oko is through the trees ahead," says Kola, and I look up to see the thinning of the forest, the path to the village just visible.

It isn't far, they could have made it, I think, allowing a small relief to bloom. And then I see it to my right. Curled delicately, fingers loose. The hand is splayed palm up, lined with blood that pools in its dipped center.

I stop. My chest tightens as I follow the line of the wrist to the elbow, pausing to see the rest hidden behind a tree thick with wild pears.

The night feels colder now, the crush of earth beneath my feet rough with stones and the roots of trees. I take a shaky step toward the hand, unable to breathe.

"Simi!" Kola's voice shatters the quiet, but I don't turn around.

I can feel the grief rising in me before I really know who I am looking at. Sucking in a breath, I move closer, walking around the side of the tree, my soles on fire from running and my heartbeat throbbing in my throat.

Folasade is lying on her back, her head turned in my direction. Her eyes are open, but they are not focused on anything other than her journey home to Olodumare. Blood spreads beneath her, crowning her short black curls in a dark halo.

A sob rips through me as I fall to my knees. I crawl forward and take her hand, pressing my fingers where her pulse should be. Her skin is still warm, but that is all. I cradle her hand against my cheek, closing my eyes as the tears course down my face.

How can Folasade be dead?

A wail escapes from deep within me. I shouldn't have told her to run; she would have been safer with us. All I thought about was protecting the soul song in her sapphire.

My eyes spring open and I sit up. Folasade's hand is still in mine as I force myself to look at the ruin of her body. I swallow down bile, and another sob echoes in the air.

Images of the delicate fan of her tail flood my mind. The time she always had for me when I was first re-created by Yemoja, when I didn't want to accept that I was no longer the same as humans. Her scorn, but also her understanding as she pleaded with me to embrace who I was. The gentle touch when she would hold my hair away from my face in the deep so that she could look into my eyes, to show me how much she cared even if her words were sometimes barbed.

Folasade.

Always wanting to please Yemoja.

To do her duty.

And now look at her. Her body cooling in the earth of a forest far from her home and the sea. Surrounded by blood and moonlight, and the stars that witnessed her murder.

"Simidele." Yinka is dipping down beside me. She clasps my chin, forcing my gaze to hers. "We will give her the burial she deserves, whatever you want. But right now, we need the soul song."

Yinka's gaze locks with mine and I see pain and shock in her eyes.

The soul song. I nod and sniff, wiping my face with shaking hands. We can't let Folasade's death be for nothing. I know this. After gently placing her hand on the ground next to her, I run my cold fingertips over the still-warm skin of her neck. Inhaling deeply, I fumble over the drape of her collarbone, feeling for the golden chain that matches mine. Ignoring the blood that is gathered in the brown hollows, I search for the sapphire that glows purple with the Mokele-mbembe's soul song. When I don't find the links or the facets of the jewel, I force myself to look more closely, holding in a sob as I tip her head gently to the side, but where the gem should be hanging like a glittering strange fruit, there is only Folasade's blood.

· · ·

A hoot comes from above us and I flinch as Yinka lifts her axes. But it is only an owl, its piercing green eyes shining from a white face, beak sharp over black-and-gray chest feathers. The bird perches on a high branch, staring down at us.

"The necklace isn't there," I say, staring down at Folasade in a blur of tears.

"Idera has done this. She must have it," hisses Kola. "Where's Ara?" He looks around the forest, his movements mirrored by Yinka.

Ara.

I clamber to my feet, head swinging wildly as I rake our surroundings for my oldest friend, lips moving as I say a prayer for her safety and her life. Please don't let her be lost, too, I think as I stumble around the tree that looms over Folasade's body. The prayer reverberates in my mind as I search the ground and the leaves, but it's only when I see a red handprint on a tree trunk that my stomach falls, and I stop. A trail of blood on the fallen leaves loops around before petering out.

"She's been taken." Along with the soul song. I think back to Ara escaping the Nupe Kingdom and the hardship she faced there. And I couldn't protect her. Again.

Kola spins and runs in the direction of Oko. "Come," he shouts over his shoulder. "We need the guards. We can search."

"What about Folasade?" I ask, my voice cracking.

"We'll come back for her," says Yinka, pulling at me. "I promise." She yanks me again and I follow them both as they sprint through the trees, finding the path that leads to Kola's village. They were so close, I think as we run through the last of the forest, our feet slamming against the dirt road. A jolt of pain bursts through my soles but I keep going, using it to feel something other than the numbness that is starting to creep in. Folasade is dead, and both Ara and the soul song have been taken. A sob rises in my chest, but the burn of running keeps it at bay.

I let Yinka tow me through the concealed entrance before I collapse in the earth, hands going to my lips as a cry escapes. Yinka speaks to the newly stationed guards at the gate, barking orders.

"Simi." Kola crouches down next to me, his voice as soft as the way he slides his arms around me. "Simi. Listen to me. I'm going to get the guard. We're going to look for Ara and bring Folasade's body back."

I don't answer. I can't. But I nod and Kola slips away, replaced by Yinka's hand held in front of me. I sniff, taking a deep breath before letting her pull me to my feet.

We reach Kola's compound and a small room off the cooking quarters, where Yinka eases me down on a blue-and-purple woven mat. I can't stop the tears that come as she strokes my hair, her other hand warm on my arm.

"What do we do now?" My words are tiny, sorrow shrinking them.

"You rest. I'm going to look for Ara with the others." I peer up at Yinka, at the fierce glint in her eyes, her own pain showing as anger. "Kola has sent a messenger to get Bem and Esu from the babalawo's."

I sit up, her words scorching like fire. Esu. Perhaps he can help somehow. "I'm coming with you." My grief will do nothing. I should be out there searching, too.

Yinka shakes her head, pressing me back down. "You need to rest. I'll get a guard to bring Folasade here and together we will pay her the respect she deserves."

"What if you don't find Ara? What if Idera somehow manages to use Folasade's sapphire?" The thought of the iyalawo freeing the ajogun with the soul song makes it hard to breathe.

"If we don't find them?" answers Yinka, standing up, her jaw tight as her hands go instinctively to her axes. "Then we're going to the Nupe Kingdom to get them back."

CHAPTER TWENTY

I DON'T WANT to sleep, but I feel my mind shutting down and soon I slip into fractured dreams filled with blood and death. When I jerk into consciousness, it is to Yinka hovering over me, her eyes flashing in the gloom. She tries to smile, but her lips only form a grimace that makes my stomach dip. Yinka turns away from me to light a lamp, her arms and back shining with sweat in the flickering glow. I open my mouth to ask her if they found Ara, but the words get stuck when Kola walks through the entranceway.

His arms are full of a white wrapper tucked around brown limbs. Kola's eyes are on me as he pauses on the threshold. A tear slips down his cheek as I stand up, legs shaking, my heart beating so loudly that I can hear each thud. I swallow as he takes a step, his gaze darting around the room.

I make myself move, allowing Kola to lay Folasade down on the sleeping mat. A bare toe peeps from the end of the material and I swallow a sob, fingers twisted tight as he lowers her. Gently, he tucks the white cloth around her, settling the girl before me.

"What . . ." But he never finishes his sentence, his mouth tightening in grief as he straightens up.

Yinka takes my hand as we gaze down at the shape of my friend. I think of Folasade rolling her eyes at me in the water, annoyed when I used to change to human form unnecessarily.

She didn't need to come with me. I should have told her to stay with the other Mami Wata.

"Thank you," I say. "For bringing her."

Kola nods. "The guards couldn't find Ara, but they found tracks and . . . the signs of a struggle."

"Idera has her, then," says Yinka, her lip curled. "And the soul song, too."

"It looks that way." Kola rubs a hand over the back of his neck and squeezes.

I knew it, but still the confirmation shatters the hope I have been silly enough to cling to. Folasade is dead and Ara has been captured. And I could do nothing to stop it. Despair creeps through me as I hold out a hand to the ivory fabric wrapped around Folasade. The cotton is soft as I gently take a piece between my thumb and forefinger.

Kola frowns, his empty hands in fists now, and looks down at me. "Would you like help with the funeral rituals? We can bury her in Oko."

"No, but thank you." I kneel beside Folasade, my hands trembling as they hover over the white cloth that covers her face. "I'll take her back to the sea. Where she belongs."

"I can stay and help you prepare her," says Yinka. "I'll get some fresh water and oils."

Kola murmurs about meetings with his father, his words washing over me as he leaves. I stare at the shape of Folasade when Yinka follows him out, my unfocused eyes then catching on the altar against the wall. Resting on its surface are two coconuts, rooster feathers, and corn. Offerings to Oko, orisa of crops. I blink slowly as the room fades.

The altar takes up an entire corner, the same height as me. I sit as close as I can without jostling all that it holds, mesmerized by the rainbow of light that flares through the crystal necklace in the center. I tilt my head, watching as the colors project onto the white petals of the flowers next to it, giving them vibrant shades of freshly cut mango, watermelon, and the grass after the rains. When ìyá tells stories of Yemoja, she wears it nestled against the folds of her wrapper, but when her tales center on other orisas, it stays on the altar.

"Good morning, little one." I feel a gentle touch on my shoulder and the smell of shea butter envelops me.

"Morning, ìyá."

She hands me fresh white-and-blue flowers, the seven silver bracelets she wears to honor Yemoja jangling on her wrist. "Would you like to help me?"

I nod, eyeing the lilies and the small platter of àkàrà that my mother holds. She gives me the fresh blooms and I'm careful not to crush the petals as I place them in the terra-cotta pot that is patterned with the curves of the sea. If I peer close enough, I can make out the blowhole of a whale and its spurt of water. I take my time, arranging the flowers so that they are spaced out equally, checking that there is enough water in the pot. Ìyá places the bean cakes next to the gourd rattle, which is bound with strings of blue beads, and we step back.

"Yemoja will be pleased," says my mother, pulling me to her side, her warm hand wrapped around my shoulders. "Would you like to lead the prayer today?"

I look up, nerves coiling in my stomach. "But I've never done it before." What if I stutter or forget an important word and Yemoja takes offense?

"You know it, Simidele. I see you mouthing it every time I speak the words." Ìyá crouches next to me and smiles, her dimples deep in the glow of her brown cheeks. "Besides, even if you make a mistake, it is fine. Mistakes are very important. They are there for us to learn from."

I take a deep breath, looking at the altar, thinking of the cool water of the river. Ìyá takes my hand and squeezes.

"Yemoja, mo bu olá fún o pèlú àwon òdòdó wònyí . . ."

Yemoja. The first orisa I remember praying to, my mother's ancestral deity and therefore mine. I owe her so much, more than my worship before can account for.

I open my eyes, my gaze falling on Folasade again. All this time, and I am back where I started, trying to fix what I have done wrong. It is time to go back to the reason behind my creation, behind the creation of all Mami Wata. Once I have helped Esu, I will return to Yemoja. Gather the souls and bless them upon their release. Do all that Folasade was proud to do. All that she did with fervor and compassion.

Yinka returns with a large copper bowl and muslin cloths. She sits next to me in silence as we contemplate the lifeless body before us.

Sister, friend, Mami Wata.

I lean over her and hold my breath as I draw the cloth down to reveal her face. Her lips are parted, a brown-and-pink that reminds me of my own. Lashes lie delicately on her full cheeks. I bend down, cupping her face with my hand.

A way to survive.

A way to serve.

A way to save.

But she could not survive Idera's attack, and I didn't save her.

"You didn't deserve this," I whisper as my silent tears drip down on the white fabric, darkening the cloth. "I will be better. I'll do what you cannot."

Yinka and I wash Folasade's body. I imagine her asleep, not willing to think of her never smiling or chiding me again. As I wipe at the skin of her neck, I fume at the absence of her sapphire. We received our jewels when Yemoja first re-created us in her image, and we never took them off. And now Folasade has had hers stolen along with her life. I force the anger down, wanting these last moments to be of peace and respect.

We oil her body in silence and I cross her arms over her chest. She took to her duties with piety, showing me the way when I was first remade. I know she would want to be in the sea, not spending a moment more than she had to on land. In life as Mami Wata and in death.

"When would you like to take her?" Yinka's voice is soft in the dark of the room.

"Now." The sooner the better, I think.

Yinka lays a hand on my arm, warm fingers squeezing. "The elders and officials will be busy discussing the Nupe Kingdom for most of the night. If we leave now we'll have privacy."

Together we fold a clean white cloth around Folasade's body. Yinka offers to carry her and I say yes, knowing that I don't have her strength. Not on land, anyway.

"We'll come with you." Kola emerges from the doorway. "I've told bàbá all I can. Besides, it's not safe to go on your own."

The iyalawo already has what she wants, I think bitterly, but I agree anyway. When we step outside, I see Bem waiting with Esu, his face solemn.

"Simi, I am sorry," says Bem as he steps forward and wraps his arms around me. I let him squeeze me once before I pull away.

The orisa doesn't move. "This was a loss. One that will be felt by both you and Yemoja." Part of Esu's face is still cloaked in the dark, but he bows his head once and holds his right hand against his chest. "The ajogun will be bound."

I notice that he doesn't profess any sadness of his own at Folasade's death, but I nod back at him anyway.

"I told the council what happened," says Kola. "We'll join the contingent of warriors that will be sent from Oko to fight the Tapa at Rabah. And then we will find Idera and recover the soul song."

"You make it sound so easy," I say, trying to keep the sharpness from my tone.

"It won't be. We know this." Kola moves closer to me, one hand reaching out for my arm. "But what's the alternative? To give up?"

Perhaps, I think, but I don't say this out loud. I pull away and look back at Folasade's body in Yinka's strong arms. "So much has been lost." My voice is a whisper.

"Which is why we have no choice."

He's right. Kola's words spark something in me, a blaze against the flood of grief. I take a deep breath. "Let me return Folasade to the sea, and then we'll do whatever it takes."

The pathways of Oko are full of shadows cut through with bright shafts of moonlight. We move silently down the main street and through the gates swept open by Kola's guards, until we reach the fields that lead to the sea. I sense the water before I hear it, feel the pull of it deep in my gut. The swish and rush of the sea soon surround us as we near the beach. Yinka stands in the last of the grass before passing me Folasade.

Clouds drift across a dark sky as I stand at the edge of the sea, clutching Folasade tightly. As a human, I was afraid of the open water the first time I saw it, so unending did it seem. Now I feel the tug of home as I look at its shifting surface.

Home, where Folasade belongs.

Tears slide down my cheeks as I walk into the place where the waves lap at the land, their sudden frill cold against my changing skin. Scales prick their way through as I sink into the shallows. I head deeper until I am swimming with Folasade held against me, my tail propelling us farther into the sea.

She does not change her form, cannot in death. But as I hold Folasade's body steady, I loosen my grip, letting her float just ahead of me. If only her legs would fuse together, scales peppering her skin, the sea reviving what the land couldn't. But she does not transform, and I let my misery free, sobbing into the pleats of the water until I know I must let her go. To honor her properly.

Holding my sapphire, I lift my eyes to the moon as it bathes its cool glow on the gentle swells of the nighttime tides. "Olodumare ń pè, pẹlú àdúrà yìí, á ṣe ìrìn-àjò rẹ padà sí ilé ní ìrọrùn, adẹ́dàá rẹ, ìbẹ̀rẹ̀ àti òpin in rẹ." My prayer spirals into the breeze as I close my eyes and whisper it again. "Olodumare is calling, and with this prayer, we ease your journey back home, to your maker, your beginning and your end." I repeat this five more times, seven in total, my voice breaking only on the last one.

Folasade's body, limbs gleaming in the white light from the moon, begins to shine brighter. My tail waves in the water as I watch the glow consume her, bound in a light so strong that I am forced to narrow my eyes. The sudden explosion of radiance sets the sea alight in a scorch of silvery ivory. Folasade's body shimmers, slowly changing from its clean glossy softness. I give thanks as the girl merges with the glitter on the sea, my tears flowing, slipping down into the water.

"I'm sorry. Àláfíà ni tìrẹ báàyí," I whisper as Folasade becomes yet another layer of foam upon the sea, its delicate froth lacing the waves in beautiful filigrees. "Peace is yours now."

...

I fight against the urge to let the currents snatch me, take me back down to the deep, where I can nurse my sorrow in the icy dark. I let the blues of the sea wash over me, the weight a slow balm. Eventually I swim back to shore.

The others watch me emerge from the water. I step onto land as my scales shift into smooth skin, bones arranged so that I can walk. My wrapper glimmers golden in the muted light. Kola reaches for me, but I don't let him get close enough to touch, veering away toward Oko. I won't take refuge in someone I will have to leave. Not again.

"Simi, we can use the cover of the battle to get into the capital and then the temple," says Yinka, walking to my side. "This is not finished."

"Ara spoke of the city's arrangement to me," adds Kola. "We can do this."

I say nothing. The grief has a ragged rawness to it that eats away at everything else. I sigh, feeling my shoulders slump, tears prickle again.

"Good. Then I will be able to get a few hours' sleep yet," says

Esu. "Since I was rudely awakened earlier. I am greatly inconvenienced by lack of rest."

Yinka snaps, reminding him of the loss of the soul song, growing angry as the orisa yawns and flaps his hands at her.

"Yes, yes. I know all this. It's merely a minor setback."

"I like your confidence," says Kola with an edge to his voice. "But war with the Tapa was what we were trying to avoid."

"Psht. It is but one battle." Esu ambles toward Oko's gates. "The rest will be resolved once the ajogun are bound."

"But before then?" Kola matches his pace. "What other creatures can Idera call on to fight for them?"

"We shall see," says the orisa, his words marred by another yawn. "However, they will most likely be no match for me."

"And what of the men and women of Oyo?" I say as they all turn to face me. "What match will they be? Their lives are what we are fighting for."

"You are right. But to do this, we need the soul song that you lost. And so, in order for us to get it back, there will be some casualties." Esu smiles, teeth wide and large in the dark. "Unfortunately."

I know that what the trickster said is the truth, but as I run my fingers over the hilt of the dagger in my hair, I make a promise to myself to put it all right.

We reach Oko in the thick of the night. The soft black envelops the village in a way that suggests peace, rather than the tensions it merely hides. Yinka and Bem take Esu to the compound to rest and I slip away, going back to the same room I washed Folasade's body in. There are only a few hours until sunrise, and I know I should spend them sleeping, but I can't relax. Instead, I slump in the corner, staring at the mat where her body lay.

After a while, Kola arrives, but he doesn't speak, just sits next to me. I say nothing for a few minutes, even when he shuffles closer.

"This is not your fault," he says. "You do know that, right?"

"I've let so many people down . . ." Pushing my hands against my mouth, I clench my jaw. "I should have done . . . *more*."

"Simi," Kola murmurs, crouching beside me. I feel as if I will shatter, as if my rib cage will crack. "There is no 'you' in any of this. There is only us. All of us. And we will do this together, bear the burden together."

I nod, but his words don't stop the ache inside. Kola's eyes flicker over me, and then he pulls me against him, holding me carefully.

"We will honor them," Kola says, his voice firm in the dark. "The ones we've lost. And we will fight for them all."

I draw in a trembling breath, allowing myself the comfort of his scent and the warm press of our skin. I think of Folasade lying on the forest floor, her sightless eyes on the stars. I think of Ara, terrified at being back in Rabah. And I think of Issa, the way the yumbo was snatched by the sasabonsam at Esu's palace.

"We had a vigil for Issa," says Kola quietly, as if reading my mind. "I sent word to the yumboes, but the messengers couldn't find them. I failed his grandfather." I tip my face to his, seeing the guilt folded in his expression. "I told Salif I'd make sure Issa was safe."

"You couldn't control what happened." I know that my words won't stop his guilt, just as his won't for me, but I say them anyway.

Silence stretches between us, our thoughts loud in the warmth of the room. There's a faint scent of coconut oil and spice from the cooking quarters. The ordinary smells taunt me, a reminder that for others, this is just another day.

"Maybe. I've thought about it over and over." Kola closes his eyes, resting his head back against the wall. "But then I spoke to the babalawo and he told me that all we should focus on is what is right, what is in our hearts. All we can do is our best."

"What if . . . ," I say slowly. "What if our best still isn't good enough?"

"Then we do it anyway, Simi." Kola sighs and turns to face me. "It's all there is."

I take a breath, sorrow deepening it. Kola stands up suddenly, brushing down his wrapper. "Can I show you something?"

"What is it?" I ask, letting him pull me to my feet.

"You'll see." Kola smiles tentatively, and there's a light in his eyes that somewhat eases the ache in my chest. "This way."

We leave the compound and head down the back road toward a tall gate. After Kola unlocks it, he lets me through before following. Together we walk into a large outdoor space. Palm trees shade the area from the sharpness of the moonlight, and the smell of overripe bananas is strong.

Kola lets loose a low whistle. A small group of trees in the corner shakes and I take a nervous step back.

"It's all right," he murmurs. "I just wanted to make sure that the attack hasn't scared him."

I stay close to Kola as he moves farther into the open space, just as a large part of the darkness detaches itself and charges straight for us. I whip the dagger from my hair but feel Kola's hand on my arm and lower the weapon. "Wait."

Any words I have are cut off when the gray trunk curls toward us, large ears flapping once in the cool of the night.

"Tunde," whispers Kola as the elephant uses its trunk to pat its way around the folds of his wrapper. "Here." He holds out a banana. Tunde grasps the fruit eagerly before tucking it into his waiting mouth.

The creature towers above us, chewing loudly. Kola turns to me, smiling. "He's not fully grown yet."

"Really?" I ask. I have only seen an elephant once, in Oyo-Ile, in the Aláàfin's birthday parade. I eye the gleam of Tunde's tusks nervously as Kola pats the animal, rubbing behind the elephant's large fanlike ears. "He's huge!"

"I found him slumped in a patch of mangrove trees. He was wasting away from lack of water and food. I was surprised that he was still alive. His mother was dead, arrows in her body, her tusks sawn off." Kola's face clouds, his mouth pulled down, before Tunde's trunk curls around his shoulders, producing a small smile. "Bàbá said I could keep him as long as I trained him, and he's been doing very well. He is fiercely loyal. He even trampled one of the òyìnbó we came across last month."

"Your father . . . I should have asked before. How is he?"

"He's been teaching me about the running of the village." Kola pats Tunde's side. "I've made changes to the Oko guard, our patrols and defenses. He's listened."

"He knows that you will follow in his footsteps. I remember the way he looked at you when you returned to Oko." I smile.

"As if he had seen a ghost!" laughs Kola, but there is a forced edge to the laughter.

"No. As if he had just found the most precious thing he had lost."

Tunde nudges Kola again, nearly pushing him over. We laugh as the elephant wraps his trunk around the boy's waist, hauling him upright. Kola pretends to be injured, but Tunde lightly nudges him again until he fetches some tree bark and a bundle of grass. "Here, greedy."

As the elephant eats, we sit together on a carved bench in the dark, content. I shiver in the cooling night and Kola runs to get a blanket.

"Thank you," I murmur as he drapes its softness around my shoulders. I'm glad when he once again sits next to me.

I look up at the brightest star in the sky, remembering when we rested under it while Kola was recovering from the Ninki Nanka's attack. The courting star. If we were just . . . us, just Adekola and Simidele, perhaps he would turn to me now. If there were nothing else, no Mami Wata, no Tapa or ajogun, perhaps he would put a hand on my jaw and raise my lips to his. Or perhaps he wouldn't. He's barely spoken to me since I arrived. Sneaking a look at him, I wish I knew what he was thinking. The blanket slips at my movement and I twist, fumbling for it.

"What will you do after?" Kola pulls the cover back up, his fingers skimming my arm. I suck in a breath at his touch. "What I mean is, have you ever thought about going back to Oyo-Ile?"

I welcome the distraction, taking my time to consider his question for a moment, thinking about my parents.

"You know that as Mami Wata we gave up our human lives as well as our memories," I explain, measuring my response carefully. "I always had flashes of memories whenever I took on this form. It's why I changed even when I didn't need to. Those bits of my life would come back to me. But every time I went back to the water, they used to just . . . dissolve."

"What changed?"

"I think it was remembering what happened to me. Why and how Yemoja saved me." I think of the wild sea and the terror I felt after jumping from the òyìnbó ship, and swallow. "I've kept every part of me, and my life, since then. Even in the Land of the Dead."

Kola looks at me intently. "And now that you fully remember yourself—will you go back home?"

"I want to go and see them." I think of my mother's wide smile and my father's laugh. "I'm not the same, though. I'm not the daughter they lost. I hate the thought of them grieving for me, but would they have to mourn all over again when I tell them what I am? That I'm not human and I can't stay with them?" I pull the blanket tighter around me as if it can ward off my sadness as it does the night's chill. "I think that would be worse."

"You'll always be their daughter, Simi." Kola's voice is soft, and I find myself blinking at the prickle of tears. "That's not something you should ever worry about."

I twist my fingers and think of my home—the red curve of the walls, my father's leopard pipe and the many wrappers my mother has, a special one for each story she tells. "I'll think about it," I whisper.

"And after? Do you think you'll return?" Kola clears his throat and looks down at his feet. "To the sea, I mean."

"It's where I belong." I force a stiff laugh. "Where else would I go?"

Kola pauses for a moment before turning to me. "You could stay here, you know. I mean, after we help Esu."

"In Oko?"

He nods, his eyes on me. I turn to Tunde to give myself more time before answering. Kola wants me to stay. The thought settles and spreads as I take a step toward the elephant. Tunde stills as I approach, folds of gray skin almost metallic in the moonlight, small black eyes watching me. The elephant holds out his trunk and tentatively, I let him snuffle my hand, jumping when he blows some air out. Tunde sways from side to side, mouth quirked open. I keep my palm flat and join in, taking pleasure in this simple joy.

"I'll bring you breakfast when the sun rises," murmurs Kola to Tunde, stepping forward and pressing his forehead against the animal's side.

The elephant allows another pat from us before he ambles back to the trees, melting into the shadows. Kola faces me again, moonlight reflected in his gaze. I realize I was silly to wonder how he felt about me. It's in the way he looks at me now, the nervousness at asking me to stay. I don't want to hurt him again, but I know that the only answer I can give him will.

"I can't stay here. With you."

At my words, Kola's face smooths into a careful blank as he takes a step away from me, putting space and shadows between us. His hands swing in the night breeze before he speaks, voice made tiny in the dark. "I understand."

"Do you, though?" I ask, frustrated at his shutting down. "Your place is here. One day, you will lead Oko. I am of the sea. And now Yemoja has lost Folasade." My voice cracks and I pause.

"That wasn't your fault."

"I know. But it's shown me where my place is. I want to see ìyá and bàbá, but Yemoja needs me. I owe her. More than my life now." I think of Folasade's loss and the souls she might have gathered. I drop the blanket, moving toward the gate. "Once we have helped Esu bind the ajogun, I'm going back to the sea. I have to. It's where I belong."

I turn away from Kola, and the moon that drenches him in silver light, knowing that I am making the right decision. There is no other way.

CHAPTER TWENTY-ONE

THE FAINT BEAT of drums wakes me from sleep. For a moment, I take in the sun that streams through the window of the twins' bedroom, where I settled after leaving Kola, bathing my feet in a soft yellow warmth.

And then what happened last night crashes in and the loss hits. Folasade dead, her body returned to the sea. Ara and the soul song taken by the Tapa iyalawo. I close my eyes again, wanting to sink back into a slumber where none of this is real.

"Is she awake?" I hear the small whisper next to me.

"I don't think so."

I look up into two sets of brown eyes, a grin, and a smile that has a front tooth missing. "You're awake!" The twins lean down, and I am smothered by coconut-scented curls and the sweet tang of fried plantain. They hold out a bowl to me as I sit up and rub my eyes. Taiwo and Kehinde wind their arms around my neck, squeezing before letting go. I smile into their hair, feeling blessed, comforted by their presence.

"I am now," I say, feeling myself smile. "Why aren't you with your parents?"

"Taiwo wanted his bow and arrow," says Kehinde, pointing to

her brother, who clutches a miniature weapon made of light sapling. "And so ẹ̀gbọ́n ọkùnrin took us. He said we could see you."

I sink back down into the nest of blankets as the twins sit, one on either side of me, their hands clasping each of mine.

"We've missed you," says Taiwo, and the lisp caused by his missing tooth makes me give him another little squeeze.

"I've missed you, too."

"We brought you some breakfast." Kehinde moves the bowl closer to me, but I don't want to let go of them.

"I'll eat it in a minute," I say, drinking them both in. "Tell me how you are and all that's been going on."

The twins both begin to speak at once and then stop, staring at each other crossly. I laugh and they stop frowning, talking in turns to tell me things important to them. Tales of swimming in the sea, of healing a baby white-faced monkey they found, a ride on Tunde. Kehinde speaks of how they have been helping to keep their father comfortable after a recent illness and I reach out to wrap my arms around them.

When the twins scamper off to find arrows, I eat the slices of fried plantain.

The children return just as I finish. "Come, can we get breakfast now?" Taiwo holds his stomach and eyes my empty bowl. "This hunger is killing me."

I laugh at his solemn face. "Did you not eat?"

"Well, yes. But that was my first breakfast." The small boy rubs his belly. "I'm ready for my second."

"I am, too," echoes Kehinde as she grabs my hand and tries to haul me to my feet, staggering with the effort. "Taiwo, help me."

"I'm coming," I say as they pull me up. They wait as I tighten my wrapper. I run a hand over the plaits at my crown, the bump of my dagger giving me comfort as I follow the children out of the room.

The open courtyard receives the coming day in a flush of light. It's still relatively cool as I walk through the fading shadows, following the twins, who head for the central open space. Bem and Yinka sit close to each other on woven mats decorated with patterns of fish swimming in repeating loops. They add more cooked beans to their plates as they speak of weapons and battle formations. Esu reclines opposite them, eyes closed, hands folded behind his head, empty bowls scattered around him. As I approach, he looks up.

"Oh, it's you, little fish," the orisa says. "I was hoping for more food." He rubs his stomach and tips his head back to rest on a folded-up blanket.

Kehinde and Taiwo give the trickster a wide berth, seating themselves next to Yinka. She wraps an arm around each of them and drops a kiss on their curls. Kola strolls from the cooking quarters with his own bowl and pauses when he sees me. For a minute I think he might walk back out, but he nods at me before sitting down next to Bem.

I accept a small plate of eggs fried with chilies and onions from Yinka, sitting across from her, trying not to think about how Kola must be feeling after last night. How I feel after last night.

We eat quickly, and just as I work myself up to stealing a look at him, Kola rises, beckoning to the twins.

"Come on, you two, I'm taking you back to bàbá and ìyá." Kola looks over at Esu as he says this, and I tense when the orisa waves lazily at the children. To Taiwo's and Kehinde's credit, they do not flinch. Instead, they merely lift their noses and hold on to their brother's hands as they sweep out of the courtyard, waving at me as their brother leads them away.

I place the half-eaten eggs, now cold, on the ground. Yinka looks up at me, worry in her gaze, until I roll my shoulders and offer her a smile. I want to be doing something that will set things right, not mourning over something that never really was and never can be. There are bigger things than me and Kola.

"What's Oko's plan? And what's ours?" I ask, keeping my voice even and strong.

Bem grins as he reaches around Yinka to clasp my shoulder. "I'm glad you asked," he says, and begins to outline what Kola's father has agreed with the council members from Oyo-Ile. "We'll leave in a few hours and join with the Oyo regiments. Other villages are sending fighters, and we'll gather in the dip of land before Rabah."

"We attack at dusk," continues Yinka. "And hope for the element of surprise."

"Why aren't we leaving now?" I ask. I drain a cup of water, watching as Kola slips back into the courtyard. I think of Ara, hoping she's still alive, wondering if she's hurt. I take a deep breath and blow it out. I just want to get moving.

"Bàbá has arranged an Egúngún ceremony." Kola approaches us, picking up a cup of water and sipping. Outside the walls of the compound, there are faint calls as the drums rise to a crescendo. "It's not the usual days-long festival, but a short one to bless those who are leaving to fight and those who are staying behind."

"For courage and strength," I say, nodding, glad that he is still speaking to me.

"Exactly," says Kola, a faint smile ghosting his lips. I think of the way it felt to have his arms around me last night. Heat flushes across my chest as I rise with Yinka and Bem. Esu is once again sprawled out in the growing sunlight, snores ripping through the clear air.

"What about him?" I ask, gesturing to the orisa.

Kola waves his hand, lip curling. "He can stay here."

"I'll stay and watch him," says Bem, eyeing Esu.

I nod at Bem and squeeze his arm in thanks before I follow Yinka and Kola. We leave the compound and join the streams of people heading to the market square. Stalls full of star apples and coconuts are set up on the edges, people layered around the space left empty in the center. The scents of roasted goat and fried fish mingle in the air. Directly at the back sit Kola's parents and the elders of the council. The officials from Oyo-Ile stand to their left, and their familiar indigo wrappers with white concentric circles make my stomach lurch in recognition. The dress of the Aláàfin's scholars, councilors, and advisers. I think of my father when he wore his, the shine of his smile mingling with my pride.

Peering closer, I falter as one of the men turns. I want to see my father's scar running from his forehead to the top of his left cheek, where it will disappear into his black-and-white beard. But there are only round bare cheeks, a smattering of scars on both, and a wisp of hair on the man's chin.

I push away the disappointment and follow Kola to where the twins are seated, just in range of their parents and the Oko guard.

"Will you be all right? I need to sit at bàbá's right side."

I reach forward and tickle the twins, smiling when they giggle and turn to me. "They'll keep me good company," I answer as Taiwo and Kehinde wrap their skinny arms around me.

"Ẹ̀gbọ́n obìnrin!" exclaims Kola's sister, her eyes sparkling. "Come, sit with me."

"No, sit with me," counters Taiwo, trying to push Kehinde out of the way.

I appease them both by settling a twin on each side of me, my arms around them. "I'll sit between you. That way it's fair."

The twins glare at each other before placing their hands in their laps, the gleam of their obsidian rings on their right hands the only reminder that they are both children and also something more.

Kola greets his father by touching the ground at his feet as the man rests one hand on his son's shoulder. He is thinner than when I last saw him, nearly swallowed by the royal-blue folds of his wrapper. Kola's mother gazes proudly at them both as her son settles himself between his parents.

"This morning we have come together to look to the ancestors for guidance. Through the Egúngún ceremony we will seek the wisdom of those who came before us, accept any blessings they honor us with." Kola's father pauses, adjusting the blue fila on his head, golden rings flashing in the sunlight. A thick chain hangs from his neck, set with polished gems glimmering in orange, red, and blue. "We face a threat that has been growing for generations. They have taken people before, encouraged by the trade with the òyìnbó."

Dark muttering breaks out among the crowds of Oko. Many more than Kola have been taken over the last year or so. The òyìnbó have influenced these lands already, even in such a short space of time.

"Whole villages have been wiped out, with some even moving

from the coast, deep into the thicker forests inland, as far away from the òyìnbó and the warring kingdoms as they can get. Oko has always stood firm. Protected what is ours and as many others as we could." The villagers shout in approval, stamping feet and staffs on the ground. "But recently, the attacks from the Tapa have been more frequent, more . . . violent, and dark. The Aláàfin has decided that enough is enough!"

Shouts ring out across the square, but I also see unease on many faces. War will bring more loss, more death.

The leader of Oko gestures to the elders who sit around him, their faces drawn with both age and the weight of difficult and important choices. "Those who are on the council have agreed to give our support. United with the whole of Oyo, we will not allow the Nupe Kingdom to threaten us anymore!" Kola's father's words are met with roars and a pounding of feet. He nods, scanning the crowd. "We are rejoicing in our strength and seeking more. As you know, without music, there is no way to celebrate. And today, we will celebrate as we honor the Egúngún and accept the blessings they see fit to bestow."

The people of Oko mask any trepidation with a furious clap of agreement. Kola's father gestures to his son and Kola stands tall, taller even than his father now.

"May Àyàn, the god of drumming, protect you!" Oko's leader calls out, turning to a semicircle of men who line the empty space, each one seated before his bàtá drum. He nods once at them. "Àyàn ó gbè ọ́!"

The largest musician hunches over the mother drum and pounds on the ìyáàlù slowly. The beat that pours forth is then matched by the others in a rhythm that holds the crowd in thrall.

Bàtá drums are only used for special ceremonies, ones that command a use of belief and magic. As one, the people of Oko listen carefully, paying the beats the respect they deserve. Some villagers sway, while others smile.

Kola watches the drummers, a fierce determination lighting up his face. I see his mother with her eyes on him, her smile slipping, and I know she's drinking in the sight of him in case it is her last. I see the same all around. The people of Oko are imbued with passion, but they also know all that they have to lose. I already know what is at stake, but seeing everyone like this only makes it more real.

A collective gasp rises into the morning heat as the beat of the bàtá drums slows.

The Egúngún bursts through the circle of villagers, stalking into the center. Segments of leather and cotton contrast with panels of silks in colors of red, blue, and yellow, all stitched together with metallic thread. The fabric cascades down to the ground, each bright section representing a different ancestor. A small carved head, adorned with a flaring headdress, sits atop a shoulder platform, representing the ancestors and giving the figure an unnatural height. Whirling, the Egúngún spins, fabric splayed and blurred in the sun, each turn cleansing the area, as the villagers begin to sing and cheer. The figure slides and jerks before us, their movements sharp and powerful. I catch glimpses of the face veil, studded with cowrie shells, and although it represents the collective ancestors of Oko, I can't help but be reminded of Yemoja and the pearls she wears over her face to disguise her scars.

The villagers keep back, showing caution around the powerful spiritual forces that the Egúngún embodies. Yellow-and-red-striped slippers stamp on the earth from underneath the costume; colored glass beads, stitched in the edges of the panels, glitter as the Egúngún draws closer. Beside me, Kehinde and Taiwo grip my hands, excitement making them lean forward, eyes fixed on the Egúngún as they pause before us. With a low bow, nods are given to the children, and a hand gloved in white cotton hovers over each of their heads. Prayers muffled beneath the veil are spoken, and then the figure is pulling back to the middle of the marketplace. The drums pick up their speed, matching the movements of the ancestors incarnate as the Egúngún spins, whirling so fast that the colors of the cloth become a blurred rainbow. The Egúngún takes the center of the open space, twirling slowly until the figure freezes. The drums die away, palms held above taut skins.

A gloved hand is raised, the gold-and-silver thread on each finger catching the sunlight. And then the figure is jumping up, twisting and jerking as it spins toward the leader of Oko. Kola's father lowers his head, waiting for his blessing, but the Egúngún does not pause in front of him. Turning away from the head of Oko, the figure draws close to Kola, the cloths licking at the boy's skin as the Egúngún writhes in front of him.

Kola's eyebrows rise and he looks to his father, who smiles. The Egúngún stops, raising both hands to let them hover in the air on either side of the boy's head. I see Kola close his eyes, aiming his face up at the sky, and then, in the silence that is strung like a web between the villagers, the Egúngún speaks.

"Orisa?" The word echoes in the ears of the people, the Egúngún's tone powerful as it rises at the end of the word.

Kola looks down, his lips parted, eyes shining and wide. I think of the way he cut through the adzes, the power and speed that seemed unnatural even then.

"Yes," the Egúngún says. "Orisa." The figure leans forward and whispers a prayer to Kola, and I see his expression fall apart and then come together again, his features arranged in an understanding that makes his mother and father fall to their knees in front of him.

Taiwo and Kehinde look at each other before grinning and standing. They move past the Egúngún, who waits, perfectly still, in front of Kola. Standing on either side of the figure who embodies their ancestors, the twins reach up to hold Kola's hands.

"Welcome, ẹ̀gbọ́n ọkùnrin."

The beat of the bàtá drums begins again, and so does the song of the people of Oko. Their voices rise together in a harmony that weaves identity and belonging and power. I think of how Kola swam so deep, pulled Olokun back by the lengths of his thick golden chains. It all makes sense now, with the Egúngún confirming it.

Kola is orisa.

...

The whirl and dance of the Egúngún give Kola and his parents time to compose themselves, their cheeks wet with tears but lips in joyful smiles.

I watch Kola as he stands next to his family, face calm. Only I can see the little things that betray his stillness, the muscle in his jaw that twitches and the forward set of his shoulders.

Orisa.

What will this mean? Not just for Kola and Oko, but for us? If he is no longer human, then can we . . . ? I quash the thought immediately. If Kola is orisa, then Oko and the Oyo Kingdom will be protected. He is needed. Kola catches my eye and we stare at each other. The pull I felt in the sea and on the beach is there again.

When the Egúngún dances toward the edges of the market square, the villagers follow, continuing in their song, taking the lead of the ìyáàlù drum with its strong pulsing beat. The procession swells as more join in, all hoping to be blessed by the Egúngún, but also jumping out of their way in respect. Kola and his family are left with their guards standing at a suitable distance and I hover, unsure whether to approach.

"Simi!" Kehinde runs over to me and tugs me toward her parents.

Kola stands still as his mother embraces him, murmuring prayers of thanks to Ogun and Olodumare.

"We are blessed." The leader of Oko stands before his son, hands thrown up in praise, diamonds sparkling. "Thrice now."

"Bàbá, I don't understand." Kola looks over at me, eyes wide.

"Sit," says his father, patting the velvet-covered stool beside him. Kola sinks down as the twins sit at his feet and his mother stands behind him, her hands rubbing and squeezing his shoulders.

"Do you remember the story of Sango?" she asks.

"Yes, ìyá. The fourth Aláàfin of Oyo," Kola recounts. "Stories tell of him being able to breathe fire from his mouth and command the lightning from storms."

"That's right. But he was originally human, not orisa. There were many rumors about his death. Some say his council turned on him, while others say he ended his own life." Kola's mother leans down, her words strong and clear. "His actions as a human were so great that upon his mortal death, he was deified by those who revered him."

"And became the god of fire, thunder, and lightning." Kola's father pats his son's knee.

The boy opens and closes his mouth, sneaking a helpless glance at me. I wish I could reassure him. I think of the courage Kola showed, the risks and then the price he paid on Esu's island—giving his life in order to save the twins. I blessed his soul, kept it there while the twins used their rings and their connection to health and life.

"We brought you back," says Kehinde.

"But you were not the same," adds Taiwo.

I look at the children gazing up at their brother and I realize that they must have known. "Why didn't you tell him?"

"We couldn't be sure." They exchange glances. "And it was not for us to reveal. We had to wait for the ancestors."

Kola whips back and forth between the twins, listening carefully. I can see the frustration in the frown lines that mar his expression.

"You are not the same as the twins; you are not the embodiment of an orisa," explains his mother. "You are new. The Egúngún has spoken, and now it is time for you to begin settling into your power."

"But what is it?" Kola's tone is panicked, his eyes darting between his family. "I don't feel any different."

"Your power is not yet defined, but it will be revealed in time." Kola's father offers an encouraging nod to his son. "You are orisa, and the power that comes with that is already slowly forming."

I step forward, lowering my gaze and touching the ground in

deference to both his mother and father. "You may not realize it, but I've noticed the changes in you." Moving to stand in front of Kola, I smile. "Perhaps you haven't had much time to consider them. But you've tracked and hunted the Tapa in ways never seen before."

"Because there are more encroaching on our lands." Kola holds his hands up. "I am head of the Oko guard. It's my duty."

"You fought the adzes as if they were nothing but insects."

"I—"

"And you swam deep enough and long enough to yank Olokun back by his chains," I finish. "The Egúngún is right. You are orisa. There's no other explanation."

"And with you, the Oyo Kingdom will win against the Nupe." Kola's father rises from his chair, pulling his son with him. He embraces him fully and then lowers himself to the ground slowly and touches the boy's feet. "I am honored."

Kola stares down, his face still smooth with shock. And then he is kneeling next to his father, helping him up as the man wraps his arms around him. His mother joins them, and then so do Kehinde and Taiwo. I watch the love and joy and hope that they spin, feeling it myself as they repeat prayers of gratitude.

Kola's family take him back to their compound to gather his weapons and supplies, but I choose to stay with Yinka, who has arrived with her horse. She hands me a full waterskin before being distracted by the sight of the bultungin pouring out of a nearby compound. They stretch in the sun, their limbs a glossy dark brown, glistening hair coiled or plaited in a single chunky braid. Aissa brushes dust from her short fur wrapper before catching sight of Yinka. She grins and raises a hand in greeting.

"We won't need horses," Aissa calls, wrinkling her nose.

Yinka laughs as she passes me the reins. "In that case I'll travel with you and the pack." When she reaches the girl, she embraces her, squeezing tight. She kisses her on both cheeks, ignoring Aissa's embarrassment. "Thank you again for trusting me and helping Oko."

"Where you go, we all go." Aissa smiles as Yinka releases her. "You know this."

I fiddle with the leather straps of the horse, not wanting to appear as if I am eavesdropping. The sight of Yinka with those who love her fills me with happiness. Bem turns the corner of the marketplace, checking it is clear before he enters with Esu just behind him. "The official guard will take the horses," he says. His face is unlined but his giant shoulders are tense. Sliding a fourth dagger into a leather weapons belt over his waist, he manages a small smile for me. "They'll be able to issue orders more effectively."

"What of the rest of Oko?" I ask, looking around at the spiral of compounds.

"The remaining guards will stay. Those who have volunteered will come with us."

I take a deep breath, but Bem leans closer. "Don't worry, they'll be protected by the walls and the rest of our fighters."

Nodding, I can't help but think of the adzes and their red firefly bodies. But Idera will be focusing all of her power on freeing the ajogun, and the Nupe Oba will be concentrating on protecting his kingdom.

The best way to ensure Oko's safety will be to stop the iyalawo and bind the ajogun.

Gradually, the main street of the village begins to fill, lined with those who are ready to fight for Oyo and those who are seeing them off. A woman bends down to her small daughter. I see the girl press her face against her mother's chest. When the child raises her face, there are tears but also a fierce look of pride. I watch as the woman adjusts her black wrapper before strapping a goatskin quiver of arrows on her back. She has shaved her hair as Yinka has done, and patches of white are scattered across her brown skin, gleaming with shea butter, enhancing her beauty even more. A boy runs from a nearby doorway with a bow as big as him. He nearly trips on the end and is steadied by his father. The man takes the bow from his son and hands the weapon to his wife, their fingers touching. He brings his lips down to her forehead, kissing her once, his eyes shining as he steps back. The woman tips her head before pressing her fingers against her mouth. And then she is turning from her family and joining the other warriors who are waiting, lining the street.

Bem and the other official Oko guards weave throughout the people, words of courage and gratitude flowing between them. The faces of the people of Oko glow with faith and defiance as they say good-bye to their loved ones. I stop myself from trying to count how many will march with us and join the Oyo Kingdom in attacking the Tapa, knowing that I will do my best to save as many as possible.

Even though I try to push away the thought of death, my mind curdles with worry until a sudden shaking of the earth stops me. The people around me pause, hands going to weapons as the sound of pounding grows louder.

CHAPTER TWENTY-TWO

THE TIPS OF my fingers go to the emerald of my dagger instantly as I watch the leaves of the trees shaking. Could Idera have sent something else to attack us? My panicked thoughts turn to how many people we can get to safety—just as I see Yinka grin. From her position, she can see something that I can't, and as the earth continues to shake, a laugh breaks free from her. Those around begin to smile, too, hands slipping from hilts and handles of bone and leather as the pounding grows louder.

Footsteps, I think, just as Tunde rounds the bend. The thuds are the sound of footsteps, and the elephant towers over the people scattered before him. If he is indeed not yet fully grown, then I see how truly huge he will be one day. He pauses, swinging his great head from side to side, a golden headdress with spiny ridges stretching over the tops of his ears. Tunde raises his head, shining metal articulated down the center of it and rippling along his trunk as he lifts his gaze to the sun. Golden light cascades over the matching plates of armor that hang around his chest, and as he stamps one foot, I see that the metal circles his legs, spikes protruding from each wide band. With a loud trumpet, he rakes the ground with tusks tipped in points of gold, and it's only then that I see the figure perched on top of a large saddle.

Kola slithers from his opulent seat to the gasps of those near him, dropping to the ground and landing on one knee. As he stands, the crowd erupts into cheers and whoops of admiration. Seeing the thick golden chain around his neck and the matching trimmed brace for his sword, hanging just above his fresh dark blue wrapper, I feel like joining in. I know he sees the smile that splits my face as he makes his way to me.

"That was an entrance," I say, watching as a small boy offers Tunde a green banana. The elephant accepts it gently and the child clasps his trunk shyly before backing away.

"I aim to please." Kola adjusts his necklace.

"One fit for an orisa," I add, striving to keep my tone light.

Kola frowns but smooths it away with a smile at the boy who fed Tunde. The child bows low to the ground and then scampers off through the crowd.

"I'm not entirely sure I understand, but the ancestors are never wrong."

"You're still undecided? Despite the story of Sango? You met him. This is not out of the question." I face Kola. "It makes sense to me. I knew you were different when we met again. I just thought it was . . ." Something to do with how I feel about you, I think.

"It is true." The babalawo stands beside me, a tall staff of mahogany clutched in his grip, his words firm, despite the quaver that only age can add to a voice.

The priest's skin hangs from wiry arms, wrists draped in curls of gold that match the chain at his neck. An emerald peeps from the top of his wrapper, the same color as the one in the end of my dagger. I bend to the ground in greeting, hand on my chest as Kola does the same.

"It is good to see you, child of the sea." The babalawo pats my arm, a faint smile on his lips. I feel the calmness radiating from him. "Take heart in the faith I have in you. I knew you would succeed." He turns to the boy at my side. "Which brings me to you, Adekola. I imagine you must have questions."

The babalawo beckons Kola to the side, and as the boy bends down to listen to the whispers of the priest, I think of the strength I have already seen. With his status as orisa, he is an important part of the attack, especially since there is no time to summon other orisas and persuade them to aid our side against the Nupe Kingdom. I think of Oya and Sango, wishing for their strength and power but glad that they are likely still chasing and attacking the òyìnbó ships, freeing as many of the taken as they can.

"We need to leave if we are to arrive in time to meet the other factions of the Oyo fighters," calls Bem. He strolls toward us, eyeing Tunde nervously.

The elephant blows air at the giant boy and I have to smother a grin when Bem flinches, jumping slightly. He purses his lips and raises a fist to the creature, shaking it. Tunde repeats his snuffle but this time, he coils his trunk about Bem's shoulders in a quick squeeze.

Kola bows to the babalawo before loping over to Bem to discuss supplies. The priest draws me to him, his familiar scent of bitter leaf filling the air. "You will need more strength, Mami Wata. There will be more choices, ones you thought you wouldn't need to make." The old man pulls away but keeps hold of my hand, his gnarled fingers grasping mine. "Although you have lost much and stand to gain little, you always do what is right. I have faith in you, Simidele. I know that you always do your best."

The babalawo squeezes my hand once and then limps off in the direction of the council's quarters before I can speak. I take a moment to think about his words. There are no real choices, I think. None but getting the soul song so that Esu can complete the binding, and then returning to serve Yemoja.

The trickster watches me from a white stallion, standing heads above the others. Around him, the warriors sneak guarded looks. Bem has told them he is fighting on our side, but some are worried it may be a trick, that Esu is allied with the Tapa. It took Bem a while to convince them, but even now they shift away from the orisa, muttering prayers and cutting their eyes at him.

The official guards mount their horses, leading the way as the new gates of Oko are opened. The warriors, women and men from all walks of life, follow behind, and despite their proud stature and array of weapons, I feel a twist of unease. I hope the Oyo Kingdom has other trained fighters, and that the Aláàfin is not merely relying on farmers and fishermen of surrounding villages.

"Simi?" I turn to see Kola looking at me from the height of Tunde. "Come."

I feel my mouth fall open before quickly shutting it. "Up there?"

Tunde regards me from the cocoon of his golden armor, swishing his trunk gently from side to side.

"Unless you want to walk." Kola shades his eyes from the sun. "But it'll take most of today to march to Rabah." He gestures to my feet, smiling. "I'd rather not have to stop to find some wild lettuce. Although you know I would."

The elephant stands completely still, watching.

"How do I . . . ?"

Tunde answers me by lowering his head, offering his trunk. I step forward tentatively and look up at Kola. He nods and I climb onto the golden armor that encases the creature's long nose.

"Whoa!" I gasp as Tunde lifts his trunk, swinging me up and around so that I am level with Kola.

Shaking, I accept the boy's help as I clamber onto the velvet saddle behind him. Kola looks over his shoulder and grins, but I only cling to the tassels that frame the seat. I can't remember ever being so high, and definitely not on an animal this big.

"Let's go, Tunde." At Kola's command, the elephant begins to walk, swaying from side to side, taking up the rear of the procession. His armor gleams, the golden plates shifting seamlessly around his tough gray skin. I clutch at the side of the seat until Kola sees the clench of my fingers. "You'd do better to hold on to me and roll with Tunde's movements. It's just like riding a horse, but slower."

Tentatively, I put my arms around Kola's waist, forcing myself to relax. My hands slide around the hard muscle of his stomach, and I lace my fingers together. I can feel my face burning as I press against his warm skin. Sneaking a glance up at Kola, I spy the bulge of his cheeks as he smiles. It doesn't matter, I tell myself, it's just a necessity.

We follow the people of Oko for hours, winding our way through the forest, heading northeast toward the grass plains that border the kingdoms of Oyo and Nupe. The sun burns down on us, but there are no stops, just water shared. The heat has me slumped in my seat on Tunde, my body covered in sweat. We are high enough to see some of the way ahead, and I use the advantage to scan for anything out of the ordinary. Bem doubles back often to update Kola on our progress, his gaze warily on the forest until we are past it. Even then he doesn't settle, and the two agree to keep pushing forward, planning to rest only when we meet the main Oyo contingent in the lands surrounding the river Ogun.

Taking a sip of my water, I think about Kola's words with the priest before we left Oko. "What did the babalawo say to you?"

Kola stares ahead, and for a moment, I think he hasn't heard me. Then he answers.

"He said that Esu will bind the ajogun."

I touch the ruby, its golden chain wrapped several times around my wrist. I remember its burn and the different warlords it has shown me.

"He also forewarned of lives lost."

The battle looming ahead only gives credence to the babalawo's warning. "What else? Did he speak of the Egúngún's prophecy? That you are orisa?"

Kola dips his head, Tunde's reins held loosely in his fist. "Yes."

I wait but he doesn't say any more, shifting uncomfortably.

"You're not . . . worried, are you?"

"Only that, if I am—"

"You are."

"*If* I am, how will I know what my strengths are?" He turns to face me, eyes half-closed against the sun. "If I don't know what powers I have, how can I use them?"

"Remember the adzes?" I say. "You fought them in a way I'd never seen before. You were faster, stronger. I could barely follow your movements."

"Hm. I don't feel like an orisa."

I laugh a little. "And what would that feel like?"

"I don't know." Kola shrugs, a sulk tugging at his mouth.

"Are you expecting to have bigger muscles? To be able to spew fire like Sango? Every orisa is different, you know this. If your power is yet to be revealed properly, then so be it. It doesn't mean it's not there."

Kola is silent, blinking, a hand on the back of his neck squeezing at the hot skin.

"And you said yourself you had successfully fended off several Tapa attacks." I sit up straighter. "It seems to me that fighting is definitely a strength. And there could be more. Sango has many."

Kola sits back, but his shoulders are not as slumped now. "People will still die."

"That may be," I say, even though the words are painful. "But you can help us get into Rabah and get the soul song back. Ara, too. Then we can stop all of this."

"I know you're trying to make me feel better."

I shake my head, curling my hands. "It's not just about you, Kola. You are orisa and that is a gift. That's the way you need to see this. Think—you can help everyone in so many more ways."

The boy nods, a faint tilt to his lips transforming into a nervous twist. "The babalawo spoke of . . . other things." The catch in his voice makes something in my stomach coil and tighten.

"What?"

Kola leaves a moment of silence that sears the air between us. He clears his throat and angles his face away from me. "He said that from the moment I died and you and the twins brought me back, I was changed." Kola pauses and slides a look at me before facing forward once again. "That it means I am no longer completely human. That I am no longer completely . . . me."

I turn his words over in my mind, remembering how, when Yemoja remade me, my memories having all but disappeared, I felt not like myself, but like something *other*.

"You'll always be you," I say carefully, thinking of my own struggle and not wanting to dismiss his. "Nothing can change that." But even as I say the words, I think of all the things I have done as Mami Wata that I wouldn't have done before. Kola won't truly be the same.

Bem rides back to our position, face wide open with hope. "The Oyo army is gathered just beyond the next bend. I've seen the colors of the soldiers, and many other towns and villagers have already joined them." His voice rises with excitement in the heat of the afternoon. "There are more than we thought."

Kola's gaze stays on me for a few seconds, and then he slides from Tunde's back. Before I can say anything else, I see Esu's white stallion nudging its way through the milling fighters. Kola gives the orisa one long stare, his eyes dark, mouth curled, before melting into the crowd. The people gather into small groups, nervously eyeing the trickster as they pull supplies from their bags. Some begin to assemble small meals of dried beef and corn once he has passed, prayers on their lips as they avert their gazes.

"Little fish," says Esu in greeting. His skinny plaits swing and graze the tops of his shoulders as he dismounts and holds a hand out to me. "Would you like some help?"

I purse my lips and ease my legs sideways, slipping from Tunde with a grace that surprises even me. The elephant snuffles loudly and I take this as congratulations; I stand up straighter and neaten the folds of my wrapper.

"The plan is to attack Rabah once everyone has arrived. The Tapa have destroyed villages in the Oyo Kingdom, and so the Aláàfin has decided to strike back hard and at its center."

Esu raises his eyebrows. "I am surprised. It is a strong move."

"And one that allows us to get inside." I imagine Ara back in the temple under Idera's control, and my stomach turns.

Esu nods and looks down at the ruby glistening on my wrist.

"Keep it for now, but I will need it to fully bind the ajogun." He watches me touch the gem, his voice turning gruff. "I hope its possession has allayed any feelings of mistrust you had for me."

"It has," I agree, and then think of the visions it has also tormented me with. I feel as if I've been tricked. I frown, sliding the ruby along my wrist. "But you didn't explain what it would do. The things it would show me . . ."

"Ah," Esu says. "The ajogun have revealed themselves to you."

"Why didn't you tell me?" I ask. "Or did the thought of what it would do to me please you?"

The orisa waves his hand. "Nonsense. It is not an easy burden to bear, but I didn't know if it would affect you or not." Esu leans closer to me, a hint of palm wine on his breath. "It has shown you the warlords, what may be, what could be. You cannot let anything, not even grief, weaken you, little fish."

I pull away, hating that he is right. The visions of the ajogun linger still and I think of all the dead they showed me. The ajogun must be bound. By any means.

Kola returns with Bem and Yinka, Aissa stalking behind her. The bultungin mix in with the Oko warriors, sharing strips of dried beef and checking weapons.

"The Oyo leader says they will wait for a few more villages to arrive and then attack as the day ends," says Bem. His face is stern, muscles flexing as he readjusts his grip on his sword. "We'll use twilight for more cover."

"The Tapa are in for a surprise," adds Yinka.

Aissa smirks at her, canines a touch too long in the light. They both look up to the moon that shares the sky with the sun, and then back at each other, matching hard smiles on their faces.

CHAPTER TWENTY-THREE

THE OYO CAMP is nestled in the grass plains just before a hill that conceals it from Rabah, the Nupe capital. There is an expectant quiet about the sprawl of warriors who check weapons and rest in preparation. The Oyo commander, who leads the cavalry, has four groups ready, one to maintain the camp's position and three to strike at the entrance and side gates. The gate to the east provides the easiest route to the temple, and Kola and Bem direct the Oko warriors there.

The day begins to leave us, the sky flushed in shades of coral. As night draws its veil from the east, enfolding the plains and forest behind us in soft swathes of charcoal, Kola edges Tunde behind Esu and his stallion. Bem has corralled the fighters from Oko in preparation for them to ease toward the right, along with us.

A chilled breeze blows from the south, lifting my curls. I watch a girl around my age as she adjusts her hold on a spear tipped in copper, her hands shaking. When she catches me examining her, I hold my fist to my heart and she bows her head, mirroring me.

Together, we will make this count.

When the dark clouds above us fill the twilight sky, we surge forward, silent in the sway of the long grass. I stay close to Yinka, blood rushing in my ears as I keep up with the loping gait of the bultungin. They stalk through the grass behind Bem, their wrappers camouflaging them in the approaching night. Kola remains behind us, and the thunder of Tunde's steps makes me feel just a bit more confident.

As we rise up the slope, I try to keep my breaths even. It's hard to know what lies in wait, and a tightness in my chest spreads until we crest the hill, the capital of the Nupe Kingdom finally revealed to us.

Rabah sits in the dip of the land with a shallow forest of trees behind it. The city is completely circular, with all the sandy stone buildings gleaming in the last warmth of light. In the center of the city is the temple, its dome topped with gold.

"It is beautiful," someone murmurs, and I agree. But the more I stare at the uniform roofs and pathways, the more I see a perfection that looks unnatural. Forced.

I glance at the young girl whose hands shook, and her face is open with awe. The golden roof of the temple glimmers in the first light of the moon. Majestic, the building rises above all others. Despite its beautiful façade, I think instead of the ajogun and the power that Idera wields.

"Remember," I hiss as loudly as I dare. "This is the kingdom who attacks us. Who carries off people to use as they please in their cities. Who trades our people to the òyìnbó." The girl stands taller at this, her lip curling. Around her, the warriors do the same. "They have chosen violence over peace, time and time again. They have slaughtered entire villages in the Oyo Kingdom." I slide the dagger from my hair and raise it, thinking of Folasade's body. Of Ara, dragged back to the temple she escaped from. "It is time for us to end this. To show the Tapa that we are not afraid. To show the Tapa that we will not have this from them. Not anymore!"

The people of Oko gather around me, their faces snarling with rage and determination. With bows and swords and spears raised, they add their own hisses and curses. Kola's eyes glow as he joins in, nodding at me in approval.

As we move into our formations, a horn sounds. Silence falls as all faces turn toward the city below us. The long low call emanates from Rabah, growing louder as it echoes around the basin.

"Be ready!" shouts the Oyo commander as he starts down the hill. "It looks as though they know we are coming!"

He gets halfway with his cavalry, the rest of us descending behind, before the main gates of Rabah open, spewing forth the Tapa. They swarm from their city, the first wave on horses. The Oyo cavalry dash to meet them as archers stand back, bows strung with arrows, their metal tips blazing in the last rays of sun. They aim upward and release, driving arrows through the air. Some meet their mark, toppling the Tapa riders from their horses or thudding into the glossy flanks of the mounts, but more warriors pour out of the main entrance, their ranks swelling.

The two outer gates are thrown open, releasing a stream of fighters on foot, all wearing wrappers of yellow and black. They streak toward their Oyo counterparts, making me think of a swarm of bees, their blades vicious stingers.

"This way," calls Bem as he veers right of the onslaught, thundering toward the Tapa men from the east gate.

Kola gives a command and the archers behind us fire into the line of the fighters, and at least a dozen fall to the ground, the arrows striking limbs and shoulders and chests. The rest leap over the wounded and sprint toward us, faces twisted into fierce expressions.

"Cover!" screams Yinka as a line of Tapa archers by the gate release yet more arrows.

Wooden shields are hefted into place and arrows pepper the air. Yinka pulls me to the side just as one whistles past my ear.

I tighten my grip, whirling to slash at the side of a Tapa woman who bears down on us. But it's a weak strike, and the blood I draw does nothing to stop her as she snarls, teeth bared. Yinka steps in front of her and raises her axes, sweeping them together in one smooth chop. The woman falls, her head cut clean from her body.

Esu leaps from his horse to my left, plunging his long sword into the chest of a Tapa man. He lifts the impaled fighter up, swinging his body around and pressing the blade into another man. The orisa watches as their blood mingles and their souls rise into the air. He places a foot on the dead man on top, pulling his blade free, eyes glittering. Four Tapa come at him from behind and Esu turns, body changing, wrapper transforming from red and black to red and yellow. He holds his hands up, mouth downturned.

"No, brothers, not me!" Even his words have changed in cadence and tone, adopting a high quirk filled with fear.

The men falter, their axes and swords sharp, gripped tightly. Esu runs toward them, hand held out in supplication, playing on their confusion.

"Who are you?" asks one of the Tapa, reaching for Esu. The orisa makes as if to grasp his hand but then lifts his sword and brings it down in a silver blur, severing the man's arm.

The trickster barks with laughter and changes back to his

usual height, plaits hanging in his face as he lowers his head and stalks toward them. The three Tapa don't last longer than five seconds as Esu thrusts, lunges, and cuts them down, still smiling as he stands in their cooling blood.

Ragged screams and dying gasps mix with battle cries, and though each kill draws us closer to our goal, my heart lurches with every soul I see released. It strikes me how senseless all this death truly is, and a sharp despair fills me. At people who follow their leaders and the ajogun, manipulated into slaughter and death. For a moment, I stand still, the clashing of blades and the cries of the dead and dying echoing all around me. Wherever I look, glittering souls of gold and silver climb and twirl into the air. So many lost. I think of my visions of the ajogun and shudder, my skin growing clammy. There is only one way this can end so that the sky will not be full of souls reaped by the eight warlords.

"Little fish! We need to hurry," shouts Esu. He looks up at the fat moon inching its way higher in the sky. "The ritual can only be done when the moon is at its peak."

The orisa spins away, transforming once again. He waits until he infiltrates a formation of Tapa before reverting to his usual form, using his size and strength to slaughter the small contingent in under two minutes.

I stay behind Yinka as the bultungin and Oyo fighters cut a steady swathe toward the east gate. Tunde bellows behind us, and I turn to see him kicking out at the Tapa who try to attack him, the spikes of his golden cuffs digging into their flesh, tearing blood and screams from them. The elephant snatches at a man who tries to slash at his flank, picking him up in his armored trunk and throwing him against a nearby tree. There's a loud crack as the man's spine breaks, and his body lands in a crumpled pile among the grass. The Tapa archers target Tunde, but their arrows bounce from his armor and Kola ducks around each one. He urges the elephant onward, not even wincing when the creature tramples two men underfoot as he stampedes past us toward the east gate.

We follow in Tunde's wake as he scatters Tapa in every direction, but halt when the elephant stops. He rears up on his back legs and trumpets loudly. The whites of his eyes gleam with fear as his gaze skitters around him.

"Tunde! It's all right," says Kola as he clings on tightly. "It's all right."

But the elephant sways his head from side to side, his gold-tipped tusks glinting. When Tunde won't be soothed, Kola slides quickly from his back and begins rubbing the animal's flank. I see a Tapa man running full pelt toward the boy and I open my mouth to scream a warning, but Kola thrusts his sword backward, catching his attacker without even looking at him. Relief flows briefly as the boy continues to soothe Tunde, who stamps nervously, rocking back and forth.

I start toward the elephant and Kola, but before I can reach him, the ruby at my wrist grows hot once again, scorching my skin and lighting up like a red star. I gasp as the battlefield around me disappears.

Cries fill the darkness until the moon, nearly full, sheds enough light for me to see the cages that stretch as far as I can see. A forest of hands reach from between wooden bars, moans seeping into the night. Ewon, warlord of imprisonment, stands before the captives, his back to me. He yanks a man from the nearest cell; the prisoner falls to the ground at his feet, his gibbering pleas ignored.

Ese steps into view, shoulders thick with muscles and shadows. He carries a sword that drips with blood as he stalks toward the man. Ese looms over him before bringing his blade down again and again, until even the other prisoners are silent. As the blood of the dead seeps into the earth, the ajogun of affliction raises his weapon and points at the rest of the imprisoned.

The darkness slips away, leaving me staring at the ground, gasping as I try not to fall. I won't let this happen, I think as my hand shakes, the dagger wavering before me. And then I see Kola. He moves toward me, cutting down any Tapa in his way.

"I'm all right," I say, feeling a steadiness from his presence. And then the earth quakes beneath us.

We stagger, as does everyone around us apart from one.

Idera.

She stands just in front of the east gate, her copper-bound locs rippling in the night breeze. With her eyes closed, Idera's lip curls as a rumble begins beneath our feet, stopping me and others in our tracks, weapons at the ready. And then the ground erupts as the Tapa back away, grins slicing their faces.

The grass shakes beneath us, soil spraying as gaping holes appear in the ground. Stumbling, we look down as rocks are pushed up from the open seams, and a few of the Tapa begin to laugh. The warriors of Oko stare at the earth warily, and then there are screams as a hand rises from the dirt before us, followed by an arm corded with strings of muscle and rotting skin. Hands plant themselves on either side of the growing hole, hauling out a body made from grass and old flesh and the roots of plants. There's a chest of blackness and thick green roots; eyes pits of obsidian. The bultungin back away, their curved swords hanging at their sides, mouths open.

Obambo.

Ghosts.

The forgotten.

Said to be created from those slain, their bodies abandoned after death. The creatures rise from the earth, their shadow-wreathed jaws opening to emit chitters and screeches that chill my soul. Black fingers as long as my arm claw at the air, ending with fingernails as honed as daggers.

Idera looks up, her gaze locking onto mine before she turns and saunters back toward the east gate. More obambo fight their way from the earth, backs hunched, sunken empty eyeholes in their sharp faces. They unfurl themselves, a mass of dark flesh and spines of teeth.

"Cut their heads off." Aissa stands before us, head bent forward, unafraid. "Or carve their hearts from their chests. It is the only way to stop obambo."

The warriors of Oko falter in disbelief, faces full of horror as they watch these creatures of nightmares and stories. They turn to look at Bem.

"You heard her!" he shouts. "Take off their heads or go for their hearts."

The closest rakes out a hand, swiping at the giant boy. Bem dodges to the side before swinging his sword in a hurried strike as the creature is joined by more obambo. Long fingers and twisted bodies rise up around us, revealing evidence of the many lives that the Tapa have taken, their bodies buried beneath their lands. Forgotten until now.

Esu charges forward, sweeping through them in a whirl of steel, plaits flying in the air as he slashes out at each obambo. But for every one he cuts down, another rises. The stench of rot and blood sticks in the back of our throats, giving our terror a taste. Bem calls to the rest of Oko's fighters and they join, blades flashing in the moonlight.

An obambo lunges, grabbing Bem around the neck, decomposing fingers wrapped tight as a Tapa man heads toward them, sword held level with his hip.

"No!" Yinka runs at the man and cuts him with her axe, cleaving a heavy gash in his side so that he drops to his knees.

The obambo tightens its grip as Bem scrabbles at its rotting fingers. The monster's claws gouge his flesh, drawing blood that trickles down his wide chest. And then Yinka is leaping through the air, skin shimmering as it turns to fur, her bones cracking loudly as her limbs grow, her fingernails turning to claws. A growl splits from her jaws as she grabs the obambo, ripping its arm and loosening its grip from Bem's neck. He spins, carving his sword into the creature's chest. With a jerk, Bem rips the creature's rib cage open. Maggots wriggle from the cavity, and he holds a hand over his mouth and nose as the stench of dead flesh rolls over us.

Bile rises in my throat as I watch Bem kick the obambo away and block a Tapa attack, the clash of his sword loud in the dark. Panic claws its way through me and I scan the area, my chest heaving as I see how many Tapa there are, how many obambo are still rising. I watch the archer from earlier draw the string of her bow, but before she can release it, hands shoot from the earth, grabbing at her legs. She screams as she goes down, and I run toward her, only to feel arms wrap around my chest.

"We need to keep moving while the east gates are open." Esu's voice is a calm slick of silk in my ear, and I wrench away. "You won't get to her in time."

"Watch me," I snarl as I sprint toward the archer.

The obambo has pulled her closer now, still only half emerged from the ground, and it opens its mouth and shrieks. I run harder, ignoring the burn in my soles, my dagger ready. The archer uses her arrow to stab at the obambo where eyes should be, but it has her in a tight grip, drawing her closer to the black maw of its face. I arrive to see the charcoal spines of its teeth, small razor-sharp spikes that line its mouth, as it screams again, the shriek this time edged with a low snicker. Seizing the head from behind, I bring my dagger across the rotting skin of the creature's throat. Its head falls to the ground.

The archer scrambles backward, untangling herself from the loosened fingers. She nods her thanks, then quickly climbs to her feet, retrieves her bow, and aims at a Tapa man whose blade is drawn tight against an Oko warrior's.

More yowls sound now as the bultungin also shift, skin exchanged for fur, limbs sleek as they leap at the Tapa and the obambo.

"Simi!" Kola is cutting through the fighters at the east entrance, Esu by his side. The men try to shut the tall wooden panels, but Esu jams himself between them. Heaving them open, Kola joins him, and together they spin and thrust, muscles glistening, killing all those in their path. "Come!"

I begin to run toward them as they clear the gate of the last of the Tapa guarding it but am yanked backward by my hair. Sweat and rot make me retch as I see blackened flesh grasp around my chest, squeezing the breath from me. Bucking wildly, I try to break free, but I can't even bring my blade up, let alone fight my way out of the grip. I scream in frustration just as something slams into us and I am thrown to the ground, the pressure gone.

I'm on all fours, trying not to vomit, as I hear the snarls behind me. Pushing myself away, I scramble to my feet to see Bem and Yinka attack the obambo. They work together, and as the hyena bites at the monster's arm, the giant boy swings his sword around in a large arc, lopping the obambo's head from its shoulders.

"Go, Simi!" calls Bem, wiping his forehead. Drying blood is splattered across his chest, but apart from the gouges from his attack earlier, he appears unharmed. "Before more come." Yinka pauses beside him, her lustrous fur and eyes glowing in the light of the moon.

"We can hold them. Look. Look at what the Oyo Kingdom, united, can do!" Behind Bem, I watch as the archer from before bends to her knee, letting an arrow fly quick and fast through the air. When she reaches for another from her quiver, a Tapa lunges toward her, blade bright. A bultungin slams into his side, knocking him to the ground before it clamps its jaws around the fighter's neck. Beyond this, the people of Oyo clash against the fighters from Nupe.

Yinka runs forward, her breath steaming in the cooling night. She lowers her head and pushes me closer to the gate. I smile, my vision blurred with tears. I don't want to leave them. Not to this.

Yinka butts me again and I snatch another look back. Bem runs to join the Oyo contingent, calling the Oko warriors to him. It's impossible to see who has the upper hand, but I know only one thing will end this all. I run toward Kola and Esu, toward the temple where Idera plans to usher in the ajogun.

CHAPTER TWENTY-FOUR

SHOUTS TEAR THROUGH the night air as we reach the walls of Rabah. They rise up high, with slim thatched roofs that prevent them from being washed away by the rains. Dull red and smoothed into horizontal ripples, the thick walls have been an effective defense mechanism. Until now.

The carved panels of the east gate depict lions and wild boars, both in flight but with arrows in their sides. Tall figures loom over them, draped in the skins of their kills, long blades held high. Esu digs his fingers into the seam between the closed gates and pulls. Kola joins him, and together, they claw and dig at the widening gap. Slowly, the gate cracks open, giving us just enough space to slip inside. Kola and Esu heave the panels shut behind us, ramming their shoulders against the carved wood. I run forward and push the heavy bar down, locking the gate.

A grunt and a cry come from behind us and I turn to see Kola standing with a hand over the mouth of a guard, his sword deep in the man's gut. Another four men bleed into the earth, their eyes sightless, their souls already gone.

"We need to move. Now." Kola releases the body as the man's essence spirals up into the night sky. "There are more coming."

As we sink into the shadows that line the compound, I don't ask how he knows more are on their way, how he managed to kill so many men in seconds. Instead I press my back against the ridges of the wall, and when Kola's hand grazes my wrist, his fingers grip mine tightly.

"Stay close," he murmurs. Moonlight glows on the sharpness of his cheekbones. Once again, I find myself memorizing the shape of his mouth, the brown of his eyes. Just in case.

The streets of Rabah are wide, with palm-oil lamps that cast pools of light at regular intervals. We keep to the dark, the gilded dome of the temple just visible above the compound roofs. Warriors swarm the streets, heading toward the gate we have just come from, their faces drawn shut in anger and purpose. Kola and Esu could have taken them all on, but the moon is still climbing and time is running out.

The sounds of battle beyond the city walls are carried on the breeze, each cry a scar on my heart. Be strong, I think as we run down the orderly pathways, or more will die. The streets empty as we get closer to the temple, making my gut twist with unease. No doubt many warriors have been held back to protect the Oba and the Nupe council. And then I see the guards who flank the temple doorway, and my shoulders slump as we flatten ourselves against an adjacent wall.

Giant lamps blaze along the temple's façade, throwing bright arcs of light that beat back the shadows. The men who guard the entrance are shoulder to shoulder, clad in wrappers and leather and copper. They hold spears twice their size, and swords are strapped to their waists.

Esu glances at Kola, gesturing to the left. "You start there and I'll take the other side."

Seeing them work together feels strange, and as the two orisa peel away from the dark, weapons held low as they sprint toward the temple guards, I know the Tapa do not stand a chance. Kola cuts the throat of the one he reaches first, gutting the next and then sliding his sword free. Esu slits the throats of two guards in one deadly slice before facing the others.

I ease my way from the gloom, dagger held in front. With the guards responding to the attack, I can just make out the temple entrance. Carved into the double doors are eight marks with concentric circles on top. The same emblem I saw in the sea on the dead men's armor.

Idera's temple. A place to worship the anti-gods whom she is intent on releasing.

As I approach, Esu decapitates two more guards in a row with one large sweep of his long sword. The rest of the men form a defensive formation, but the two orisa are a blur of blades and death. The gray souls of those pledged to the ajogun dissipate in quick succession until Kola and Esu stand on the steps of the palace together, chests heaving, bodies splattered with blood.

Picking my way around the corpses, I reach out for the copper handles of the doors. Before my shaking fingers touch the metal handles, I pause. I think of the power of the iyalawo, the jaws of the adzes, the clawed hands of the obambo.

"Let's go, Simi," Kola urges as he flanks me, Esu by his side.

I open the doors with both hands, pulse thundering in my ears. I tense, expecting more guards, or something with teeth and talons to slither or leap at us, but the entryway opens onto a passage lit with golden light in evenly spaced wall sconces. Eight giant masks are hung on either side.

Arun is depicted opposite Ofo, disease and loss opposite each other. Their carved faces are followed by those of Egba, Oran, Epe, Ewon, and Ese. I shiver at the careful grooves of their eyes, shaped as if narrowed. Noses are pointed, spread across the tops of mouths that vary from snarls to roars, teeth sharpened. But it is when I come to stand in front of the last mask that I stop, small bumps rising on my arms.

Iku.

Death.

Known as the collector of the ultimate debt, which cannot go unpaid, one of the ajogun we must all face eventually, sacrifice or not. He is the only warlord who is unconfined, coming and going as needed, but not allowed freedom on a grand scale. However, there are times he has run amok, and those are the moments in history of great famine and wars that ravage whole countries. Iku's mask is larger than the others, hung over another set of double doors, which shimmer in copper and bronze, red silk wrapped around the handles.

Shuddering, I turn away from the ajogun. "We should look for Ara," I say. I think of how hard it must be for her to be back here in a place created for the worship of warriors of death and pain.

"No, there is not enough time." Esu flicks his plaits from his face, his eyes hooded. "We will do what we came here for."

"He's right," Kola says, avoiding the surprised look I give him. "We can find her afterward."

I take a deep breath and nod, knowing what they say makes sense. Esu steps forward, grasping the silk-wrapped handles. When the orisa eases the doors open, it is to a wave of decay that makes us gag. The scents of decomposing flesh and ash flood the air as we struggle to breathe. With my hand held against my nose and mouth, I gaze around the room, forcing down a wave of nausea. Thoughts of more obambo press their way into my mind as I adjust my grip on my dagger, trying to quell my panic.

The chamber is a large circle, topped with the shining dome above that reaches impossible heights. But it is not the ceiling that captures my attention. Directly in the center of the space is a tree that stretches up to the gold of the roof, long thick branches with even, fanlike leaves. The vast trunk plants the tree's largest roots deep beneath the marble floor. Lights are woven through the greenery, gilding the stalks and casting the branches in a honey brown.

"What is this?" I whisper. The tree's vibrancy fills the space, the vivid lime green of its leaves glittering in an unsettling show of life. The ruby pressed against my wrist blazes once again, burning hot enough to make me flinch. I hold in a cry but look around as my unease builds. The dazzle and scorch from the gem can only mean ajogun power.

Esu strides around the room, wide shoulders bunched with tension. "Where is the iyalawo? That's the question we should be asking."

The lower branches of the tree sway, and there's a flash of bronze just beyond it.

"No need to ask." Idera's voice is a low growl as she emerges from behind the trunk. She holds her slim sword at her side and behind her, head down, is Ara. "I am here."

"Ara?" I ask, taking a step toward her, scanning her for injuries. "Are you all right?"

"Ara is here to serve me. As is her place." A sneer carves the iyalawo's lips apart as she folds her hands in front of her.

The girl nods but doesn't look up. My fingers tighten on my dagger, but Kola's hand on my arm stops me.

"And where's Folasade's sapphire?" he asks, his eyes darting around the chamber.

Idera's lips stretch farther apart as she grins at me, her mouth full of tiny teeth. "The sapphire that contains the soul song?" She lifts heavy twists of hair, pushing them back over one shoulder so that we can see the blue jewel, the fleck of red in its center, hanging just below her collarbone.

"Thank you for gleaning it, Simidele. Without you this would not have been possible."

Folasade. I think of her bravery, the way she killed the Mokele-mbembe and gathered the soul song. I clench my fists, the bone and skin tight as fury floods through me. "You killed her."

"No, I did not. Her death was a mistake. My orders were to bring any Mami Wata and her necklace. I needed her to release the soul song. For too long I have endured prayer and rituals to give the Oba what he craves. But what of me? What about what I need? The power I could have." Idera pauses a moment, her nostrils flaring. "Beholden to none, the Nupe Kingdom expanded under my leadership. The Oba is a weakling!" she hisses. "He accepts the warriors and the powers I can give them without even asking what it takes to produce them. The sacrifices I must make, the time, the ceremonies I must prepare and undertake. And all for that fool to show off." Idera stands before the tree, stroking the sapphire at her neck. "That is not true power. It is only a fraction of what could be. Even now, the world is changing, and I will not be left behind." The iyalawo shakes her head, the copper strands wound around her locs flashing. "Not with the trouble the òyìnbó bring."

"Releasing them won't give you what you want," I say, but even I can hear the desperation lacing my words. "You can't control the ajogun. They have only one purpose, and that is to ruin the world."

"They will listen to me if I command them." There's a wild belief in Idera's tone. "Their energy can be harnessed. Look at what I have been able to create, to command—the adzes, the obambo! After I summon the ajogun, I will have power that even orisas cannot imagine!" Idera glares at me, the milkiness of her damaged eye gleaming. "I just need the soul song to release the ajogun. And then I will bind them to me."

"You will not," says Kola. He and Esu creep closer to the iyalawo.

Idera lifts her face to the golden dome above her. She lets out a hard laugh full of malice. "I would like to see you stop me." She lowers her head and regards the boy coolly. "Or do you think that as a village leader's son, you can do as you please?"

"It is not a matter of doing as I please, but what is right, what must be done."

"Let this be over with," drawls Esu, his tone calm, almost honeyed, as he moves closer to the iyalawo. "Her words are tedious and she does not know what she speaks of."

Kola takes Esu's lead and together they advance on Idera, swords held ready. I look around, checking to see if there are hidden guards, wondering how many steps it would take me to get to Ara. The girl shuffles back, her eyes widening in a growing panic as the iyalawo watches the orisas, the same dark smile still on her face. She begins to murmur, and she glances at the tree.

"Wait!" I manage to choke out. But the orisas lunge toward the iyalawo, swords a sharp blur as they attack.

The priestess brings her hands up and continues to chant. There's a sudden rustle of green and brown and Esu's and Kola's attacks are caught, arms frozen, held in place. Idera crows when the orisas look down, confusion creasing their faces as they try to move their hands. More tentacles shoot out from the tree, joining the others and wrapping around the orisas' waists. I watch as Kola kicks out at another vine, but it twists around his ankle, holding his foot still. Esu thrashes beside him, his sword clattering to the floor beneath them as a thick tentacle twines around his shoulders.

I lash out, hacking at one of the vines, but three more glide out from the body of the tree and I skip backward, barely escaping their grip. Without missing a beat, they wrap tighter around Kola. More tentacles unfurl from the tree, tangling themselves around the orisas until they are lifted from the ground, bare toes dangling, their limbs wound tight with vines.

"Simi—" Kola's words are cut off when a vine slithers over his face, wrapping over his mouth and chin.

Idera watches as the two orisas are hoisted above her. She moves to the tree, caressing the trunk and bending down. As she runs her hands through the spaces and gaps at the base, I see what is cradled in the curve of the shadows.

Skulls.

Nestled at the base of the tree and half buried in exposed roots. Idera reaches, strokes her fingers over many more craniums crowded in the dark. She turns, another vicious smile on her face.

"Ya-Te-Veo—'I see you.' The Mkodo people offered sacrifices to the Ya-Te-Veo for thousands of years," says the iyalawo. She straightens up, pushing the twist of her locs over one shoulder. "But none have been squandered. Growing deep in the forest of the large island I was born on, the Ya-Te-Veo has always been revered by those who see its power, its potential. Spores of this tree have spread across the land in one way or another. But this one? It was sown when I was still learning the ways of Ifá, just as I was realizing that there was more power than what I was being told."

Stepping forward, I hold my dagger ready, but a slither of branches swipes at me, forcing me back. I blink away tears of frustration as I gaze up at Kola and Esu, who dangle above me, struggling against their restraints. I want nothing more than to slice the lips from Idera's mouth so she can't speak.

"Look." She gestures to the trunk and I see the bark ripple. "See. It is the perfect gateway for the ajogun."

I take a tiny step closer and then gasp, hand flying to my mouth when I see what the iyalawo is talking about. The sides of the bark roll like the taut skin of a pregnant belly, pushing outward before snapping back in. A sudden hand molds the shape of the bulging trunk, and then a face, mouth open, lips peeled back in a snarl, can just be seen. My visions crowd in, my stomach roils.

"The ajogun have been fed with the conquests of the Nupe Kingdom, and soon they will be released and I will have the power I need. The power that I deserve." Idera watches the tree expectantly, her good eye shining with reverence and excitement. "Do not worry, these deaths will be worthy ones."

I glance down at the skulls at the tree's base, my throat tight with revulsion. I can't move, terror leaving my limbs frozen.

"The lives we have taken have helped me gain the power of the ajogun. Sacrifice was needed, and sacrifice it will be for both these orisas. Unless . . ." Her words trail off as she slips closer to me. "Unless you release the soul song from the sapphire. If you do that, then I will spare the boy."

The jewel glints at the base of her throat. Kola tries to wriggle, but even that small movement is constrained. The iyalawo smiles, a slow spread of lips and teeth that are curved with victory.

Behind her, Ara looks up at me. Her expression is clearer now, and she takes a small step toward Idera, her hand trembling as she reaches for the iyalawo's sword.

"I'll do as you ask, but you need to let Esu go, too. He is Olodumare's messenger," I say.

"He has no role after this," rasps Idera. "There will be no need for him to balance the ajogun and orisa—"

Her sentence goes unfinished as Ara grabs for Idera's blade. The iyalawo starts to turn around and Ara tugs on the sword, hitting at the woman's hand and snatching the weapon from her grip. Idera roars with rage, but Ara brings the sword up in a fast arc, plunging it into the priestess's back.

Blood fills Idera's mouth as she looks down at the blade protruding from her chest. Ara yells as she yanks the sword out, a shout mixed with anger and fear. The iyalawo staggers. Her lips move as she tries to speak, but only red bubbles froth from between her white teeth. Idera slides to the floor, landing in a crumpled pile. A blackened soul escapes her chest, a twist of silver in its midst, fading as it rises into the air.

CHAPTER TWENTY-FIVE

THE IYALAWO RESTS in a growing pool of blood. I look from the corpse to my childhood friend, her chest heaving, arms splattered red. Ara stands above the body, knuckles tight as she clutches the hilt of the sword. Blood drips from the blade, a constant patter on the hard floor. Slowly, she bends to pluck the chain from the iyalawo's neck, clutching the sapphire in her fist.

"Thank Olodumare!" I say, rushing forward to embrace Ara. When she doesn't move, I pull back, scanning her body. "What's wrong? Are you all right? Did Idera hurt you?" My questions sound shrill, and I force myself to take a gulp of air, trying to calm myself.

"No." Ara is shaking her head now, her eyes becoming more focused. She smiles at me, but the corner of her mouth is crooked, and I press a hand to her cheek.

"Come away. I need to cut Kola and Esu free." I tug at the girl, but she remains where she is, still gripping the sword. "You've done so well. I'll take care of this part." I curl my hands gently around her shoulders and try to steer her away from the Ya-Te-Veo, but Ara plants her feet and shrugs me off.

"Come," I repeat. "The sooner we get them down, the sooner

Esu can bind the ajogun and we can put a stop to this war." I take a step around her, eyes on the Ya-Te-Veo. Kola and Esu have gone limp, the vines wrapped around them still slowly squeezing. The thought of them being dead gnaws at me.

Then the ruby burns brightly again, and this time it feels as if it is searing the skin from my flesh. I cry out, clamping a hand around the gem. The pain fades, but the stone stays lit in a furious shade of red. Sweat pours down my forehead as I wait for the fog or mist of another vision. Could the ajogun be—

My thoughts are cut short as a blade stings my throat.

"Stop." Ara stands in my path, holding the weapon to my neck. Her eyes are bright and hard now, a feverish brown in the flickering light of the wall sconces. "Stay where you are."

"Ara, what—" I am forced into silence as she presses the blade harder into my skin, and I swallow as I feel a trickle of my blood escape. Ara snatches the dagger from my grip, throwing it away from us.

The girl's hand does not waver, and I feel her sword slice deeper into my skin. She fumbles one-handed with the clasp of Folasade's necklace, wrapping it around her throat before managing to snap it shut. The sapphire hangs from her neck, chain dripping with blood, a dark smear on the jewel matching the small red glow in its center. "I wanted to tell you before, when we first saw each other. But as time went on, it was clear where you stood."

I say nothing, thinking of the moment I set eyes on Ara again. The dimple I knew would be there when she smiled, the memories of lying in the sun together, hiding in the arch of the seventeenth gate as we avoided our chores. I knew then that things weren't the same, but I'd put that down to all we'd been through, and our time apart.

I think back to killing the Mokele-mbembe and Olokun. I understand now. He knew that someone was acting on behalf of Idera. He was trying to warn me."

"Ara, this isn't—"

"Me?" She laughs, a harsh bark. "Shall I tell you what is? Taken by the Nupe Kingdom. Used by the iyalawo." Ara brings her face closer to mine, teeth bared. "While you were splashing about in the sea complaining about your lack of humanity—" She breaks off, her words stuttering as anger courses through her. "Let me tell you this, *you* could not comprehend any part of how it was for me."

Ara stops and straightens but still holds the weapon firmly against my neck. I don't move, thinking only about what she has said. And the fact that it stems from my own mistakes. Mistakes I can't seem to stop making. Frustration and hurt flood through me.

"Time spent here has shown me what we should have had in Oyo-Ile," continues Ara. "The kind of power that would have kept us safe." She shudders and the sword wavers for a moment before she presses it harder against me. "We would have been protected if the Aláàfin and the babalawos had dared to try to possess the ajogun's energy."

"But they didn't! And for a good reason." I don't attempt to disguise my pleading tone. "I won't pretend to understand what it has been like for you. But this isn't the answer. The anti-gods can't truly be harnessed. You know this."

"We're not going to go back and forth." Ara's lips twist in a snarl and she presses deeper, not wincing when I cry out in pain. "You always want to be the one to save everyone, to do the right thing, but all it does is cause more problems. We wouldn't have been taken if it hadn't been for . . ."

Me, I think. *We wouldn't have been taken if it hadn't been for me.* The guilt rises in me, as rancid as the air in the temple chamber. Ara stares at me, her gaze filling with spite. It sits on top of the pain I see layered in her, the fury that is forcing her on.

"Look at Esu. Binding him meant he couldn't mediate with the ajogun, and then Idera was able to call to them, to draw on their power. This is all because of you. You helped this to happen. Now, release the soul song, Simi, or they'll both die."

Her words are simple yet so keen that I feel them deep in my heart. Ara holds the bloodied sapphire up to me, her eyebrows knitted together. My fingers tremble as I reach for the jewel. If I do this, then I am bringing about the ruin of the world, but if I don't do this, then Kola and Esu will die. I will die.

Think, I tell myself furiously.

"How?" I croak. "How did you know all of this?"

"Eventually Idera showed me how things could be different, that our means of redemption and protection was the ajogun. And I began to believe." Ara smiles, but I don't recognize the malice in the twist of her lips. "We heard word of you and your kind, of the abilities of the sapphires. It's why I went to Oko. Idera wanted me to find out more, and if the rumors were true, it was the perfect way to get to the Mokele-mbembe. Once Kola told me about you, I knew it was the best, if not the only, way to gather the soul song. You could glean it and your sapphire could contain it."

She used us.

I breathe deeply, sneaking a look at Kola and Esu. The twitch of a finger, an ankle rotating, tells me that they're alive. I try to work out if they're still conscious, forcing the kick of panic from my chest. How long do they have before the Ya-Te-Veo squeezes the life from them?

"We've all had to do things we didn't want to." Ara takes a quick glance at the necklace she holds. "But it's necessary. There's no way around some actions."

The sapphire glows a gentle lilac in her hands, and I think of Folasade's black halo of hair, of her pure courage and faith.

"What happened to Folasade?" My voice is quiet. "Was it you?"

Ara's lips lose their curve, but her eyes are just as hard. "At first, I thought I could persuade you to come with me. For us to use the power together, especially if I told you that it was a way you could be with Kola. But you were never going to claim the soul song for your own needs. And then Idera got impatient and sent the adzes to attack." Ara shrugs, but I see a small tremble in her wrist, the downturn of her mouth. "It was the perfect opportunity to take the soul song, but Folasade fought me. It had to be done."

I think of the swim I made with Folasade's body. Her return to the sea and the shimmer of the foam that took her back to Olodumare. Standing straighter, I try to ignore the pain of the blade at my throat, grief shaping my courage.

"I knew that you would come for the soul song. That you would think I had been taken once again and try to save me."

And she's right, I always would have. "Because you are family to me," I say softly. I keep my eyes on her, trying to work out if I could push the sword away and get to my dagger. "You always have been. You always will be. I would never have left you in such a place. You know this, too."

Ara stares at me and I think I see a waver in her eyes, but then she pushes forward, slanting the blade horizontally against my neck. One slash and more of my blood will spill.

"There is no way around this, Simi. Release the soul song now."

I know from the set of her shoulders, her hand steady with the sword, that I can't keep on distracting her. If I don't do this, then Ara will cut my throat, and the Ya-Te-Veo will consume Kola and Esu. Without Esu, the ajogun will never be pacified, and Ara may still find another way to release the soul song. I reach out, fingers touching the facets of the sapphire gently, thinking of the tangled essence inside.

If I do this now, perhaps there is still some hope of gaining control.

Ara presses the blade a touch more, and the wet, hot spill of blood slips down my chest.

"I'll do it," I whisper, trembling as I take Folasade's sapphire into my hand. A tug of dread and revulsion winds its way through me, and I double over. I feel the slither of terror and death that releasing the ajogun can bring, and I grit my teeth at the pain of it. The world might not be the same, and I can feel the horror that awaits deep inside me.

"Simi . . ." The dagger digs into the skin of my neck, slicing deeper this time.

Closing my eyes, I breathe out, using the pain to focus myself. "With this prayer, we ease your journey to this realm." I choke back a sob as I grasp for words that will release the soul song. Though they are similar to the ones I used to return a person's essence, this time I know I am not ushering in peace, but chaos instead. "Mo tú u ẹ sínu aiyé."

I release you into this world. The words are simple, but when I open my eyes, it is to the wisp of soul that begins to seep from the jewel. The essence is gold, interlaced with the red strands of the Mokele-mbembe's song. The soul song shimmers in the air between us, as mesmerizing and dangerous as a flame.

"The gateway is open. Come, now is your time." Ara smiles

and draws the weapon away from me, raising her arms as she continues to chant. "Ẹnu ọ̀nà wà ni ṣíṣí. Wá, àsìkò ẹ rèé."

The essence hovers a moment before streaming toward the Ya-Te-Veo, where it drapes itself among the uppermost branches. The red-gold twist of the soul song shimmers among green leaves. Kola and Esu are still bound by the monstrous vines, but now they hang to the side as the tree opens its branches to reveal a maw lined with teeth. The Ya-Te-Veo vines snake out, dragging the body of Idera into the yawning hole. Deep within, something thrashes around, the trunk bulging and stretching.

"O ti bọ́!" cries Ara, her voice rising with a fervor that heightens the pitch of her voice. "You are free!"

I edge away from her, eyes on the gold of my dagger that glints on the marble floor. A scream splits the air as the tree breaks open even wider, and a head emerges from the mouth of bark and serrated teeth. The figure unfurls from the maw, standing straight and raising its head. Its face is flat, with black holes for eyes and a deep slash of a mouth that reveals the flicker of red tongue. The ajogun screams again, climbing from the tree on long spider-like limbs. Scars and boils decorate its body, and I recoil.

Arun. The warlord of disease. One of the only two not shown in my visions.

"Who calls me?" The ajogun scuttles free of the gateway and stands on his bowed legs, glaring down at Ara. "Who has set me free?"

"I have. Aramide."

"Aramide. 'My family has arrived.'" Arun laughs, a rough sound that rattles the darkness of his chest. "And have we? Do you seek us as your people, as your *family*?" The last word ends on a sneer.

"I do." Ara lifts her chin, raising her voice. "And I am ready to receive your divine sanction in return for freeing you. You will be under my command." Her words hover in the air for a moment, strong and full of belief, but such emotions mean nothing to the anti-gods, and Arun skitters forward, stooping so that his face is level with Ara's. She stands her ground, but I see the tremor in her hands before she presses them against her sides.

"You would like my blessing?" Arun laughs, a crooked viscous sound that spreads from his blistered mouth. "Are you sure?"

Ara nods, her eyes fixed on the warlord. I hold my breath, edging my way slowly toward my dagger. Arun lowers his face so that it is close to the girl's, their lips only a space apart. One more step and I snatch up the weapon, the emerald digging into my palm as I grip it tightly. The ajogun presses his long fingers against Ara's cheeks, tipping her chin upward as he mutters words that I can't quite hear, their sharp tone peppered with hisses.

Kola and Esu dangle from the depths of the tree, held aloft by its vines. I creep to the Ya-Te-Veo, placing a hand gingerly against the trunk, stomach turning at the heat of it, as if warm blood is flowing through the bark. Kola is the closer of the two, and as I slip the blade under the green tentacles, his eyes inch open, and relief courses through me.

I move quickly, slicing through the bindings around his mouth and neck, and he gasps. Soon his hands are free, and he hacks at the remaining vines around his legs. We work together to free Esu, scrambling backward as the tree oozes a black sap from the vines we have cut.

With the iyalawo dead, the Ya-Te-Veo seems almost placid. Or perhaps all of its energy is flowing to what is being conjured from its depths. The soul song still glows from its tips, and I nurture the hope that Esu can control it. And then a hand with nails like blades emerges from the maw. I stop for a moment, dagger raised as fingers claw at the bark. With Arun already summoned, my blood runs cold at which ajogun is next.

But then a scream rings out, and as I turn, it peters out into a gargle.

Ara.

The warlord of disease clutches her close to him, breathing over Ara's face in a heavy exhale. Something flows from his mouth to hers, a spray of red-and-black mist.

"No!" I scream, spinning to run to her. But Kola's arms stretch around me, holding me against him.

"She accepted," rasps Arun, releasing a wily chuckle.

The girl sags in his grip, her gag cut off and replaced by a beatific smile.

"Ara!" I call again, but as she turns to me, I recoil in Kola's grip.

Her grin is a slip of red that stains her teeth, her black pupils grown to swallow the white. She appears to regain control of herself, standing straighter and holding her hands out to me, palms up. "You see? I told you." But even as she speaks, the red stains that blight her body shift to black, turning her smile a shade closer to obsidian.

Ara peers down at the rot that spreads over her skin. She looks back up at Arun. "I command you." But her tone shakes, and I can hear the unease in her words.

The ajogun laughs, his snicker rising in the air as Ara scrabbles at the spores on her skin. Pustules of yellow and green pepper her limbs as she staggers away from the ajogun, her mouth open. The braids on Ara's head turn to gray, and then white. Her fingernails lengthen and thicken into yellow talons. Her spine twists, bending her over so she can only gaze at the floor, a weak keening seeping into the air.

"No," I moan, sagging against Kola as the girl crumples to the floor.

Arun swivels toward us, his split tongue flickering out from a grin that cleaves open his face. "What is a blessing for some is a curse for others."

Kola pushes me behind him as I see Esu look up at the soul song spun between the top branches of the Ya-Te-Veo.

"We have not asked for a blessing," the boy hisses, sword raised.

Arun lowers his head, neck bent at an impossible angle, and glares at us. "No, you have not. But I'm sure that one of my brothers will bestow upon you one of theirs nonetheless."

Another head appears from the mouth of the tree as an arm emerges, beginning to pull its body from the pitch-black hole. I tremble, my chest slick with cold sweat.

"Can you still use the soul song?" I ask Esu.

The orisa tears his gaze away from the branches and nods once. "Give me the ruby. It is part of my power, of what is needed."

My fingers go to the golden chain wrapped around my wrist, the guarantee from Esu that he would do as he promised. What if I give it to him now and he betrays us?

Kola draws me to him and whispers in my ear. "He fought next to us earlier. If the warlords break free, he won't be able to do as he pleases any longer. He needs this as much as we do."

I slip my finger under the heavy clasp, letting the chain slither from my wrist, and I cup the ruby in my right hand. Taking a deep breath, I hold the gem out, its crimson shine dangling from the golden chain. Esu takes it from my hand, and as his fingers brush mine, there's a spark of electricity and the orisa smiles.

"You can feel the energy. You've felt it before." Esu drapes the chain around his neck and turns to face Arun. Raising his eyes to the soul song, he begins to chant, the slip and sway of his words echoing around us.

Arun opens his mouth and roars, bony feet clicking forward on the stone floor of the temple, heading straight for Esu. But Kola is there, sword held high between the ajogun and the trickster. He thrusts the blade into Arun's stomach. The warlord jerks to the right, contorting his body in unnatural angles, laughing while he does so. His cackles are cut off, though, as Kola brings his blade up again, catching the ajogun's thigh and then bringing the weapon down, drawing the same black sap that ran from the Ya-Te-Veo.

As Arun growls and rushes for Kola, Esu holds the ruby in both hands, his voice rising into a melody of prayer and song. He presses his hands around the jewel and lifts his face to the essence of the Mokele-mbembe, his voice a surprisingly sweet tone that floats toward the domed ceiling of the temple, filling the chamber. The soul song twitches, untangling itself from the vivid green leaves and vines, floating closer and closer to Esu.

I dart around the orisa as Kola drives the warlord of disease back toward the open mouth of the tree. Seven other faces press against the bulging trunk, two sets of hands reaching upward, sharp nails scoring the bark as the ajogun try to drag themselves free. Kola sees this and lunges forward at Arun. I join him, slashing at the warlord with my dagger so that he presses his diseased back against the Ya-Te-Veo.

While Kola continues to force the ajogun toward the tree's open maw, I drop to the floor next to Ara. The girl is sunken into the folds of her wrapper, tufts of white hair sprouting from a patched skull.

"Ara," I whisper softly.

Ara's head turns, a hand spotted with red sores rising from the ruin of her body. She lifts her face to mine and I suck in a sharp breath.

"Simi?" Ara's voice is as cracked as the skin on her face. Two clouded eyes peer sightlessly up at me, her mouth a toothless concave hole in a heavily lined face. "Simi? I . . ."

"It's all right," I say, drawing her to me, letting her rest her head on my lap. I remember the way Ara used to braid my unraveled hair, her fingers always cautious, never hurting me. I remember when we would wake up before everyone else in our compounds, sit outside, and watch the beginning of a new day, chatting quietly about what it would hold. I remember her silly impressions of those who annoyed her.

I take her hand and clasp it in mine. Her fingers are cold, the knuckles swollen and twisted, the bones brittle, and as she opens her mouth to speak, I see the weak rise and fall of her chest. "Rest. I'm here."

Ara attempts to speak again, but she only manages a low croak before her head tips back, resting against my stomach. I tighten my grip on her hand as the last of her breath flows from between withered lips.

CHAPTER TWENTY-SIX

ESU'S VOICE GROWS louder, singing of life and death and the balance between the two. Of the stories of mortals and orisas, of the earth and the sea and the sky that surrounds them all. He sings about love, greed, peace, hate, and war, and with each note, the soul song descends through the brown limbs of the Ya-Te-Veo, its tendrils growing redder and thicker.

I cradle Ara's body as the wisp of her essence rises, choking on a wail of grief that builds in my throat, burning my chest. Her soul is silver with thin threads of gold and a delicate vein of black spun in its center. Before I can stop myself, I raise a hand to her essence, fingertips touching the metallic edges. Ara is tiny, sitting on her mother's lap, looking up into her bright eyes, touching a chubby finger to the flare of her mother's nose. Love enfolds them both, cushioning them. Then Ara is older, sitting in the earth, poking at the roots of the mahogany tree in our compound. I'm there, squatting next to her. Together we squeal at a marching line of ants, our fingers stained with the juice of Ara's favorite fresh mangoes.

My cheeks are wet with tears, and I don't have a chance to pull back as the black crackle in the center of Ara's soul brushes at my fingers. Hate rolls through me. I see the òyìnbó, the slash of their mouths on their pale faces. Then come the Tapa, the greed and violence of the Nupe Kingdom, and Idera. Prayers that carry darkness within them; the lurking power of the ajogun.

Spreading.

Influencing.

I jerk back, away from the shadowed part of Ara's soul, a sob caught in my throat as her essence dissipates. What she has done is unfathomable, but so is what has happened to her.

"Àláfíà ni tìrẹ báàyí," I murmur as I ease her body from my lap. Gently, I undo the sapphire necklace, sliding it from Ara's neck and holding it tight. "Peace is yours now, sister. I'm sorry I didn't protect you."

Kola forces Arun back toward the tree, his blade parrying the clawed swipes of the ajogun as he resists. I run to Kola's side, thrusting at the warlord as he tries to slip to the right. We keep him in place, only managing to land a few blows before Esu draws closer to the tree, the ruby at his chest burning a brilliant red, matching the soul song's vibrant hue.

Ofo, the warlord of loss, is partially emerged, attempting to climb free. He screeches as the essence hovers closer to the opening, the flares of red and gold burning his raven limbs. The antigod whips his arm away, sinking back down into the depths of the tree. Kola lunges forward, leaping into the air, kicking out at Arun's chest, pushing him after Ofo, back into the mouth of the Ya-Te-Veo.

Esu's words become a scream, and the soul song grows in response, a broad twist of red with threads of crackling gold woven throughout. The energy descends, hovering over Arun, searing his skin and forcing him deeper into the gateway of the tree. The scent of fire and ash fills the air as Esu's howling voice reaches fever pitch, the power of the Mokele-mbembe's essence brightening, as the ajogun cowers from it, dipping down so that just the top of his head is visible. The blaze of gold in the soul song grows, searing the cracked mouth of the tree, serrated teeth retracting, drawing down into the pulsating trunk.

"A ti'lẹ̀kùn gbọigbọin. Mo dè ẹ́. Ò lágbára mọ́ ní ibíyìí." The ruby ignites, mimicking an incandescent sunset as sweat runs down Esu's chest. He brings his fingers to the gem, holding it aloft as he repeats the prayer. "Sealed and closed. I bind you. You have no power here anymore."

The energy of the soul song lowers further, ringing the maw of the Ya-Te-Veo. The gateway begins to shrink, its bark darkening until there is nothing left but an ashen and misshapen seam.

Esu leans against the trunk, more sweat dripping down his forehead. His plaits hang forward, concealing his face.

I return to Ara, gazing down through the blur of tears. When I look up at Kola, he just wraps his arms around me, letting me sob against his chest as grief rises, threatening to consume me.

Shouts outside and the distant clang of weapons can be heard, reminding us that the battle is still raging.

"We need to go," says Kola gently. He turns to Esu. "Is it done?"

"I will need to perform other rituals to continue to appease them. There is much to make up for." The muscles in Esu's back ripple as he heaves in breath after breath. "But they are bound for now, and this particular gateway to our realm is closed."

"Can anything else be done in Oko?" asks Kola, his gaze skittering over the Ya-Te-Veo. "Perhaps the babalawo can help."

Esu turns away from us, the ruby settled on his chest, back to its crimson hue. Strands of the soul song cling to the sealed gash in the tree, beginning to fade even as we watch. "It can be done elsewhere."

I step closer to the Ya-Te-Veo. Its trunk flexes, and a bulge presses against the bark. I think of all it has brought, the power it leaked from the ajogun's nearness, the greed it created and added to. The skulls that glint among the roots, all the lives lost to its hunger, to the craving of the humans who nurtured it, to the anti-gods it nearly gave passage to. Next to its monstrous roots, Ara's body is slumped. My stomach curdles at it all.

"Burn it." My voice is small but I steel my tone. "You sealed it, but we should burn it as well."

Kola stands close to me, his eyes going to the skulls picked free of flesh and hair.

"We need to leave," says Esu as he moves to my other side. "The ajogun are bound. They can't enter our realm now."

"I don't care if you claim this gateway is closed." I can't take my eyes off the Ya-Te-Veo, hands flat against my thighs as I try to stay calm. "It must be gone. All of it."

Kola sees the look on my face and rushes to the sconces, wrenching two from the wall and stalking to the tree.

"Wait." Esu lifts his hands as his ruby flares once more. Shreds of soul song cling to the tree, and at his touch, they jump up like a fire revived. He curls his fingers as the redness spreads, heat and ribbons of gold at its core. The orisa controls the essence, the ruby glowing against his chest as he grows the soul song once again. It spreads, scorching the trunk, sweeping to the branches and vines, scalding leaves and igniting the tendrils that begin to writhe.

We watch as the Ya-Te-Veo bursts into flames, out of reach of the burning branches that try to snake toward us. As the fire licks at the skulls and the flames reach for the ceiling, I look up, following the billow of smoke. Consumed in the red-and-gold inferno, the dome above us is painted in black cinders, revealed for what it truly holds—the rot and greed of humans and the entryway for darker forces of the world made incarnate.

Kola pulls at me as the heat grows closer. We turn to the door, the chamber behind us alight with the fury of the Mokelembembe's soul song.

"It will burn now until nothing is left!" shouts Esu as he brings up the rear. "Go!"

We sprint through the corridor, the stark depictions of Arun, Ofo, Egba, Oran, Epe, Ewon, and Ese glaring down at us. As we pass each mask of the ajogun, they ignite, bright fire eating away at the wood. Kola wrenches the main doors open to a stream of cold night air.

I turn to watch as the passageway behind us is consumed. The only mask that has not burned is Iku's. The warlord's large, pointed face has deep grooves of a frown above eyes thinned into flat black holes. The mask stares blankly at us as the walls on either side of it collapse and the great doors blaze a violent black and red.

• • •

The night washes over us, and with stinging soles, I stagger onto the path, Kola gripping my arm to stop me from keeling over. The loss of Ara and the stifling heat of the fire make it hard to breathe. I pull away from him, taking a few seconds to draw in cold breaths that chill my seared lungs. Above us hangs the full moon, round with a yellow light that shines down on the city and the surrounding terrain.

Uncurling my fingers, I allow myself a look at Folasade's necklace. When the grief starts to surge, I push it back, clutching the sapphire in a tight fist. There is no time now.

"We may have pacified the warlords, but there are still the Tapa," Kola says.

Esu stalks away from the blazing temple, his ruby now a dark burgundy, glimmering against the skin of his chest. "Even without the adzes and the obambo, I do not particularly want to be caught next to the smoldering ruins of their temple."

The streets are quiet, but the echoes of battle are carried to us on the night breeze.

"Can you walk now?" asks Kola, his hand hovering near my waist.

I nod and draw myself up straight. "I'm all right." Each breath is becoming easier. "Let's go."

We move quickly through the streets of Rabah, pressing against the walls of compounds, avoiding the tall burning palm-oil lights. Men and women pass by us, many heading to the temple to attempt to put out the fire, but others are securing the gates. The Tapa are retreating behind their walls.

When we reach the gateway, it is to find a large group attempting to fortify the wooden panels. We pause, hovering in the ink-dark shadows. Kola lifts his sword, but I block his way, my hands pushing the boy's weapon down.

"There is no need for more killing," I say softly. "Please."

Esu steps forward, nodding once at me before leaving the shadows. We watch him go, his hair transforming into the shorter cut with a folded braid on top favored by the Tapa, wrapper changing color to black with yellow triangles. The trickster calls out a greeting and then joins in the effort to barricade the gate, helping to hammer in a thick bar of wood. He accepts the thanks of the weary Tapa and tells them that help is needed at the central gate. With his back to the wall, and promises to defend the entryway, he waits until the Tapa have left before beckoning us over, his tall figure and swinging braids forming once again.

Ripping off the fortifications with ease, Esu opens the gates and ushers us through before drawing them closed behind us. With the sapphire digging into my palm, I step outside Rabah's walls and into a fresh graveyard. Mounds of bodies, both Oyo and Tapa, dot the earth, and as I take in the fallen, I see a few wisps of souls that quickly spiral into the cool night air.

The dead surround us.

It didn't have to be this way.

But power leads to corruption, and as we ease our way past the bodies, this is at the forefront of my mind.

Ara.

She really did believe that she could command the ajogun, something she would never have considered when we were younger, but her time in the Nupe Kingdom stole more than her freedom. It took her goodness, her logic, her faith in Ifá.

As we pick our way through the corpses and the gouges in the earth where the obambo emerged, I think of all the lives lost in the pursuit of power, and then I see a vision not of the enemy corpses around me but of men and women who became lost. Each one trying to maintain their way of life, loyal to their leader, putting their trust in the elders and council of their kingdom. Even though they chose violence, was this really their free will?

"Olódùmarè, gbà àwọn ọmọ yín ti wọn ba dé'lé. Ẹ jọọ́, ṣàánú wọn. Dáríjì wọn." There are too many to say separate words for, and their souls have already moved on, but I murmur my prayer over and over. "Olodumare, receive your children when they return home. Please show them mercy and forgiveness."

Esu and Kola move toward the hill where we made camp, and when I see the cluster of people at the top, I feel the spreading glow of faith. A tall figure looms over them, wheeling his arms as we begin to run.

"You're here!" Bem wraps his arms around his friend before releasing him and sweeping me up in a giant hug. "I am so glad that you're all right." I lean into his chest, closing my eyes briefly.

Kola clasps his friend to him again, thumping his chest before leaving us to weave between the survivors, hope and grief vying for control of his expression. I see him counting how many are left, only half of those who set out. The people of his village are resting or aiding those who need to be healed, but their spirits are strong. An Oyo victory has been declared. Tunde charges toward us, scrapes and smears of dried blood streaking his armor, but otherwise unharmed. The animal curls his trunk around Kola and blows softly as the boy rubs his hand down Tunde's flank.

"Where's Yinka?" I snap my gaze around the group huddled together. "How many of the bultungin survived?"

"I'm here." Yinka's voice comes from my left. She limps closer, holding her right side. "The pack is whole."

"What happened?" I gasp, rushing to her.

"It's nothing."

"It is not *nothing*," argues Aissa as she moves to Yinka's side, hand on her arm. "She fought three obambo on her own."

I open my mouth but my words are stopped by the archer I

saw when we left Oko, the one saying good-bye to her children and husband. She leans forward, touching the ground in front of Yinka before straightening up. Her brown-and-white skin shines with sweat and she rubs at a smear of blood on her cheek.

"My thanks. Over and over, Olayinka." The archer trembles before us, tears running down her cheeks as she holds a bloodied fist to her heart. "I would have died."

Yinka reaches out and places a hand on the woman's shoulder. "Stop, sister. We are all we have. And we fight for each other. Always."

"To the end," chants the archer.

"To the end." Yinka smiles as the archer retreats and Aissa fusses around her, checking her side and forcing her to sit down.

"Is it done? Esu has bound the ajogun?"

I nod, sinking down, accepting a waterskin from Aissa and drinking deeply. The taste of ashes is still there and I tip my head back, trying to drown it. Yinka grins, clapping me on the back once.

"Did you find Ara?"

Her question is simple, but when I begin to answer, I find that I can't. Instead, I hunch forward, staring at my feet as Yinka wraps her arms around me.

CHAPTER TWENTY-SEVEN

OKO WELCOMES US as the sun breaks free from the skyline, bursts of orange and red that frame the tops of trees. The gates are thrown open, cheers and the spicy tang of roasted goat rising through the morning air. Drums and singing begin as prayers of thanks are offered through wide smiles and tears.

I watch as a small girl and boy run between the compounds, bare feet slapping hard on the ground. The archer weaves through the crowd of Oko warriors and runs to her children, sweeping them up and clasping their tiny bodies against hers. Others find their families, sobs and laughs and smiles mingling with the sorrow for those who have been lost.

The wounded are laid on stretchers as healers rush forward and Bem coordinates. Kola slips from Tunde's back and asks the animal to kneel so that he can help the few wounded he carried on the walk home. The boy walks among the villagers of Oko, smiling and accepting their thanks, stopping to speak with several elders who are gathered on a corner.

He's a natural. It's quite clear that his people love him. A girl not much older than me approaches him, dropping to touch the ground in front of him in respect. As she rises, she averts her eyes, but a smile lights up her face.

My heart beats a little too hard, but I try to ignore it. Kola's place is here, after all. I back away slowly, letting the sea fill my mind. I think of what I will say to Yemoja, to help her understand that I am more than ready to fulfill all of my duties. Even now, the sea calls to me, a small need that grows with every day I spend out of it. I think of cool waves, slips of currents, and the way the water enfolds me, welcoming me, blessing me. I've taken a few steps, turning to the still-open gates, when two hands take mine and pull me to a stop.

"Simidele!"

I turn to the outraged faces of Kehinde and Taiwo. "Where are you going? You're going to miss the celebrations."

"I . . ."

But the twins don't let me finish, turning me around and yanking me toward the marketplace teeming with villagers. Laughter rings out and I can't help but smile at the joy, proud and grateful to see that Oko and its people are safe.

Kola is already there, greeting his parents. I watch as he gently hugs his father before his mother throws her arms around him. When she finally lets Kola go, I see him look around again, his gaze raking through the crowd until it lands on me.

The twins pull me toward their brother. Kola stands still, taller than those around him, skin burnished and glowing in the sunlight. I still can't believe how much he has changed since I took him from the sea—from the wide set of his shoulders to the short beard that peppers his chin and cheeks. But it's not just that. Kola has done whatever has been needed to keep his people safe. It is as it should be.

I muster a smile and walk toward him as the crowd clears for dancers. As fabrics of white and blue whirl around us, Kola pulls me to the side. "Come, the others are waiting."

He turns to the path that leads to his compound, holding my hand tightly. I run to keep up with him, ignoring my aching feet, light at the heat of his touch. "Where are we going?" I ask.

"You'll see."

We veer past his compound and head down the back of the guards' until we get to the gate of Tunde's enclosure. A laugh rings out and then Kola is tugging me inside. Trees hang over the clearing, their palm leaves affording us shade as I venture forward. Yinka is dabbing at the few gouges Tunde received while Bem hauls a large bundle of grass over.

"I found her," announces Kola, nudging me toward them.

Yinka straightens up and grins at me, wiping her hands and bounding over. She wraps me in a crushing hug and then releases me. "Kola wanted to celebrate with just us first."

"We'll join the villagers after," he says. He slips inside Tunde's food store and returns with a flask of palm wine and four copper cups.

"Yes, after I've washed." Bem lifts his arms and wrinkles his nose. "So that I properly look the part of a hero. And smell like one."

"I think I'm more heroic," says Yinka as she lays down a large woven blanket for us to sit on. "I definitely killed more of the obambo than you."

"Hmph. Helped by the fact that you can change into a huge hyena," grumbles Bem as he lowers himself onto the ground. "An unfair advantage. In fact, I knew you'd pull that one out sooner or later. Use it to try to make me feel inadequate."

"Would I ever do that?" asks Yinka, batting her lashes and laughing.

Smiling, I sit down next to them and take the cup Kola offers me. My shoulders relax as my grin grows. To be here, like this . . . no sense of urgency or worry. I can't quite remember the last time I felt this way.

"You were all magnificent," adds Kola, beaming at us.

We sip our drinks and talk through the battle and what happened at the temple, until Bem complains that his cup is empty and demands a refill.

Once we all have more palm wine, Kola raises his cup, his eyes glowing ocher. "Thank you. I want to say thank you to you all. For always putting Oko first. For helping me even though it meant you might be hurting yourself. For being by my side no matter what." Kola looks at Bem and Yinka in turn before his gaze lands on me. "I wouldn't be here today without you. Any of you. And I know that when I am Oko's leader, it will be as much because of your loyalty and sacrifice as it will be because of mine."

Yinka and Bem cheer and then we are drinking, finishing the small cup of palm wine in one swallow. Yinka smacks her lips and jumps to her feet, pulling Bem to his. "Go. Go and get that wash now. You smell worse than Tunde. I don't think I can take it anymore."

"I could say the same. You smell like one of those wild dogs that stole our chickens."

They bicker as they head to the gate and I am left with Kola, who is gathering the cups and avoiding my gaze. I lean forward to help him, but he stops.

"I saw you about to leave."

I don't answer but fold my hands in my lap. "I need to let Yemoja know that the ajogun are bound."

"You won't come back." It's not a question and I don't answer. Instead, I stand up, feeling dizzy at the blood rush to my head as Kola does the same.

Nothing has changed, I want to say. I am Mami Wata. But I shake my head and turn to the gate.

"Your place is in Oko and mine is with Yemoja. I told you before—"

"But I'm orisa."

"And you are still needed here." I thought that Kola as orisa might be a way for us to be together, let possibilities slide around my mind. But it doesn't stop Oko from being his home, nor does it end my duty to Yemoja. "It's not just that. You belong in Oko. And I don't."

Kola frowns, trying to pick his away around it all. I reach for him, standing on tiptoes, the earth warm beneath my feet as I twine my arms around his neck. Kola's arms do not go around me immediately, but when they do, he squeezes tightly.

"So much has happened," I whisper.

"Well then, can't we somehow . . . I don't know." He tenses beneath my touch. "Can't we . . . try?"

"What's expected of us, what is needed from us, has changed, though. It's bigger. You'll be Oko's leader." I force a smile. "A brilliant one." I rest my chin on his shoulder, and then I let go. "And I am needed by Yemoja."

"Simi . . ."

But I don't answer. Instead, I turn away, vision wavy, holding my breath in. It has to be like this, I tell myself, hurrying out of Tunde's enclosure before I can look back and see Kola's face. Sometimes we have to choose something other than what we want. I think of Folasade's sacrifice and the many that Yemoja has made, and I keep walking.

The sounds of singing and laughter accompany me as I wind my way through the streets, heading for Oko's gates, wiping my face roughly. My feet are hurting, each step a stinging pain. I know that the sea will soothe them—my heart, I'm not so sure.

"Little fish, are you leaving?" Esu steps out from the cool shadows of a compound on my right.

"I'm returning to Yemoja." I pause, sniffing once and lifting my chin. I will not let this pain rule me. "Where I truly belong. Where I'm still needed."

The trickster leans against the wall and I brace myself for a clever reply, but he merely nods. His response throws me off and I look up at him, trying to see if there is any other meaning.

"And you?" I ask. "Where will you go?"

Esu taps his nose and grins, his eyes flashing silver. "I will do the necessary rituals to keep the ajogun at bay. Although that gateway is destroyed, they have never been so close." He lifts his hand to stroke the ruby hanging from his neck, eyebrows raised high. The gem flashes once, a scarlet glimmer, a mere whisper of its power. "Let it be known that I do not shirk my duties. Journey well, Mami Wata."

• • •

I'm limping by the time I reach the edge of the sea, relieved as I stand in the shallows and my scales start to form, cutting through sun-darkened skin. The water welcomes me, caressing me in cold waves of blue as I sink beneath the surface.

The swim to Yemoja's island only takes a few hours. I emerge on her shore as the rain starts to fall, tangled drops from a sky ripe with the coming night, the shade seen on the seven indigo-and-white blooms I offer to the water. Yemoja's summoning wave of water rears up, scraping the sky, the same hue. This time I don't wait for it to crash against the beach; instead, I stagger forward on the feet that swap skin and bones for a caudal fin, and plunge into the sea. The fan of my tail bursts forth from transformed legs, gold scales flashing in the muted light. My entry seems to break the swell and the water pushes against the land, forcing me to swim deeper against the sudden pull.

Sand swirls with crabs, stones, and silt but I ignore it all, fighting through the waves until I see the shine of white gold, the thick twist of black hair, and the silver slash of Yemoja's gaze.

"Simidele, what is it?" Her voice grazes me, as rough as the sand and the rocks beneath us. "You could not wait?"

I don't answer. Hanging poised in the water for a moment, I think of the soft arrangement of Folasade's dead body, of the ruin of Ara's. And then I am rushing forward, bubbles peppering my skin, the clean scent of the cold water cutting through me, scoring my bones as I reach the orisa. Snaking my arms around the scales of Yemoja's waist, I press my face against the hot skin of her stomach and let out the wail that I've kept trapped inside me for too long.

The orisa wraps her arms around my back, her large hands moving in circles against the bones of my spine. I cry until the sea has swallowed all of my tears and only then do I pull away. Yemoja holds me carefully, her long fingers around my arms.

"Is it done? Are the ajogun bound?"

I nod, but still I do not raise my gaze. How can I tell her that Folasade is gone?

"Well done, Simidele." Yemoja places a hand to her heart, smile flashing like a curved bone. "I am honored." She releases my arm and looks beyond me, into the layers of black blue. "And what of Folasade?"

I want to hold on to her praise, but I can't. Trying to push my shoulders down, to find the courage to tell her what has happened, I squeeze the necklace tighter in my right hand. The words slither away, sticking in the soft thickness of my throat, refusing to be coaxed forth. Shaking, I bring my closed fist between us, slowly opening it until the blue gem sparkles before us, another hue of indigo that the sea recognizes, currents swirling at the power the stone holds.

Yemoja's intake of breath is sharp, her lips bitten between pointed teeth. Gently, she takes the jewel from my lined palm, the golden links of the necklace bright in the depths.

"Folasade's?"

Trembling, I raise my eyes to the orisa's. "Yes."

Yemoja draws the sapphire to her chest, pressing the gem against the beat of her heart. With her eyes closed and curls spiraling around us, she opens her mouth and keens. It is filled with the pain and rage and sorrow that curdle within me, threatening to burst out.

"She suffered." I bow my head at the orisa's words, shamed by their plain truth. "But the courage she showed was immense?"

"Yes, Mother Yemoja." Nails scrape at my chin, lifting my face to Yemoja's. "I'm sorry. So sorry. I should have—"

"There are no 'should haves,' my daughter. What's done is

done." The orisa gazes above us at the sun that splashes the waves, but she still clasps the necklace to her chest, knuckles tight. "Did you return her?"

"I did. She will be forever at one with the sea." My gaze is drawn to the surface, to the light that dapples the shifting mass. I think of the delicate frill of foam, Folasade's final form.

"Your fortitude is admired." Yemoja faces me now. "You have shown again your love for all."

I hang my head, the shame too much; it destroys any of the words Yemoja chooses for me. They will not bring back Folasade or unmake Ara from the person she was in the end.

"I would ask that you allow me to return. To do all that you created me for. I want to do what is right. Since Folasade . . ." I gulp, trying to find the right words. "Since Folasade is gone, I want to make sure there is no lack in gathering souls." I look up into Yemoja's black-and-silver eyes. "And perhaps find a way to see my parents. To check that after all the Oyo Kingdom has endured, they are well."

"Simidele." The orisa says my name only once before tilting her head to one side, scales and skin glimmering. "Your curiosity and questions have always been unlike the others'. You follow your heart, and that is what has saved so many, time and time again." Yemoja's long curls drift in the currents around us, coils as black as the deep. "Do not let your sorrow or guilt destroy you. Be proud of all that you have done. All that you are. Mami Wata . . . yet more." The orisa holds her arms out to me and I swim into them. "I release you."

Yemoja's simple whispered words have me drawing back in confusion, water swirling between us. The orisa lowers her head, her veil swaying.

"What do you mean?" I ask, eyes wide in the chill of the sea.

"That you will always be Mami Wata, that you can return to fulfill those duties when you so wish. That after all you have done, you deserve something more. Now that you have all of your memories back, not knowing how your parents are will eat away at you, just as your guilt has done." Yemoja smiles, the tilt of her full lips framed by glistening pearls. "Simidele, I would not see you unhappy. I am giving you the gift of choice. You are free to follow your own path."

My hands slide through the water, resting on my scales as I stare at the orisa in shock. "But . . ."

"This is your freedom. Just as I offered you salvation, a way to survive, when I first found you, I am offering you something more now."

Freedom to be who I choose, go where I want? I open my mouth to answer just as a shaft of bright light penetrates the waves and shines on Yemoja, spreading its warm glow to me. When the water swirls around us, a tug deep inside me pulls my gaze up to where the smooth wooden hull of a ship cuts through the waves.

"And now you will be faced with another decision." Yemoja tips her head to the tops of the waves and pushes me gently away from her. "But remember, you must choose what is right for you, not just what you think you desire, Simidele."

"What other choice is there?" But even as I ask this, I know who the ship belongs to.

"He has come for you. He never gave up his search when you were in the Land of the Dead. You have been connected ever since you helped guide his soul back to his body."

Kola.

Yemoja lays a hand on my cold cheek. "Do not deny your feelings."

"He is orisa now. The babalawo has declared it." I peer up through the water. "But it doesn't matter." Even saying it hurts my chest. Leaving him again was always a certainty, even though I fought against the knowledge of it. "Kola is of the land . . . where he belongs."

The orisa keeps her black eyes on me, serrated silver in her pupils. "That is untested and undefined as yet. And so are his strengths."

"How so?" I turn away from the surface to face Yemoja.

"Orisas caught powers that Olodumare rained down on the earth. This you know. But Adekola is deified only now, and so his powers are not yet confirmed." Yemoja slips a look upward. "We do not know whether he is of the land, water, or air."

The ship above slows, and something in me wants it to be because of what Kola senses beneath the layers of currents. A sliver of hope plants itself deep inside my heart.

Yemoja holds out the sapphire necklace to me. "You could help him make that choice."

The gem hangs at the end of the thick twist of golden chain. Identical to mine, one of only seven. Yemoja's number. Offered to the first of those taken by the òyìnbó who ended up in the water far from home.

I reach for the jewel, my hand shaking. "You would give him the same as Mami Wata?"

"You have renounced so much. But every sacrifice has its reward." Yemoja leans forward and places the necklace in my hands. "Not only am I offering your freedom, but I would also give Kola whatever power the sapphire brings, and you the chance to be with him."

CHAPTER TWENTY-EIGHT

"ONE DAY, SIMIDELE, you will have to make a decision that will determine a great part your life."

I look up at the sky. There are only two clouds, small and wisplike. Against the deep blue, they look as if they might fade away at any moment. I turn my head to my mother, who is sitting beside me on the riverbank, eyes closed, face tipped to the yellow sun. Her hair is braided tight in rows of repeating patterns that follow the curve of her head. She leans back, her arms corded with muscle, a light blue wrapper with white swirls tucked around her chest. I smile at the tilt of her lips, the peace in the smoothness of her expression. Tenderness blooms inside me and I raise a hand to her hair, fingers grazing the end of one of her plaits. She catches my hand and presses a kiss to my palm.

Laughing gently, I turn to the water that roars around us, already thinking about slipping beneath its surface, sinking to the bottom where the light will barely reach.

"What choices do you mean, ìyá?"

She shifts, letting her soles dip into the cool water before she turns to me, a hand shading her eyes. "I mean love."

We have marked my seventeenth birthday at the river Ogun as we always celebrate the day. Full with the deep-fried dough balls we brought with us, we laze in the sun, enjoying the sounds of the water and nothing else.

"Love?" I snort. "I don't need that." All I want at this moment is to explore the riverbed, my hair a wave of stretched-out coils, cold currents on my sun-soaked skin.

"That is what you think now. There are many different kinds. But one in particular will catch you when you least expect it." My mother laughs and lies back down, one hand cushioning her head. "And then you will have to choose whether to fight it or embrace it."

Curls ripple across my face. Yemoja's eyes are on me, wide with silver light and the hint of a smile. I pull my hair away so that my vision is filled with her pearls and coils of gold, her skin luminous in the shine of the sun-filled water. The thunder of my blood fills my ears as bubbles pop around us, churned by Kola's ship above.

"But why? You said that—"

"I said that you could not let yourself feel for a human." Yemoja pauses, stroking the sapphire around my neck. "Now? Kola is changed. And with this sapphire, there is another choice to be made."

The necklace nestles in my cupped hands. I close my fingers around it once again and glance up at the sky, wavy through the sea.

"Simidele, I would rather Folasade's gem be used for this." The orisa's voice lowers now, as smooth as a ribbon of black silk that winds through the water. "Something just as pure as she was. You can present it to Kola, and the rest is up to you both."

A thick beam of sun pierces the water, lighting us up as a sudden panic rips through me. I swallow, trembling as Yemoja looks down at me. "What if it doesn't work?"

"The sapphire's essence is one bound with love, not destruction." Yemoja hesitates, her pearl veil clicking gently in the current. "I cannot say what it will fully bring for Adekola, but it should enhance his strengths. But remember, daughter, you must choose your own path. And what is best is not always what we think we want."

I clutch the gem to my chest, feeling the thrum of my heartbeat just as the ship begins to move on, its wooden hull a dark shadow above. My eyes follow the bottom of the vessel.

The want for him was planted a long time ago. In the sea filled with Kola's blood and bravery. In the way he looked at me and saw more than Mami Wata, more than the girl I was. I press my lips together and nod once at Yemoja.

"I will ask him."

I rise in a white shaft of light, the necklace clutched so tightly that the sapphire digs into my hand.

The sea rocks in a shifting plane of gray-blue as I slit the surface, rising to the late-afternoon sun. I gasp, sucking in a deep breath of warm air. Sunlight slants on gentle waves that cradle me and push me closer to the ship that has turned back, heading toward land.

My heart pounds against the clasp of my fist pressed to the pink and gold of my scales. I look down to make sure I still have the sapphire, even though its sharp edges are scored into my flesh, and then I begin to swim.

The sea is a whisper of sighs and gentle caresses that push me against the roll of water, carrying me closer to the vessel. I follow the ship, gaining on it as it slows, the wind falling. When I reach the hull, the sun blinds me as I raise my face. A head appears over the side, wreathed in yellow light, features blurred by the dazzle of an already hot day. I squint until my eyes refocus on a brown gaze that I would never be able to forget.

Kola bends so far over the side of the ship that I think he will fall. There is no ladder for me to climb, and this seems to enter both our minds at once, for he stands on the rail of his ship, his hands outstretched, silhouette like a cross, skin burning dark against the bright sky behind him. And then he is bringing his arms forward, leaning into the light and air, aiming the knife of his body at the sea.

The water receives him, enfolding his limbs in a cool swirl. I dive beneath the waves, following Kola's bubbled descent as he opens his eyes to my world. This time, there are no curls of blood in the sea and the flash of his eyes doesn't disconcert me. There are no òyìnbó ships or sharks lurking, tasting his near death and wanting more. I reach for Kola, my fingers brushing the satin of his skin, still warm from the sun above.

Kola smiles, not caring about the cold water that slides over his teeth. As I draw him to me, his arms loop around my waist, palms resting on scales until they slide down to the base of my spine, pressing my chest against his. I rest my forehead against Kola's, letting my curls tickle our faces, to envelop us in clouds of black.

When he pulls me toward the top of the sea, I let him, the necklace in my fist still, heart beating harder at the thought of what it means for us. We burst into sunlight and a breeze that steals my first breath.

"Simi," murmurs Kola, and the shape of his lips with my name in his mouth makes me shiver. "You need to stop leaving me. How many times must I say this?"

"What are you doing? Why are you here?" I ask, even though I know the answer.

Kola kicks to keep himself above the waves but water slops into the smile he offers me. "I came to find you. To tell you that I know you're set on helping Yemoja, but it doesn't mean we can't be together."

My eyes meet his, heart a quick thrum in my chest. Kola's skin glows in the sunlight, his cheekbones sharp and gilded.

"Even though you are of the sea, I am orisa. There must be a way." He reaches out to touch one of my curls, droplets of water sparkling as they fall from his fingertips. "We can try. We can find it."

Yemoja's words repeat in my mind as I stare into Kola's eyes, holding on tightly to him. She's given me my freedom—and with it, a decision.

The thought of all the possibilities burns through me. Love. And home. Oyo-Ile flashes through my mind, the mahogany tree that shades my home from the midday sun, the hot earth and the light that bounces off the shining compound walls.

"What if there's a way already?" I whisper, and open my hand to reveal the sapphire. The jewel sits in my palm, glittering in all the colors of the sky and sea.

"Folasade's?"

I nod, keeping my hand open, the gem's edges dark blue. "Yemoja said I could offer it to you. It would mean the sea claims you in some way." Raising my gaze to his, I catch the flash of his surprise. My hands quiver, the chain glinting. "She's not sure what it would mean . . . for you as orisa, but she said it could make you stronger."

"Would it also mean that we could be together?" Kola's voice rises with hope, his hands encircling my waist. He holds me in place as I trace fingers over his jaw, trailing them upward into the black kinks of his hair.

"This is what she thinks." My voice is low, want and fear tangled up inside me. "But—"

Kola releases me, icy water swirling where his warm grip was. I only have a moment to miss his touch before he plucks the necklace from my open hand. He holds the golden links against the wet skin of his neck, feet kicking, keeping him above the waterline.

He closes the clasp, the sapphire sparkling against the gleam of his muscles and brown skin, seawater sliding from his shoulders.

"What do you feel?" I ask, even though he smiles at me, the light brown flecks in his eyes glinting.

Kola doesn't answer, swimming closer. His large hands reach for my face, cupping my cheeks. We sway in the sea, eyes on each other as the waves whisper quiet secrets and the sea gulls call out overhead. His thumb slips down, running over the corner of my lip; his other hand shifts underneath wet hair to cradle the back of my neck. I don't move as he brings his head down, his parted lips so near to mine.

Kola draws me closer as I tilt my face to his. The air and sea fold around us, heat and coolness, a witness to whatever will happen. I think of the day I found this boy in the sea, the frantic feeling of wanting to save him, to make sure he was safe. That has never left me, and even now, knowing he has accepted the sapphire, I want to pull away, to ask him again if he is sure.

Sure of me.

But I already know the answer, feel it, deep in my very bones. I brush my mouth above the corner of Kola's, feeling the same pull I felt when I saw his ship. He stills beneath my touch as my fingertips skate across his shoulders, holding him steady.

"Simi," Kola whispers, hands splayed on my back. He holds me carefully, his gaze never leaving mine.

I look up into the brown of his eyes, his lids heavy, sure that he must be able to feel the crash of my heart against his chest. Slowly, Kola leans down, lips parted. I stay very still, breath caught and held. And then Kola fits his mouth against mine and, for a moment, it feels as if the sea stops, pausing in its incessant tides, currents frozen, waves captured in the crush of what is happening. I slide my hands around his neck as the warmth of his lips spreads to mine and the breeze whips my hair into a black storm around us. Closing my eyes, I taste salt on the brown pink of Kola's bottom lip, feel the heat of his skin as his hands squeeze my waist.

I have wanted this for so long that my chest feels tight, as if my heart might burst. But with my freedom, the gift of the sapphire, and Kola's kiss, I wonder . . . Could I be more than someone who loved a boy she shouldn't? Could I also be the daughter my parents think they have lost? Someone to help stave off the òyìnbó, to make our lands more secure. I could be more, I know it.

Kola draws away and I instantly miss the heat of him against me. When I open my eyes, it is to the blaze of the sun. The sea moves once again, lifting us up on its white-foamed back, offering us to shredded clouds and the heavens above.

"I choose you and you choose me," he whispers, leaning forward to place his lips on mine again.

Choice, I think as our kiss turns into a press of teeth and salt and sea, as waves frill and pleat around us, my tail holding us just above the water. I have the gift of choice, now more than ever. And the decision rises in me, new and raw and burning with possibilities.

When I pull away, I look to Kola's boat. "I want to go back."

"To Oko?" he asks, hope lifting his words, mouth stretching into a grin.

I take a deep breath and hold his hand, bringing it to my mouth, kissing the twist of our fingers. I know now what I want, what I must do. Kola sees my expression and tightens his grip as he leans closer to me.

"What is it? Are you not coming with me?" A sliver of worry lines his tone.

I swallow, my heart thudding. "I will," I whisper as I let go of him, hands slipping from sea-slicked skin. "But not now. I choose you, but I also choose me."

Kola doesn't say anything, his eyes skating over mine. He frowns, a small groove marring his expression. "I don't understand."

"Now that I have every memory, every part of me back, I choose the freedom Yemoja has given me." I smile, and my hands sink under the water, finding his again. "I need to go home."

"To Oyo-Ile?"

I nod, ìyá's soothing voice and bàbá's laugh rising in my mind. The richness of my mother's stories and the crisp smell of the many parchments my father studied. "I want to make sure my parents are all right. To let them know that I am . . . still here. Still alive. They most likely think I'm dead," I say softly. "I hate the thought of them in such pain."

Kola pulls me closer, fingers clutching at mine. "I can come with you . . . ," he says, voice cracking. "I can help."

Shaking my head, I lift my hands, holding his face, drawing him down to me again, our foreheads pressed against each other's. Wanting to remember it all.

"I need to do this. I want to do more." My eyes dart to his, willing him to understand. "If I go back to Oyo-Ile, I can tell them everything I know about the òyìnbó, about the patrolling ships.

About Sango and Oya." I squeeze Kola's hands again, our fingers interlocked. "It doesn't mean that I don't choose you. I do. Just not right now. You're needed in Oko and I . . . I have to do this."

Kola stares down at me as a cloud passes overhead. My stomach drops at his expression, but then he wraps his arms around me.

"You'll find me?" he asks, his voice lighter than his words, eyes glittering.

I smile once before pressing my mouth carefully to his, the sun burning down on us. When I pull away, I lift the sapphire that hangs on his chest, holding it gently.

"We are bound now, no matter what," I say as the gem at my throat blazes the brilliant shade of a clear sky. "And I will always find you."

I let go of Kola as the waves push between us, cold water replacing warm skin. The afternoon light bounces off the shifting surface of the sea as the tide tugs at me. I smile, gripping my sapphire. I can still see the glow of Kola's matching gem as he bobs in place. He lifts one hand, nodding once at me, his mouth curving into a smile that matches mine. I know that this is not the end, that this is the right decision. We were brought together for a reason, one that has us returning to each other even when it seems impossible. Belief in this lets me dive back into the chill of the sea. I swim through shades of blue, heading for currents that will speed my journey home. I will find Kola again. But only after I have done what I need to.

I am Simidele and I choose to follow no one.

I choose to be me.

I choose to go home.

AUTHOR'S NOTE

Skin of the Sea was a book born of yearning to see magical beings with African origins, and it was an honor to return to that world with *Soul of the Deep*. This story continues to build on my passion for Black mermaids, traditional spiritual beliefs, gods, goddesses, legendary creatures, and the excellence of fifteenth-century West Africa.

As always, I sought to include details that not only add to the world of the story but also celebrate Black people, specifically Black women, in their talents and their creativity. Water drummers are one such aspect in *Soul of the Deep*. When I first heard about the Baka musicians who live near the Cameroon-Congo border and how they play the river like a drum, I was immediately intrigued. Seeing footage of women creating a beat and song with water . . . it crystallized in my soul. This music! The beauty and talent! It immediately became crucial for me to add this to the story.

In the vein of traditional spirituality, it was important to me to include an Egúngún ceremony, where a person masquerades as the ancestors, bestowing guidance and blessings and sometimes imparting warnings to the living. The performer and costumes bond as one—a physical embodiment of ancestors, gatekeepers to Olodumare, and those who have passed. There are different Egúngún to perform separate functions, with each possessing a powerful spiritual strength. The Egúngún are significant culturally and traditionally, and ceremonies are still performed today.

I also loved learning more about the orisas of the Ifá spiritual belief system. Orisas are a range of deified personalities with different stories and powers. But where there is light, there is always dark, and the opposite of orisas is the ajogun. In *Soul of the Deep* we encounter these anti-gods: the warlords of ruin, intent on the destruction of the world. They are kept at bay by Esu, a warden who ensures that the ajogun do not cause chaos. But what if Esu were not free to do this? With the orisa bound by Olokun at the end of *Skin of the Sea,* we are plunged into a world where the Nupe and Oyo kingdoms are left grappling with the malignant power of eight anti-gods.

These forces of opposition are not confined to the orisas and ajogun. Another theme in *Soul of the Deep* surrounds the Portuguese, and later other Europeans, and the ramifications of their presence in West Africa. I wanted to touch on the rivalry between different groups of West Africans and how this conflict was exacerbated by the growing threat from colonizers. Europeans often took advantage of disputes between different groups to sustain a supply of prisoners of war for them to buy. In this vein we see the Nupe kingdom, its people known as the Tapa, as adversaries of the Oyo—a historically documented regional rivalry. It was important for me to include a representation of this in *Soul of the Deep* because this encouragement of discord, and the subsequent reaping of the "benefits" it yielded, became a key part of the transatlantic slave trade.

Integral to *Soul of the Deep* is the Mokele-mbembe—"one who stops the flow of rivers" in Lingala. This creature has been called the Loch Ness monster of Africa and is allegedly found in the Congo River basin. Some say it is a spirit, while others believe it may be a dinosaur. There have been many expeditions to find the

Mokele-mbembe, with multiple eyewitness accounts and even a few (somewhat) blurry photographs. Given the uncharted swathe of rain forest and flooded areas of Congo, who can say whether the Mokele-mbembe is real or not?

My stories are nothing without the darker elements, and I couldn't resist including adzes, obambo, and the Ya-Te-Veo—vampires, the undead, and a tree that eats people. How could I not include the tales of these mythical monsters passed down through generations of people from Madagascar to Ghana? They represent a sweeping range of legendary creatures across African cultures.

Soul of the Deep is the sequel to a story that explores magic, myth, and history. It is a continuation of the celebration of West Africa, spirituality, legends, creatures, and magical beings. I hope that readers will be immersed in a world of light and dark, a story of redemption and triumph, where sacrifice may not save you, but love always will.

FOR FURTHER INFORMATION

Adebowale, Oludamola. "Significance of Egungun in Yoruba Cultural History." *Guardian* (Lagos). guardian.ng/life/significance-of-egungun-in-yoruba-cultural-history

Hebblethwaite, Cordelia. "The Hunt for Mokele-mbembe: Congo's Loch Ness Monster." BBC. bbc.com/news/magazine-16306902

"Liquindi—Baka Women Water Drumming." Baka Beyond. March 15, 2011. YouTube video. youtube.com/watch?v=C7ba1CNOLiI

ACKNOWLEDGMENTS

I love *Skin of the Sea* so much that being able to dive back into Simi's world was a privilege. In a turbulent year, I can honestly say that writing has been one of the things that have kept me moving forward. Creating *Soul of the Deep* has been a welcome immersive experience, made even more amazing by the people in my life who support me and those I have the honor of working with.

My children deserve a huge amount of my gratitude. Always there to cheer me on, jump around with me at good news, listen, give feedback, and put up with me when I'm working nonstop. They make being a mother so enjoyable and (almost!) effortless.

Thank you to Clare, who continually inspires me with her work ethic and intense motivation. The saying "Surround yourself with people better than you" really does apply in your case.

Thank you to Penny, who always takes my calls, even when she knows she won't get a word in. You listen, cajole, and advise like no one else.

Thank you to Charlene, who is one of the few people who talk as much as I do. You are the perfect person to spend ages obsessing over small details with and one of my trusted early readers. Your advice always helps, and I love that our talks often last longer than we both intend them to.

Jodi, I still think back to our first conversation and how I knew there and then that we would work well together. I truly appreciate your advice, humor, and constant support. Thank you for being there to always tell me to "scroll down."

Thank you, Namina Forna. From a random conversation in 2018 to now . . . your friendship is invaluable. Here's to many more trips together!

An author is the face of a book, and while we spend time to create it, the team behind us is integral to the finished story. Thank you, Tricia Lin. I love the conversations when we're saying the same things, often getting carried away with ideas that spark from each other. Your editorial direction and advice always hone my stories into something shinier and stunning. Thank you, Carmen McCullough. Your thoughtful and detailed comments help elevate my writing to higher levels. You are both incredible!

Thank you to the team at Random House and Penguin Random House UK, as well as Cecilia de la Campa and Alessandra Birch of Writers House, who have made my publishing journey a dream. I am immensely grateful to Mallory Loehr, Michelle Nagler, Caroline Abbey, Barbara Marcus, Jasmine Hodge, Regina Flath, Ken Crossland, Janet Foley, Rebecca Vitkus, Jake Eldred, Barbara Bakowski, Alison Kolani, Tracy Heydweiller, Lili Feinberg, Dominique Cimina, Caitlin Whalen, Sophia Cohen Smith, Emma Benshoff, Shaughnessy Miller, Emily DuVal, Kelly McGauley, John Adamo, and Erica Henegen. Your belief in me, your constant hard work, and your support help make my books magical. I appreciate you all so much.

Certain rappers defined my teenage years, and one of my favorites is Snoop Dogg. I remember listening to his speech when he received a star on the Hollywood Walk of Fame. I was in awe of his authenticity. After thanking the committee, the fans, other rappers, his loved ones, and people behind the scenes, he then

went on to thank . . . himself. He thanked himself for his hard work and dedication, for never quitting, and for being himself at all times. I think this was the first time I'd heard someone do that, but it makes so much sense. Not from an egotistical point of view, but because even with support, and especially at this time, it really is an achievement for us to stay strong, to stay motivated, and to stay positive. To consciously acknowledge ourselves and our efforts, as well as those who have helped us, is important. So, in the spirit of Snoop, this next thank-you is . . . to me. Thank you to myself for maintaining a positive mindset, for working hard but also listening to myself when I needed a break. Thank you to myself for staying strong and motivated even when it was difficult. Thank you to myself for never giving up.

Lastly, a huge thank-you for the support of readers who breathe life into the stories they read. To those who get excited and preorder, recommend books to friends, go to book festivals, make TikToks, buy special editions, check out books from the library, support their local bookstores, and so much more. Thank you. I am always immensely grateful for people who love stories as much as I do.

ABOUT THE AUTHOR

Natasha Bowen is a *New York Times* bestselling author, a teacher, and a mother of three children. She is of Nigerian and Welsh descent and lives in Cambridge, England, where she grew up. Natasha studied English and creative writing at Bath Spa University before moving to East London, where she taught for nearly ten years. She is obsessed with Japanese and German stationery and spends stupid amounts on notebooks, which she then features on her secret Instagram. When she's not writing, she's reading, watched over carefully by Milk and Honey, her cat and dog.